RAFE OROPELA

A Novel

THE PERFECTIONIST

ISBN
978-1-960197-57-3 (Paperback)
978-1-960197-58-0 (eBook)
978-1-960197-56-6 (Hardcover)

— *To Mama Ocha*

TABLE OF CONTENTS

Acknowledgments

— To Luis and Manolo they know how each contributed.

INTRODUCTION

Everyone who has met The Perfectionist, think they know his true identity.

Everyone knows a perfect crime does not exist.

Everyone knows the earth is round.

One and one half out of three is very good. The last statement is true and the second one is half true. A perfect crime does not exist because once anyone knows the crime was committed it's no longer the perfect crime. The number one and only rule of secrets is that, If you want to keep a secret, you do not tell anyone. If you must, just tell one other person; after that, it's no longer a secret.

PROLOGUE

I am The Perfectionist, I can't afford mistakes, in my former line of business any insignificant detail could blow my cover and cost lives including mine. I was an active CIA field operative, not the super spy flamboyant type who drives expensive cars and kills anyone who interferes with the mission. I was the inconspicuous type of field operative who gathers information without anyone noticing even my presence. I have only killed once and it was in self defense.

In my current line of business, I still must be The Perfectionist because an insignificant detail could cost me a ton of money. I am no longer actively working for the CIA so I lay low, under the radar so to speak. I do day trading in futures and commodities. For a while I made a good money, at least before the markets crashed. Luckily I got most of my money out on time.

I need to find a good opportunity to invest which will allow me to generate the capital needed to look for the Nazi Gold. I know the gold is out there but it costs a lot of money to do salvage work.

My problem is that I don't have a curriculum vitae that I can show. When your prior work experience is mainly covert Intelligence gathering most of what you do cannot be disclosed out side the office. That is if I even had an office, in the first place. I don't exist as a real person my cover is my only existence. Besides any regular job I could get, would only give me resources to live comfortably I need the kind of money you can get killed for in order to search for the Nazi Gold.

UNDER THE WATER

DIVING AT NIGHT IS different from diving during daylight, under normal circumstances during a night dive I would use high intensity lamps to light our way under the hull of the yacht.

However, we are installing high explosives, 600 pounds of C4, on the bottom of a yacht, and we need to hide in the darkness. We're using special equipment, Closed Circuit equipment also known as rebreathers and night vision goggles. I touch my mask and indicate NO with my hand to make a signal to him I need to remind him not take off his mask under any circumstances because that would release bubbles and reveal our presence under the yacht. He signals an OK back to me indicating he is acknowledging. The only reason we're able to see each other in the darkness is because we're wearing night vision goggles.

We need to feel our way around. Even with the night vision goggles I have to feel the bottom of the hull so that we will not get lost. My SEAL training in underwater demolition kicks in, I have memorized the positions of the C4.

My partner has no idea where he is or where he needs to go he only follows me, like a blind man, and makes sure the sled carrying the 600 pounds of explosives does not float and hit the hull as I relieve the weight when I remove some of the C4 and attach it into position under the yacht.

We dive for an hour and forty-five minutes, placing the C4 into position, where the Seabee has calculated for the maximum efficiency. After I place each charge, I give a hand signal to my partner to let him know he can continue to place and run the prima cord to the next charge of C4.

Every time I remove weight from the underwater sled, he also adjusts buoyancy then and gives me an OK signal indicating we can move to the next location.

The last item is the installation of the detonator, which I decide to locate behind the housing for the starboard propeller shaft. This will minimize the danger of having the drag tearing it prematurely during travel.

By 5:35 AM, we're already sleeping in our cabins, I remind myself we're expected for breakfast with the Cartel Boss at 8:30 AM. We will have almost three hours of rest and be ready.

TEN MONTHS BEFORE:

NOT ON THE WATER, HIGH UP IN THE MOUNTAINS

"WHO ARE YOU AGAIN?"

Who the hell is this guy and how did he find out how to contact me? The name and numbers of field operatives are not listed in any phone book. I have to calm down, I was caught by surprise when he contacted me, but the only way an Ex-CIA analyst could do that is because someone at Langley who trusts him gave him my contact info.

"I worked the analyst desk on the mission tracking the Russian-Arab deals"

"Come again. What mission was that?"

"I received all the information on the Russian-Arab deals for the oil exploration; that information was never classified."

I just will not answer any questions until I confirm what he is saying about the information on the Russian-Arab deals. If it is like he says, and it was never classified, then I can sit down with him to talk about it. Even if I'm no longer active working for the CIA, I'm bound by the secrecy laws concerning any classified information I handled.

"How did you get my contact again?"

"I know who your handler is and I called him. He told me that you are outsourced and that you are cleared to accept freelance work as long as no classified information or equipment is used"

The only way this Ex-CIA analyst would know I'm cleared to work freelance is if he spoke to my handler.

It's almost funny I have only met face to face with my handler when I have been to Langley, twice during my whole career. The first time, when I was hired by the CIA, and the second time, when I was outsourced (which is what happens when your cover no longer seems useful or necessary, but they would retain it). If my cover had been blown I would be assigned to a desk job or maybe even retired, or erased. I'm lucky I'm still collecting a retainer fee as an outside contractor with the CIA. I'm not working on any assignment and I'm authorized to freelance as long as I do not break any secrecy laws.

"OK I'll agree to meet you but only if my anonymity remains protected. No names."

"Deal. No names. I understand. All I need is info on how to contact the Russian crew who worked in Saudi Arabia."

Even If I know who I'll be meeting, it's prudent to setup the meeting in a location I can control, just in case it turns to be a trap. It is second nature, trust but verify. I work alone, there is no backup available if the meeting goes bad. I need a location which does not have many access routes so I can monitor who is approaching.

Vail is a good location. It's famous for the snow skiing resorts, for its many visitors, and, because it is high up in the Rocky Mountains, it is open most of the year. Most ski resorts have only one access route from below.

When I get to the top, I'm able to observe anyone approaching. The people managing the resorts are very concerned with personal safety so they help in controlling any other unauthorized routes. A ski resort is a public place, so it offers the additional protection allowing me to hide in the crowd.

"Let's meet in Vail, Colorado. Where can I text you the time and place?"

I'll send him the contact instructions on how to dress, where to go, and what to answer when I ask for a cigaret and a light. I'll be there early and observe and verify he is alone. Once I'm satisfied the contact is safe, I'll approach him.

TWO WEEKS IT TAKES to check him out but everything seems clean.

"Hi, do you have a cigaret and a match?"

"No, I only smoke cigars but I didn't bring any, the altitude, too high for smoking."

"Let's go inside and have a drink. I'm having Scotch. What would you have?"

"I'll have a coffee, thank you. The view from up here is magnificent. My first time here."

The bar is located in the middle of a lounge, surrounded by glass windows spanning from the floor to the ceiling, which end two stories above the bar. The view of the Rockies surrounding the resort is magnificent indeed.

"Why did you leave the Company?"

"It wasn't voluntary. I had been working in that office for so long I almost forgot whether it was day or night outside after I got in there. There are no windows, just the bright illumination and the constant humming of all the electronics. I mean, even when I went to the cafeteria, it was like the same place except with tables instead of the cubicles. I would've expected"

Now he lowers his voice to a murmur.

"that the Federal Government"

Then he raises the volume back to normal.

"would give some kind of notice instead of someone from HR just walking to my cubicle and announcing my position was eliminated! And, I know I worked with sensitive information and all that. I guess I could not expect to be able to stick around there after being dismissed but, WOW! I had just been let go and it was kind of a shock any way. Right after I was notified, my supervisor came to me to remind me I had to go to legal before leaving, to sign all kinds of documents again. And he reminded that the only information I could use or disclose was information which was never classified or which had been declassified."

Saying that he pulled a piece of paper out of his pocket and handed it to me.

"When I went to legal, I asked them for a specific written clearance for the info I need from you, here it is certified as not classified."

He knows the drill he came prepared.

"How can I help you?"

I ask him after reviewing the document.

"I asked for the clearance to be able to disclose my expertise with the oil exploration on my resumé, and I was able to land a job, with a company which is drilling for oil in Alaska. I love this new job and the pay and benefits are good. I immersed myself in the operation to learn all the ropes. I studied the strategies used for the public relations efforts to curb the environmentalist opposition. I familiarized myself with how to prepare the applications for the drilling permits. I was sure I would be able to develop new ideas leading to reduction in the cost of oil exploration."

Is he really telling me the story of his life? All I need know is how I can help him.

"Excuse me for interrupting, but I'm not following. How will I be able help you?"

"I'm getting to that. The cost of oil exploration in Alaska is way too high and continues to rise. All the modern technology available is being used, but even when new deposits are located, the capacity and extension has to be determined to plan the extraction drilling. Which means going back to square one, more permits for more exploratory drilling and more opposition from the environmentalists. On top of that, after one of the largest oil spills in history, even if it was not our oil super tanker which ran aground, the spill of millions of barrels of oil off the southern coast of Alaska has almost brought drilling permits to a halt, and the public opinion is completely against drilling for exploration. The situation is out of our hands. But we need to continue with the exploration if we're going to survive."

"I'm still not following you."

"I remembered that I met you back in Langley, that is, if I could say I met you even when I never learned your true identity."

I gave him a look clearly indicating that he would not.

"I said no names, remember?"

"I'm not trying to ask that. It was just a comment. Anyway, I remembered you were the field operative responsible for gathering most of the information about the Russian-Arab dealings. If I can track down the Russians who did the exploration for the Arabs, I should be able to contact them on behalf of my company, to see if they can help us explore without drilling. Like they did for the Arabs. The company is facing strong opposition from environmentalists for the exploratory drillings."

"Clearly, it's worth a lot for the company to locate the oil more accurately and faster. What exactly are you proposing?"

"I need to know what your fee would be for working for the company, as an outsourced contractor looking for the Russian contacts."

"I don't know how long that would take, and...."

"Just give me your number. I'll call my boss, and if he approves, it's a go. If it's too much for him to approve, he said he would have to bring it up with our upper management, and then I would have to get back to you later."

"OK, $350 per day plus expenses. If I have to travel, I'll let you know in advance, and you will reimburse me when I present my bill"

"Don't move. I'm texting my boss your terms right now."

He takes his mobile phone out of his pocket and in a minute the answer is received. Maybe I should have asked for $500 per day. What the hell! This will not make me rich even at a higher fee.

"Done, you are now working for me, or for the Alaskan Oil Company. I guess I'm now in effect your handler for the oil company."

"OK this are the rules: field operatives, by definition, cannot have the direct support of the main office for supplies or equipment. A field operative cannot go to a home base to replenish supplies, and there are no ATM machines around the world with access to company's funds. The only contact with the home office is the handler, and only to deliver or receive information when it's absolutely necessary. I don't want anybody else contacting me for anything. I won't respond to anyone other than you. I have to protect my identity."

"I understand. We play it your way. I'll be you only contact."

*I'm going to have to look up all those contacts. Luckily I can use the information without my former employer learning about it, even when I'm acting as the field operative for a new employer. I need to maintain a credible cover to blend in the background so well that it withstands any scrutiny. In my own neighborhood **everyone** knows that I'm the neighbor whose work involves traveling frequently, and even when I'm home, I'm very private and don't receive visits.*

My home provides me a place to unwind away from the stress of the field operations. A place to think and plan the strategy for my next moves. A place to store my supplies and information. I'll have to pull my files on that mission. I must have notes on the locations of the contacts who had provided the information.

LESS THAN ONE WEEK, and I'm able to identify the contacts. I need to locate. Even I'm surprised how organized my notes are. I guess this is where the training pays off.

"I'm calling to let you know I was able to pick up a trail leading to one of the Russian engineers. He's in Spain. I'm heading there right now. I'll keep you informed"

"That was quick!"

"Don't count the chicken before the eggs hatch. Looking for old contacts isn't simple. Besides, if he doesn't remember me, or rather my old cover, I'm going to have to start from scratch. Even so, maybe he isn't comfortable talking to me. This Russian was always followed around. He had a tail, who clearly was KGB; never drank, never talked except to let the others know it was time to leave, and when he said it was time to leave they all stood up and left without any complaints. I have no way of knowing if he was KGB-friendly. The fact the KGB was present doesn't mean he liked them. Maybe he was just tolerant. I just never knew. The KGB presence was intended to refrain any of the people involved in the project from jumping to the West. It was more like *big brother is watching you*. Anyway, I'll keep you informed"

NOT ON THE WATER BUT IN DIFFERENT CONTINENTS

HERE WE GO AGAIN, first time around; intelligence gathering is a tricky business. The second time around is like trying to disarm an explosive device in the dark or blind folded: you may know what you are doing, but you can't see the wires.

*Contrary to what **everyone** thinks he knows, the most successful field operatives are not Super Spies running around in flamboyant cars, jumping from fast moving trains and killing any person that interferes with their mission. In reality, the best field operatives are inconspicuous; the ones **everyone** thinks he knows are completely harmless. The ones who blend into the background so well that information is placed at their reach without the subject even realizing he was being pumped for information. I'm a trained field operative. I know how to read very simple eye movements which people cannot hide during a conversation. My training as an interrogator allows me* *to read those eye movements, and I can tell if the subject is making up a story or remembering facts.*

All the information I gathered about the Russian-Arab deals was acquired following these simple techniques, without a single shot being fired or any throats being cut; not even a broken finger. Bodily harm, even when it may be sanctioned, leaves a trail and should be avoided unless the field operative has to defend himself or protect the mission.

For good or for bad, I have no idea if the Russian will remember me.

All I know is he is now retired here in Spain, on the Mediterranean coast. This place has great weather year round; the beach must be warm, women sunbathing all daylong, the view is spectacular most of the time. There he is, the old Russian engineer still enjoys drinking and boasting about his past exploits. That is good. Let's see if he remembers me.

"I remember, you're the engineer whom I used to serve as a young bartender. I always enjoyed listening to your stories about the oil exploration."

This is it. He is looking me up and down; his eyes are showing he is trying to remember. That is a good sign. He is smiling at me; a better sign.

"How have you been all this time? I'm delighted to meet an old acquaintance, *such a coincidence.*"

"I wasn't sure you'd remember me."

"How could I forget, you always told me you wanted to go to college to study to become a *geologist,* because I inspired you. Did you?"

"I've followed your steps and was hired by an oil company exploring in Alaska. Are you still in contact with the oil exploration unit? The company I work for in Alaska is looking for help with oil exploration."

"Not anymore, why do you think I retired to warm Mediterranean? I wanted to get far from Siberia as possible. Going to Alaska would be like going back to Siberia. Besides, I'm too old and too sick to work in such a cold environment."

"Do you still have any contact with your old colleagues?"

"No, not even Mexican assistant. He taught me to speak Spanish. That helped me when I chose to retire in Spain far away from the Russian cold **and** KGB. I never liked those assholes. I had close friendship with Mexican fellow, up to moment he moved back to Oaxaca. He went back home to help his mother farm land. She is widow."

"Do you have the names and contact information available for the Mexican and the other engineers and technicians who were involved in the project?"

"It would be old information, but maybe one could point in right direction. I give you what I have."

TRACKING DOWN OLD contacts is time consuming because people move, they retire or die. In this case the contacts are scattered all over Russia and require much travel. I'll need to do the tracking in person so that I do not raise suspicions.

"Again, I'm just calling to let you know my status. I met with the engineer. He is not available, but he did give me all the contacts he had, all except one are back in Russia, and I'm heading there now."

"Where is the other one?"

"It's probably a dead end. The guy was his former assistant. He is a Mexican, the Russian believes he is probably living in Oaxaca, in his mother's farm. If I don't get anything from any of the Russians, I'll track the Mexican. I'll keep you posted"

SOMETIMES YOU NEVER KNOW what you are looking for until you find it. After a full month traveling and talking to the Russian contacts, I have reached all but three of them. I expected at least some of them would provide helpful information. However, every contact I have reached so far turned out to be a dead end. That could be an indication someone is trying to hide something.

It was as if the Russian-Arab deals had never happened. Every person I reached, denied ever being involved in oil exploration in Saudi Arabia. I know they were all lying because I remembered them all from the bar where they went with the Russian engineer. I never forget faces. None of them recognized me because as the bartender I never drew attention to myself. I was, and still am a master at blending in.

I'm still working a covert operation, and even if it's not for the CIA, the rules are the same. When you hit that kind of discrepancy, you need to back off immediately and reexamine what was it you missed, before you step on someone's toes. I need to reevaluate the strategy. Maybe even change it completely. Covert may no longer be an alternative after the initial contacts I have already made.

Now the only alternative available may be open and direct; going directly to the Russian government.

"I'm afraid I don't have any good news for you this time. I've hit a wall. I still have three more to track, but all the contacts so far have denied for some reason, that they were in Saudi Arabia."

"How do you know you were contacting the right people?"

"For one thing I recognized their faces as the crew who used to work for the old Russian, even though I didn't know their names back then, during the mission, I mean. I never forget faces. I have another strategy to suggest. After I track the last three, I'm going back to the old Russian in Spain, before going to Mexico. But in the meantime I suggest your company goes directly to the Russian Government, making an official request, to see what happens."

"Who do we ask for?"

"Do you have any contacts in the State Department? They should be able to point you in the right direction."

"OK, I'll get that ball rolling, and the first one to get anything calls the other."

"I'll continue to call you, to keep you posted. I have to justify my fees."

"You don't need to worry about that. I have been keeping my boss up to speed and, so far he's not complaining about your fees. On the contrary, he told me he was surprised how fast you got results even when they have not panned out."

TWO MORE WEEKS OF TRAVEL and visits and results are all the same. These people have been ordered not to talk about the project.

"My turn with the bad news: the Russians said they would be pleased to help."

"The only thing bad about that is that you don't need my services anymore. That should be great news for your company."

"I apologize. I stand corrected then. For you it is good news. Let me tell you the whole story. The request was unsuccessful because the Russians want to charge fees so high that the cost would be higher than what the exploration is costing us now without their help. When upper management received the response from the Russians yesterday, they told my boss to continue pursuing what we're doing. So you're cleared to go back to Spain and on to Mexico. Please get some results!"

THE RUSSIAN IS hospitalized when I get back to Spain and he looks very sick. It is hard to believe that he has deteriorated so fast in less than two months.

"Can I get you anything?"

"The only thing I'd like is a drink, and that is what is killing me, so do not."

He said that with a smirk. Eventually, the damage made to the liver by alcohol catches on to you.

"Tell me again."

"The fee they want to charge is many times higher than what the Arabs paid. Why would the Russians try to charge such high fees now?"

"Only logical explanation would be, Russians are no longer willing or able to deliver services."

"The Alaskan company would like to contract your services for locating the oil."

"Unfortunately, I'm not be able to help, look where I am. Besides, without equipment we used in Saudi Arabia, I would not be able to find any oil deposit, unless I fell into it. Yes?"

"I never asked, how did you locate the oil?"

"I was never expert in oil exploration. My background is acoustic resonance. I was told to make experiments with sonar equipment for Russian Navy. They wanted device that would detect objects underwater even when viscosity of water was changing because changes in thermal layers. The device I developed did not penetrate thermal layers. However, device distinguished material of underwater object. Russian Navy did not need such information because they knew what materials US Navy uses to built submarines. What they needed was where submarines were located."

Looking at his eyes I can tell the Russian is remembering not making up the information being relayed. Besides, when I spoke to him during the last visit, it was very clear he had a grudge against the KGB for taking over the project.

"So you used sonar in land? How did sonar equipment end up in land?"

"It occurred to me if sonar equipment could be modified to use it underground, device would find underground deposits, water or oil, because device could…How do you say?…distinguish composition of material or, where an underground deposit is located. Initial testing of device was very promising when connected to sonar equipment modified for ground scanning. Mexican assistant designed modifications from top of his head, very simple solution he devised. Did you know normal sonar equipment cannot be used for ground exploration?"

"Yeah, the sound waves don't travel through solid ground."

"Regular sonar equipment does not work in ground. Mexican assistant modified equipment to connect to two probes, an emitter and a receiver, deep into ground. So simple we did modifications ourselves. Without bureaucratic request for materials or logging of specifications."

"How did the system work?"

"Once probes are in place one ping from sonar equipment will tell if there is oil or not in target area. Solid ground does not transmit sound waves so no acoustic signal is received from emitter. However, if at least one of probes is driven into an oil deposit, the sound wave is detected and device is able to identify which probe, emitter or receiver, is within oil deposit. Moving probe which is outside oil deposit closer, allows operator to detect where boundary of the deposits. Once both probes are inside oil deposit, the size and contour of deposit's determined easily by relocating probes. Size and depth of the deposit can be mapped in 3D in very short time, allowing drillers to plan accurately where and how deep they need to drill. Process is so fast and accurate it reduces cost and time consumed in oil exploration to a fraction of cost with traditional exploratory drilling."

"How did the device get to Saudi Arabia? I'd think the KGB would not let such a device out of the national borders."

He laughed out loud, clearly remembering the KGB was fooled.

"Soon after device was developed, Russian oil explorers requested testing in Saudi Arabia because they could use data to establish parameters for oil extraction in Siberia. **Everyone** knows oil deposits in Saudi Arabia are very large. First time probes were driven into the ground, both landed inside deposit. After, was just a matter of mapping contours and depth by relocating probes. Testing was so successful, so fast, that Russian government had not taken control of project until extensive mapping of existing deposits was already underway, allowing Arabs to revise the estimates of oil reserves. Never a miss during time we explored for Arabs!"

"Surely the Arabs were very happy to pay whatever fees the Russians were charging. How in the world did the KGB agree to let the project continue in Saudi Arabia?"

"They allowed project to continue because security of project, meaning device, was never compromised. Only I and Mexican assistant, had been involved handling device. Only two operational devices, both under my control, and only prototype was destroyed in the accident. Mexican almost electrocuted, just after that accident he went back to Oaxaca. Shame, I was never able to share with him he could have used device to find water at his farm, because project was taken over by KGB. To find water, probes have to be driven into ground, much closer to each other, because water deposit's smaller than oil deposit. We did tests in water deposits after he went back to Mexico, if probes are driven at regular distance used for oil exploration, test is negative even when one of the probe is inside water. Too much soil between the probes muffles sound waves and does not work because viscosity of water is much lower than oil."

"You are saying that without the device there is no way you could help us."

"I'm afraid that is exactly what I'm saying. Even if you can locate the Mexican and he is able to make sonar equipment modifications for ground exploration. Without device, there is no way to help in Alaska."

"Why do you think the Russian government is trying to avoid giving help in the Alaskan project?"

"All designs and specifications for constructing device were confiscated by KGB, and were probably stored in secured facilities. Most certainly same place where only two operating devices were stored when project ended."

"Where?"

"In Chernobyl, where the nuclear accident occurred. I believe devices and documentation has been lost and Russia would never admit that."

THAT IS THE LAST conversation I ever had with the Russian engineer. Shortly after, he passed away. I was notified of his death when I tried to reach him at the hospital to ask him if he had another way of contacting the Mexican. The Russian engineer had provided very useful information, but it all lead to a dead end.

Possibly, the only person left in the world who has any knowledge of the device, and would be willing to talk about it, is the Mexican technician. I cannot tell the oil company anything until after I find the Mexican.

This is going to be more difficult than tracking the Russians, finding anyone in the best of circumstances is difficult. I only have a name and an address, but in rural Latin America, an address has no real meaning. I'll go around inquiring and that will alert him that someone is looking for him.

THE WATER

THE MEXICAN IS AT first glad to hear about the Russian engineer and then very sad when he learns he had died.

"You and I never met because I believe you already had the accident when I met the old man. I know he cared for you very much."

"How did you meet him again?"

"I worked as a bartender at the local bar for foreigners in Saudi Arabia, where he and his crew went"

I must give him the background he needs to start trusting me, because it's not enough that we're in his home. This place is pretty run down. Probably, he has not had any success finding underground water for his farm, or acquiring another source of income.

"He was always telling me about the exploration. He inspired me to become a geologist."

"I learned much from the Russian. He placed me in charge of modifying the sonar equipment for ground scanning. He taught me everything he could about resonance and electronics. He was a true genius! The device he developed detects different materials underwater, and oil underground. It just can't detect underground water."

"How do you know that? He told me he never had a chance to tell you, because he performed the tests after you left."

"How do I know what? What tests are you talking about?"

"The tests he did for detecting water underground. How do you know about those test? He told me did those tests were made after you returned to Mexico."

"I don't know about any tests he did. I'm talking about when I tested the device here at the farm, it didn't work, it won't find underwater deposits. I tried for several months. I even asked a neighbor to let me do a test around his well and it didn't work."

I'm listening to him and I'm almost jumping out of my skin. The Russian was unaware of some details the Mexican had discovered, but how did he? He did not have the device.

"How did you do the tests? Did you find another way of using the sonar?" *I do not want to pry. He will give me the answers. I just need to ask the right questions. I must calm down.*

"I took the equipment to my neighbor's well and I planted the sonar probes and it couldn't detect the aquifer the well is tapping."

"No, I didn't mean that. I meant how did you do the test if the device was destroyed. Were you able to fix it?"

"Fix it? All it needed was a fresh set of batteries, but it would serve no purpose because it's useless for finding water and there is no oil in this region. Pemex does not contract out oil exploration. I already asked."

"Wait a minute. What do you mean when you say only batteries?"

"The prototype was not destroyed in the accident, the prototype's casing was heavily reinforced and protected the internal circuitry from the electrical discharge. The professor and I both mistakenly concluded the electrical shock had destroyed the internal circuitry because of the extent of the external damage. The professor allowed me to keep the device as an useless souvenir after I survived the accident. After I got well from my injuries, I examined the device and discovered that only the batteries had been damaged because they were outside the reinforced casing."

The device is working, 100 alarms are going off in my brain at the same time, KGB, CIA, professor. What professor?

"Hold it. Who is the professor?"

"I call him that but I mean the engineer."

"Why do you call him the professor?"

"Because he was my professor at the university in Cuba, where I went to study electronics. I have always called him professor since."

"You went to university in Cuba and the engineer was your professor there?"

The engineer never told me where he had met the Mexican and I never asked. I did not question where they had met because the Russian told me the Mexican was who made the sonar modifications.

"I thought you said you were friends with him. Didn't he tell you about that?"

Oh, Oh! He is suspecting something, I'm loosing the connection. I need to make him comfortable again.

"I just didn't know how or where you two met. The Russian, or rather, the professor, told me when he explained he'd covered for you when you took the prototype back to Mexico. Now I know your big secret, and as far as I can tell, you didn't know it was a big secret until now. Would it be accurate to say there's no one else who knows the prototype is operational?"

"Yes, that's accurate; other than me, only you know. I never told anyone else because it never worked."

OK, I made him relax again, I have to stay on track and focused, this is just an interrogation.

"What was he doing in Cuba?"

"He had been commissioned by the Russian Navy to develop a device to detect submarines. Testing was performed in the Caribbean, while he was a professor in the university, that's how I met him. I guess the climate in Cuba, year round is a lot warmer than in Russia. The prototype didn't work the way the Russians wanted and the Russian Navy dropped the project. Then the professor had this idea of using the device to locate underground deposits, possibly water and oil he said. He had no idea on how to modify sonar equipment for use underground. When he told me about the problem, I gave him the solution for modifying the sonar equipment, and he took me under his wing from that day on. We became very good friends."

"So you met him in Cuba during the Russian Navy project. I don't think you fully realize how good a friend he really was to you. He covered for you, by listing the prototype as destroyed."

"We met when I arrived at the university in Cuba before the project was canceled by the Russian Navy. He took me under his wing and took me to Saudi Arabia. We both believed the prototype had been destroyed!"

"He told me he didn't like the KGB involved in the project. How about you? You seem to share his feelings about the KGB. Otherwise, why didn't you report to him the prototype was still operational?"

"I hate those bastards, since the project in Cuba!"

"Is that why you didn't report it?"

"In part. I did try to let him know, when I replaced the batteries. I tested the device with sonar equipment I modified here at the farm, and tried to locate water, but it never worked. I tried to reach the professor, but I was never able to contact him."

"That's probably because he had retired to Spain, and he did not have any information other than a farm in Oaxaca, it took me a long time to find you, he said he was grateful to you for teaching him Spanish."

"That would explain why he never got back to me but it does not explain why none of the others ever got back to me when I was trying to contact the professor."

"I tried contacting the other Russians, with the information and contacts he gave me before he died. No one gave a straight answer. I believe they were all ordered to conceal the information about the oil exploration in Saudi Arabia."

"How could they? That was where we tested the prototype. Hijole, Russian bastards! In Saudi Arabia was where I almost died electrocuted. Do you think the KGB might come after me?"

I can see the alarm on his face he about to become very nervous, I need to calm him down.

"I need you to trust me. So I'm going to tell you my big secret. I was CIA and if KGB ever came after you I can protect you."

Have I gone mad? Did I just break my cover with this stranger? I broke my own first and most important rule, the rule of secrets. No, wait, I have not broken it. This is the first person I have ever told outside the agency that is.

"I don't think the KGB is even looking because as far as they know the prototype was destroyed."

"What do you want from me?"

Is he trusting me? Is he calmed?

"First we have to agree on several points if we're gonna go ahead with this. We need to trust each other like you have never trusted anyone else in the world."

"Why should I trust you?...What do you want from me?"

Why do I trust him? He seems sincere, but I don't know why, could it be because he is so adamant about his hatred for the KGB. Or, is it because he has confirmed everything the professor said and more. I guess those answers will have to wait for now, I trust my gut!

"Did you know Panamá has extremely friendly banking and immigration laws?"

"What the fuck are you talking about?"

"If you deposit a minimum of $500,000 in the Banco Nacional de Panamá you can apply for permanent residency. For all practical purposes, you're a citizen of Panamá. You can buy property, register a company, and you only pay taxes on the income you generate inside Panamá. In addition, the Panamanians are very strict about not disclosing your business information as long as you can show it's legit. Geological exploration is not an illegal business."

"That is all very interesting, but I don't have $500,000, and I don't understand why that's relevant to what we're discussing."

"We need to create a Panamanian company dedicated to geological exploration. The company has to establish a client base here in Oaxaca, and other countries in Central America, locating underground aquifers. That'll generate the credentials needed to show the Alaskan oil company that the company is real. At the same time, it'll create a cover in case the Russians ever start to snoop around, if they detect anything about the oil exploration in Alaska."

"What Alaskan oil company? Where are we going to get $500,000? Orale! You have me completely lost! How are we going to do that? The equipment does not detect underground water."

"I asked you to trust me!"

"Trust you? When you could be KGB as far as I know! I just met you and you come here asking out of the blue and maybe you are just trying to confirm if I have the prototype. Are you going to kill me?"

"No, I don't even think they are looking for it. I mean the KGB and NO! I'm not KGB I'm CIA. Furthermore NO! I'm not here to kill you."

"Anyway, KGB, CIA, you guys are all the same to me. Are you going to try to sell me the fairy tale about the CIA being all about freedom and democracy, and the KGB about the evil empire. Listen to me. You are here asking for my trust, very interested in the device, but as far as I'm concerned, you're just another pinche gringo trying to take advantage of… how is it you call us?…***this spic, this wetback, this taco bandido.*** So get your act together and show me the list of the 1000 reasons I should even consider to continue this conversation with you."

"Listen, I said I used to be CIA , I'm no longer working for the CIA, I'm an outsourced covert operative, which means I still have the required clearance if they decided to reactivate me to work on classified matters. However, I'm not currently working for the CIA. I'm working independently as an investigator. Currently, I'm working for the Alaskan Oil Company that hired me to find the Russians who worked in Saudi Arabia."

"What Alaskan oil company?"

"When I met the professor, I was working for the CIA and I was extracting information about the oil exploration but the mission was cancelled. Just like the Russian Navy cancelled the project in which you met the professor. The person who received and analyzed the information I obtained in Saudi Arabia, was fired from the CIA due to budget reductions and he started working with this Alaskan oil company. The company needs our help! It's a big opportunity for us if we do it right, with your expertise and the device and my experience and my money to fund the project startup. I think we could make a lot of money from the oil company. The professor told me that he had no experience in oil exploration that he wouldn't have found oil unless he fell inside a deposit, if it wasn't for the device and you handling the equipment."

"Why should I trust you?"

"You are right you shouldn't, hell I don't know why I'm trusting you. But I'm trusting you. You're the first person I have ever told that I worked for the CIA. I don't know what are your reasons for distrusting the KGB or the CIA, but I can tell you I also distrusted the CIA before I was recruited. I started working for the CIA because I was ordered to work on a mission which I believed was necessary to save lives. However, later in my career I was ordered many times, to work missions which didn't have anything to do with saving lives. It was all information gathering for someone to take economic advantage of situations with insider information. I realized some of the information I have gathered, can be used to my own advantage. However, I need your help to make it happen. WE can sit here me trying to give you the 1000 reasons to trust me but I believe actions speak louder than words."

"What actions are you talking about?"

"Actions of omission for example, I have not killed you, I'm trusting you by telling you I was CIA, I'm willing to lay on the table $2 million of my money to fund the venture I'm inviting you to join. It's your device and expertise in acoustic resonance and my money and expertise in security and covert operations. What have you got to loose?"

"My life, if the KGB comes after us, eventually."

"That's where my expertise comes in, I doubt they ever will but, if the Russians even learn about the success of the oil exploration in Alaska, and they start poking around, what they will find is a credible trail pointing to a Panamanian company owned by Panamanian residents. There will not be any connection to Oaxaca, other than the fact the company has clients here. They may eventually catch up, but the more credible the company's credentials are, the less likely they'll find anything."

"What would we be going to explore for, if the device only works for finding oil, and there is no oil here?"

"We're gonna find water first in your mother's farm, so she may move ahead with her farming business. Next, the other farms nearby. The professor explained me the device would detect underground water if the probes are placed much closer to each other. Because you need to compensate for the smaller size of an aquifer and the lower viscosity of the water."

"No way it can't be that easy."

"You can repeat your tests at the neighbor's well if you don't believe me, I'm just telling you what the professor said to me."

"Why didn't I think of that before?"

"Let's get to work! The most important detail of a credible cover is its permanency. We need to establish it soon. I have the money to start operating immediately. We need to create a long list of contracts that are verifiable, with clients who are eager to confirm the arrangement, and more important satisfied with the accuracy of the services."

TO ANY OUTSIDER the company has become a real business, not just a front created out of smoke and mirrors. The first client was the Mexican's own farm. Water was located using the process suggested by the professor. It served as a very good practice run for the crew. After a short time, the Mexican was able to assemble a very good group of helpers, with enough technical knowledge and professional training to earn their pay.

At the same time, they were all clueless about what they were getting involved in, if they were ever interrogated, they only knew that their employers were a *geologist* and an electronic genius who had joined their skills to form a very successful enterprise.

The next clients were his closest neighbors and because they were so short on cash, the Mexican and I agreed to charge on a contingency basis. The most important thing was to create a credible paper trail.

Soon after, the company was hired by a rancher in northern Mexico, a very arid country. A neighbor rancher in Oaxaca had a relative who worked in a ranch in northeast Chihuahua. The ranch owner was paying very high fees to water his herds. The information about our company, which had established a reputation of accuracy and a contingency fee structure was a deal too sweet to pass without exploring.

After the first contract in Chihuahua was completed, the other ranchers were lining up to obtain the services. The best part was that the former water supplier was also interested, once he confirmed the accuracy of the deposits. The fee structure made it even cheaper for him to provide water to those ranchers on land where no aquifers were available.

We began to line up nothing but good references and a solid reputation for good, accurate service, and above all, we milked our contingent fee structure, which was the best deal for any cash-strapped client. The company was doing brisk business. The contingent fee structure was one cent per gallon of extracted water. In other words the clients were only paying for the water produced by the aquifers and that only for as long as the aquifer was producing.

The cover became real. We are doing real business and it is very successful. The cash flow is so good the initial investment I put in from my own funds has been recovered by the time the first contract in Chihuahua was completed.

I made a bet with the last $2 million I had left of the money that I had accumulated from trading successfully in the futures market before the economy went into free fall. The investment I made in the three penthouse apartments in Panamá was not going anywhere. However, our business grew so fast that enough paper trail and a decent profit have been generated in a short time. Enough for the credentials needed for the Alaskan oil company.

THE OIL

TECHNICAL EXPERTISE IS VERY valuable, but the knowledge of hard data is even more valuable. I have been able to combine both and increase the value exponentially. The Mexican has the technical expertise and that is great because if gives confidence to the Alaskan oil company which will be assessing our credentials.

When they look for verification of a company's track record, what they find is satisfied clients who have nothing to relay but praise for our company's expertise and the accuracy of the services received. That provides good verification. The Mexican's technical expertise reinforces the findings because **Everyone** knows that a client base and contracts cannot be created out of thin air. Such a vast clientele must be real and it is real.

"Don't worry your anonymity is still intact, I made it very clear to my boss, I'm acting as your handler and the only one who will contact you. Besides, I want to get all the credit of being the person responsible for the rescue of the oil exploration operation. The payments to an investigator have never been questioned. I thinks he knows I'm using a CIA contact for this, so he is not asking any questions."

"OK, I just have to be very careful about my cover. Otherwise, I become ineffective. I found a small Panamanian company, which owns the equipment originally designed by the Mexican assistant technician who used to work for the Russian engineer. It took me a long time, but I have been checking it out. You know that looking for old contacts isn't easy or fast, and the company isn't in Mexico. It's located in Panamá. So I hope your company doesn't mind that it took a long time to find the contact?"

"Did you check their background?"

"I gathered every document I could so your people can check what they need. I'll deliver the information I have on the contracts in Central America. The information was impressive, I think."

"Why is it that this company has never been involved in oil exploration?"

"I asked the same question and was told Pemex does its own explorations; it doesn't contract out. Also, there isn't much oil in the rest of Central America. I asked around and so far all the clients seemed very satisfied, mainly because the terms are contingent on the well's output."

"What do you mean contingent?"

"This company doesn't charge a flat fee for the exploration. The only fixed charges are the out of pocket expenses for room and board during the extent of the engagement. The company charges a contingency fee based on extraction. Once the aquifer goes dry the client stops paying."

At least that is the way we do business for water exploration and we always know the extent of the aquifer.

"Do you think they'll do the same for us? How much do they charge?"

And the fish bites, I got you! Now let me reel you in slowly.

"I wasn't able to get information on the fee. The clients never mentioned the basic fee. They just said, how much they paid in total but it seems to be about one cent per gallon, and all the clients are extremely satisfied with the arrangement. I can get the owner to fly up to meet with you if you want."

"First try to get him to confirm how much the fee would be. If we get that information I'll run it by upper management to catch their interest."

No surprises there. You don't want to show your enthusiasm. Present yourself as calm and cool as possible, but I know you are probably jumping inside your skin.

"OK, I'll make the call."

WHAT WE NEED is to send a proposal! Where is the Mexican? I think he said he was showing the guys how to calibrate the equipment so they did not have to wait for him in the field. He should have his radio with him.

"Come in field crew"

I call using the radio from the office.

"Yes, Sir what can we do for you? Over"

"Is the boss there with you?"

"Yes, I'm here OVER!"

"Yes, yes, sorry about that I forgot radio protocol. I need you to come to the office. It's about the Alaskan deal. They want a proposal. OVER"

"That's good news! Over"

"Yes, it's! Over"

"No, I meant that you've finally learned to use the radio protocol. Over"

"I'm glad you are excited about that, but will you come into the office, please. Over"

THE MEXICAN ARRIVES at the office less than twenty minutes after our radio conversation.

"They want information about the fee, but I think we should send a draft of contract. The proposed contingency fee will be 42 cents per barrel of oil extracted from any new production oil well drilled in the deposits identified by us. In addition, out of pocket expenses for transportation room and board of all personnel. The amount is just about the same as 1 cent for water, but the volume of oil production is much larger. We'll be getting tons of money."

"How long do you think they'll take to answer?"

"The decision for the oil company executives shouldn't be too difficult to make; their current cost per barrel, for oil exploration, is significantly higher than 42 cents per barrel, according to what my contact has told me."

"Did they ask about our lack of expertise in oil exploration?"

"He did, but he quickly realized the contingent fee was such a good protection they really don't have anything to loose except the investment in travel, room and board. I explained PEMEX doesn't outsource and besides he wants to get all the credit for reducing the oil exploration costs. He'll fight for us."

THE CONTRACT IS SENT and the response, as anticipated, comes back the next day. Now all I need to do is break clean with the investigation so that there is no conflict of interest.

"They agreed to fly with their equipment with one condition."

"What's the condition?"

"Their English is not too good. They want to hire me as an interpreter and a consultant. They know me as a *geologist* which was my old cover."

"Are you willing to do it?"

"I approached them as a *geologist* and started consulting with them. All of a sudden, they are offering me a piece of the action, and I went along thinking that being inside it would be easier to check them out for you. To tell you the truth, after seeing what they did with the water in Mexico, I want to get my hands greasy. I'll send you my final bill because I don't want any conflict of interests, that is if you agree."

Which you will because you want to be the hero.

"Yes, yes sure, I agree. It will be good to meet you face to face again, but without the need for code words."

Sure because you do not want to disclose to your employer I'm the person who found the Panamanian company they are engaging, no problem I don't mind you taking the credit.

"Yes, for me this is also a new feeling, working without an ulterior motive."

Other than getting paid a ton of money for the exploration fee. That will be an oil royalty.

THE MEXICAN/PANAMANIAN crew arrives with their interpreter,—guess who—one week after the contract is signed. We sit down with the oil company executives and discuss the final details. After all the locations are identified on the maps, arrangements are made to start in the newest deposit. Their drillers have not been able to assess the extent of that deposit because the exploration drilling permits are being delayed. The following day, the exploration crew is transported to the first site.

The crew has much practice setting up the equipment for the water exploration. The Mexican reminds the crew one last time that for oil exploration they would extend the distance considerably between the probes and that the probes will have to be driven much deeper. Besides that, the only difference in this job, would be the cooler climate.

"Other than that, just make sure you drink lots of water too. Even if the temperature is lower, the humidity is also lower, and you may dehydrate very easily."

"Hey, boss, we have a question..."

"Before you ask me, I have one more thing to tell you, the pay from this job is going to include, for each of us, in addition the regular pay, a bonus of one cent per barrel of extracted oil, when they start paying us for that. Now, what is your question?"

They all looked at each other and smiled. Realizing that not only were they getting a huge bonus, but the bonus would keep coming for a long time.

"Nothing, boss, you just answered it!"

"Let's get cranking!"

Nothing better than a motivated employee to work harder and faster. The boundaries of the first oil deposit were located so quickly that the oil company requested the complete mapping before moving to the second location. Nothing better than a motivated client to start paying faster. Mapping ahead of schedule meant production planning would start immediately and it also meant our company would start collecting sooner. Once the oil begins to flow from the new production wells, the cash machine also starts pumping.

THE CASH FLOW FROM the water exploration in Mexico is still good, but that is the only source of cash up to now, and the future plans I have will require much more funding. The project in Alaska goes on very smoothly and fast. The client is very excited because the mapping of the deposits has been so accurate that production is excellent. The oil production is increasing so fast, without requiring exploratory drilling, that the production drilling permits are being approved at a fast pace.

EVENTUALLY, THE CIA MAY become alerted to the deal, but by then the only trail will be accounts payable for the royalty of the extracted oil. I know the information in a bureaucratic government is shared, and I know that at some point in the future some information may reach Langley, because the statistics will start showing the sharp increase in oil production, **without** any exploratory drilling.

"You know you are the first person they will call."

I have to alert him, once Langley notices the first person contacted will be him because they know he is working with the Alaskan Oil Company.

"They can ask, but we have not done any use of any classified information, and there is nothing to hide. If Langley comes asking questions, the plain and simple fact is that we contracted a Panamanian company to help explore for oil, and the Company has been very accurate."

If you feel comfortable with that, so do I.

"I agree totally. I just thought I would let you know it may happen."

"I know the statistics exist and Langley has access to the data, I looked them up to compare with the information you were sending during the mission in Saudi Arabia. But, I doubt anyone will be paying attention soon to these stats anyway."

"I'M GLAD OUR EXPLORATION and mapping job in Alaska has finished. This place is too cold for my comfort. I prefer the tropics"

I'm going to the Caribbean.

"I hope you are using a large bank, because I saw the payments that we're already sending your company for the royalties. The executives are so happy they have no problem paying without any delay, just as the contract requires. Every month a wire transfer will be made to your designated bank in Panamá."

"If you need more exploring, the same contract will be honored perpetually"

"I'm sure you will, take care and have a safe trip"

OVER THE WATER

"BOTH THE PROFESSOR AND you mentioned that you had worked for the Russian Navy in a project which eventually resulted in the device we're using. I need you to tell me everything you can remember about that, and don't spare any details. Even if you think it's not related, I need you to tell me every detail you remember."

*I love this view, the Penthouse is great, and I'm glad I was able to acquire all three apartment, it makes it the **Perfect** safe house. No one else has access to the Penthouse. The view is extraordinary from this balcony. The only line of sight into any of the three apartments is from out at sea and unless someone uses a submarine we would see it.*

"I don't know where to begin. I already told you everything I know."

"OK, I'll ask the questions and you answer."

"Wait. Before we do this, I want to ask you something."

"Go ahead."

"Why is it that we're not looking for new contracts with the equipment?"

"We won't be doing any more underground exploration. We're going to close that shop and let the crew go, that's why I set them up with a share of the oil royalty."

"What? We're going into early retirement? Where? Are we going to Spain like the professor?"

"You said one question; that's already three."

"Come on, don't evade the questions."

"Not quite just yet, we need to learn a new skill. We're going to take open water SCUBA diving lessons. We will need that for our next project. This one will require we work without the crew. Do you still trust me?"

"Definitely, ever since I met you my life has only improved. Why wouldn't I trust you?"

"That's something we also need to talk about. I always need to remind you that a cover is very easy to loose if you're not careful. When people around you know you're wealthy, **everyone** expects you to drive an expensive car. People will become suspicious if you didn't drive in luxury. The opposite is also true, if they don't know you have money. You don't want to drive into your neighborhood in a very expensive car and start raising suspicions about how and where you got the money to buy that car. The first rule for maintaining a good cover is to be like they expect you to be, to blend in, to be unnoticed."

"You don't want me to buy the car?"

"You'd mentioned you were thinking about buying a Ferrari. If you really want to buy an expensive vehicle, I'd rather you went with an SUV, with leather seats. You don't really need a flashy sports car. Also, you don't want to buy it cash. We'll go to the bank and setup a personal account for you and you can borrow the money from your own account."

"What?"

"It's called creating the paper trail. The paper trail is needed to maintain the cover. You need to learn to protect your cover. I don't want to scare you, but your life may one day depend on how well your cover stands up to scrutiny."

"OK, I hear you. We'll do it your way."

"Let's go to the bank. We also need to set up a loan to buy a boat!"

"What? Only I need to maintaining the cover?"

"It's not going to be a luxury yacht."

PANAMANIANS TEND TO BE very reserved with strangers. However, with friends they are very open and eager to help. The Captain is the kind of friend that will help in any way he can and he is always happy to see an old friend even after a long absence. He is an airline pilot but he knows just about **everyone** in Panamá, or at the very least, he knows the person that knows the right person.

I am sure I will find him here! The Balboa Yacht Club is his favorite watering hole after a long international flight.

"Captain, how have you been? How is the family?"

"Wow! It has been a long time! How long has it been?"

He stands up and gives me a big hug and slaps me on my back with both hands.

"Let's not get into that, figuring it out alone would take way too much time."

"OK, let's have a drink. Who's your friend?"

He asks me acknowledging the Mexican's presence.

"He's my partner. We have formed a geological exploration company and we're very fortunate having dealt with an oil company in Alaska. I'll only say that the cash will be rolling in as long as they continue to pump the oil. We could retire but we have decided to buy a boat and go treasure hunting."

His face lights like a neon sign with the unequivocal smile, I know the smile means he knows someone who has a boat.

"A boat? What kind of boat are you talking about?"

"I'm thinking an old fishing troller which can be modified as needed with all the necessary equipment for underwater salvage operations."

Now he can't hide it anymore. He started laughing out loud and almost jumping out of his bar stool.

"My friend, you're so lucky! I think I can get you just what you need."

"Oh, oh, how much is this going to cost us?"

I can see that my partner is reacting to what I just said. He does not know the Captain as I do and he thinks we're talking real money here. So I motion him with my hand as the Captain continues to enjoy himself, obviously fantasizing about the deal in his mind.

"Let me ask you something first. Do you need the boat to be in the Pacific or the Atlantic?"

What difference does that make, I'm thinking, and before I can verbalize anything my partner asks in a dry tone.

"What difference does that make? When you are in Panamá you can bring the boat to either Ocean."

The Captain looks at my partner sideways ignoring the question and his comment, and most of all ignoring his tone.

"Where is this boat?"

I throw my arm around the Captain's shoulder, realizing he has had a bit too much to drink, because otherwise he would not have become annoyed by my partner's comment or his question.

"It's in Chiriquí, in Puerto Armuelles at the dry dock."

Looking at the Mexican into his eyes.

"But I'm glad they teach geography in Mexico. You are right, you can bring it across the Canal no problem. If you have the money we can get you the passage."

The Captain is not succeeding at disguising his disgust with the comments made by my partner. I have to defuse this before it goes south.

"OK, so how much for you?"

He looks at me smiling again.

"You know I would never accept any money from you. I was just thinking a family trip to Taboga when you bring the boat to Panamá."

I knew that, I just needed you to say it, so that my partner realizes you are just kidding.

"Deal. Assuming we can get our hands on the boat."

"I'm almost sure you will. Remember the Master Chief?"

"Sure I remember him. Why?"

"He's the owner of the boat I'm talking about. He suffered an accident, he busted an eardrum from a fall and he's no longer able to dive. I'm sure he would be glad to work with you and…"

Again looking at my partner sideways.

"maybe even with your partner. You wouldn't have to buy the boat, just bank roll the operation."

If what the Captain is saying about the boat is true I'm sure I can strike the deal with the Master Chief, he is like family to me.

"Who is this Master Chief?"

"He was one of my instructors at the Naval Academy. He was to me like the professor to you. He is a former Seabee!"

"What is a pinche Seabee?"

The Captain jumped in to answer that one, clearly he was not mad at my partner anymore, I don't think he ever was.

"The Seabees are the Navy's Construction Battalion guys, hence CB's. Those guys build bridges in the middle of the jungles with nothing else than the trees around them and their Swiss Army knives."

He ended the explanation by standing up in attention and saluting. The Mexican kept a straight face, but I could see now the Captain was walking in his direction. It would now be a matter of time for his charm to conquer the Mexican.

"You mean he is also an engineer?"

The Captain kept answering and I don't want to interrupt. They need to get acquainted and the best way is to let them talk to one another so the Captain has a chance to play his charming skill.

"Sort of yes, you're going to get along fine with him."

With that said, the Captain moved away to the men's room without saying another word.

In a much lower tone of voice so no one else can listen I ask

"You remember the number one rule of secrets?...You just tell one person, if you need to, because after that, it ceases to be a secret."

"Yes, I remember. Why?"

"I've never told anyone else that I used to work for the CIA. The Captain nor the Master Chief know. It's very important to protect the cover."

"Understood, (raising his voice again) I'm getting the hang of this believe me. I don't intend to make any move without checking with you first. Not even getting involved with a woman as much as I would like to get laid right now."

"I see. But believe me, in that department, it's easier on your mind and your pocket, to rent than to own. The maintenance becomes a headache, and when you have to be on the move constantly, it becomes impossible. Renting is definitely a better deal when you can't share with your significant other what you do for a living."

"I'm going to stay in Panamá City and explore some rentals before going to sea. So, you go to Chiriquí to see the Master Chief with the Captain."

THE BOAT IS IN dry dock for regular maintenance and modifications the Master Chief wants to make. We arrive at Puerto Armuelles five and a half hours after we departed the following morning.

"I always hated this drive. Explain to me again why we didn't fly."

"The same two reasons I already told you: first, I had been drinking until late last night, and the regs say twelve hour dry spell before flight, it's my license."

"Yeah, yeah, I get it. You drink and have fun and I have to endure the drive."

"The other is I need to go up to Cerro Punta and I did not want to have to rent a car in Chiriquí."

"Say no more, there he is."

"Master Chief, I brought you a visit."

The boat is huge. At least, out of the water it looks impressive. *I was expecting a 40 or 50 foot boat.*

"Capi! It's been a while. Always good to see you again. Hey, man, what are you doing back in Panamá? Of all the persons I could have thought I was going to see this afternoon you would be the last one, I'm so glad to see you again."

Again a bear hug and double hand slaps on the back.

"Master Chief, I am so glad to see you too. Fine boat you have here. Does it float?"

He pushes me away and gives me an accusing look.

"You bet your sweet ass it floats and when I put it in the water the next time it will be the fastest in its class with the modifications I'm making now. I only need to get the clients to pay for the trips and I'll be living like an Arab prince."

"How big is it?"

I ask him as we climb the boarding plank.

"Its length is 95 feet."

"Master Chief the Captain tells me that you might be interested in a deal. I came to propose one to you."

"If it can help me finish with the modifications. I'm interested! After the accident the diving business dried-up."

The Captain raised his hands asking for our attention.

"I'm going to leave the two of you alone, because as much as I would love to be part of this, I have to go to Cerro Punta and go back to Panamá to catch a plane by tonight, the drive is long, and anyway, I don't have money to invest in your venture."

"Have a safe trip, Capi, and thank you for bringing us together."

I turn to the Master Chief and say.

"I'm sure we're going to come to an arrangement but even if we don't, I have agreed with Capi we would give him and his family a ride to Taboga when the boat is in Panamá City, before going off. I'll pay for the gas anyway. Is that OK with you?"

"Sure, if you are paying for the gas, you say where you want to go and we go."

We're so going to close a deal this man has been like a father to me since the Naval Academy.

AFTER CAPI LEAVES the Master Chief gives me a tour showing me the modifications being made to the boat. This man is a genius engineer, the modifications included larger water intakes for cooling the new engines which are high output turbines, at the same time each intake double as water intake for the jet propulsion system. Each engine drives a gear box which can be engaged to drive the jet propulsion system. In combination, both engines are capable of driving the boat up to a speed of 45 knots.

The most impressive part of the modification is that the boat's original propulsion system is still in place and engaged to the gear boxes. It is a double tunnel drive counter rotation propulsion, which is extremely maneuverable at slow speeds because the thrust and rudder actions are almost parallel to the waterline of the craft. With the tunnel drive propulsion engaged the boat is capable of maintaining a fixed position in the water by rotating on its axis simply with one prop in forward and the other in reverse.

Each gear box can be selectively engaged, to a propulsion shaft with a propeller pitched for heavy duty loads, or the jet propulsion for high speed. When the jet propulsion systems is engaged to the gear boxes, the propeller shafts are disengaged and the propellers, shafts and rudders are hidden by rotating a cover enclosing the tunnel to minimize drag.

"My partner who has become a very good friend, just like you Master Chief, except that he doesn't know and I don't intend to tell him, I was a Navy SEAL. I avoid telling anyone else, so I don't have to answer any questions about the black ops. Please don't be surprised if he starts bragging about the SCUBA diving lessons we took."

"I understand not wanting to share with him about you being a SEAL but you mean **you gave him** SCUBA diving lessons."

He said that with a smile on his face, he was my diving instructor.

"No, you heard me right. He **and** I took the lessons together. It was far easier than to explain why I already knew how to dive."

Now his face wears a puzzled look.

"Are you saying you want to rent my boat to go SCUBA diving with your friend?"

"Not quite, let me explain: we made a deal with an Alaskan oil company and we are still collecting a ton of cash from that deal. The thing with oil royalties is that as much oil as can be extracted at some point, the production will begin to drop for a variety of reasons, and I want to have a substitute source of cash in place before that happens. So we're going hunting for the Nazi Gold."

All the time he was listening but with a mesmerized look on his face, finally he was able to verbalize a question.

"What does you partner do?"

"My partner is an expert in electronics. He uses sonar equipment like it was a stethoscope. He was trained by a Russian engineer who was an expert in acoustic resonance. He is a very good engineer too, even if he does not have the title."

"Hey, I don't judge, I don't have the title either so, no problem. All that you have told me sounds very good. When you go fishing for oil in Alaska, I mean, you know the oil is there in the first place, you just have to map it. However, when you go searching for a sunken treasures underwater, where do you start looking if you don't have any idea of where the hell it is? We need to have a general idea of the location, like maybe off the coast of the Yucatán peninsula, or off the coast of Aruba."

"How did you guess it's off the coast of Aruba?"

"Are you serious? Do you know where it is already?"

"Sort of, ever since my days in Annapolis, I have been studying this. At the Academy we learned the Nazi smuggled tons of gold out of Europe before the end of World War II. I have spent every free moment tracking and studying all the information on this subject that I could get my hands on, and I'm convinced that a German Hospital ship, which was scuttled off the coast of Aruba, was carrying a big part of the gold, or if not, it probably has the answer of where most of the gold is located. Why else would the Germans scuttle a hospital ship loaded with medical supplies, unless it had something else very important they needed to conceal?"

"For argument's sake I'll agree with what you are saying but first let me make sure I understand your proposition, I provide my boat, my salvage license and my equipment, you and your partner will handle any diving required and you'll bank roll the operation."

"Correct."

"How much money do you have?"

"Enough to pay for all the repairs and modifications."

"What will be the split?"

"If you accept, we're equal partners, we split any profits three ways. Your boat, license and equipment will make the salvage **legal**, and our money will make the salvage **possible**. To help you make a decision today, we will cover any debt you owe on the boat and equipment, including the repairs and modifications. You can repay us out of your cut when we split the profits and you get to keep the boat."

"It's a deal where do I sign?"

"With you, I don't sign documents. We spit and shake and drink to the success of the venture".

He smiles at me and we hug again.

"Do you think your Mexican engineer could take a look at the submersible?"

He asks, lifting a cover from the equipment.

"What's that? Where did you get it?"

"The submersible was a gift from the Navy. It's a self contained robot."

"A gift?"

"I helped the US Navy recover material from a drug-run by one of the Cartels. The material had been dropped off the coast of Texas in one of the deepest areas in the Gulf of Mexico. The Navy supplied the equipment and the ship. I provided my expertise in Gulf currents to help locate the drugs. The Navy couldn't legally pay me with anything more than regular pay as a reactivated Navy reservist. However, the skipper of the ship, the Impeccable, declared, after the operation ended, that one of the submersibles used in the salvaged had somehow been disconnected from the tether line and was lost in the Gulf waters."

"Some loss!"

"This submersible has a thruster controller board malfunction and the techs on board determined it was better to have it decommissioned than to repair it. The equipment was going to be replaced anyway and the skipper knew I'd be able to fix it given enough time, and that I'd never allow it to go into the wrong hands. Only a handful of the crew ever knew what the skipper did and they were all people who I trained"

"I'm sure the Mexican will be delighted to take a look at it, and he will also enjoy fixing it!"

TWO DAYS LATER, the Mexican arrives at the airport in David, which is the main city and capital of the province of Chiriquí. After picking him up I bring him to meet the Master Chief and the boat at the dry dock in Puerto Armuelles.

"How much longer will the boat be in dry dock?"

"I think it'll be another week or so. Why do you ask?"

"My partner wants to know. He's outside inspecting the hull. You can ask him yourself when he climbs aboard."

Moments later the Mexican comes aboard wide eyed.

"This is no boat, this is a cruise liner. How big is this thing?"

The Master Chief and I start laughing.

"Master Chief this my partner."

"The Master Chief was my professor in the Naval Academy. He taught me everything a sailor needs to know to survive in the Navy."

"I heard you're a Seabee. Is it true you guys build bridges in the middle of the jungle with Swiss Army knives?"

"That is only half true. We didn't carry Swiss Army knives. Why are you interested in the time table at dry dock?"

"Master Chief"

The Master Chief raised his hand motioning to stop.

"Call me Skipper from now on. After all, I'm the captain of this boat."

"OK, Skipper, I was thinking that if we add fuel and fresh water tanks we will increase our range without needing to refuel and replenish. This pinche *botecito* is really big, and maybe we can extend the range. That'd help us to avoid disclosing where we have been or where we're going next."

Looking at us both Skipper starts nodding his head in approval and says,

"I like the way this guy thinks. Have you been training him?"

"Yes, he has. And we also need to add a tether line dispenser with capacity for 10,000 feet of shielded fiber optic cable."

That made Skipper jump.

"What would that be for?"

"For the submersible!"

"The submersible does not need a fiber optic connection to operate. It is self contained. Besides you haven't even looked at it yet."

"I looked it up in the Internet and already ordered the thruster control board to fix it."

"Why do you want to add the fiber optic?"

"I know, the submersible is self-contained, but the fiber optic connection is not for the submersible itself. The connection is for the equipment I'm adding as part of the repairs, and at the same time, it will make a stronger tether line. So we don't actually loose it the same way the US Navy lost theirs."

What he leaves out is that the fiber optic is for the device.

"What equipment are you adding?"

Now you look at me for help? I make a face and shrug my shoulders letting him know he should continue.

"It's not equipment, it's only the sonar probes, modified to connect remotely to my sonar equipment. The detection is more accurate if the probes are closer to the target and with the fiber optic connection the signal degradation will be minimal."

"The boat's sonar will be more efficient and faster than deploying the submersible to do the search."

"I agree and we'll use the boat's sonar to locate the target. But once we've located the target we'll deploy the submersible, I'm changing its name to REMSO for REMote SOnar, it will tell us quickly if the target has the right cargo or not."

"How does it work?"

Now you are in deep water and your sonar is not going to help you. So I look at him to see what he is going to do. The Mexican looks back at me. The

Mexican has clearly lost his words and does not know what to say. I give him a nod and take over the explanation. His shoulders relax as he exhales.

"Skipper, the sonar equipment we're using was developed by a Russian engineer, based on equipment he developed for the Russian Navy after they dropped the project. They had requested that the sonar equipment be capable of detecting our submarines beyond the thermal layers underwater. The equipment didn't cut it. However, after the Russian Navy dropped the project, the engineer continued testing together with his assistant and they realized the equipment was capable of detecting and distinguishing the different materials in an underwater target."

"With this equipment we are be able to detect if there's any treasure present or not. Once the boat's sonar finds a target we'll deploy the submersible and scan the target with the REMSO."

Now you dare speak again, after I clean the path for you. I smile at the Mexican.

"If there's any treasure present we'll find it without having to get wet."

Skipper's looking at both of us, as if we just stepped down from a space ship.

"OK guys; but are you sure the Russians won't want their toy back at some point?"

"It's not their toy. We're absolutely sure the Russian Navy dropped the project because it didn't work the way they wanted. It was developed later by the engineer and his assistant."

"How do you know this?"

"The reason we know this information is because the assistant, was a Mexican who went to the University in Cuba to study electronics and became an expert working with the old Russian. You want to guess who that was?"

I say that pointing with my thumb conspicuously at the person standing next to me.

"I have one more suggestion for you. It's related to the propulsion system. Well, not the propulsion system so much as the hull configuration."

Now Skipper is making a mocking face, like wondering if the young Mexican thinks he is a boat designer too.

"I'm listening. Go ahead."

"It occurred to me that if we ever need to use the jet propulsion to get out of a jam in a hurry, we could use as much advantage as we can even in rough seas. You already modified the rear hull to eliminate the drag from the drive shafts, the propellers and the rudders. Do you think you could modify the forward hull to accommodate a retractable hydrofoil?"

Skipper's jaw drops. His face changes from a mock to surprise to a smile all in less than two-seconds.

"My God, you are brilliant! Why didn't I think about that? That shouldn't be too much trouble at all. It would lift the keel above the rough seas and give us an extra edge, indeed."

Skipper's attitude towards the Mexican changes from skepticism to joy. Respect sets in. Now they were both talking in their same mutual-benefit language.

"I haven't done any calculations on it, but I estimate that, based on the size of the boat, it could easily give us an additional 10 knots, just by raising the hull out of the water and eliminating a great portion of the drag."

"You're not too far from reality."

"I have to go back to Panamá City to place the order for the fiber optic. Can you take me to the airport?"

He asks me and then turns to Skipper.

"I need to know where can we receive the fiber optic in Panamá and have it delivered directly to the boat."

"Sure, I'll make the arrangements in the port of Panamá and will have the information by the time your flight lands. How do I get in touch with you?"

Now Skipper was not only enthusiastic but even warm and friendly as he answers.

OK, this is my queue. I must set the tone for them both. Neither recognizes the need to be security-conscious 24/7.

"We're going to use these secure sat phones from now on. There's one for each of us and the numbers for the other two are already recorded in each of them. We'll be able to keep in touch from anywhere, even if one of us needs to stay on shore and the others are at sea. Don't be alarmed. I'm not doing this because of the Russians, I'm doing it to protect the project if we hit the jackpot. I don't want other salvage companies jumping in before we can arrange the retrieval of any precious cargo we find."

"Can I use it right now? I need to call Capi to ask him to pick me up at the airport, and take me to get the fiber optic."

"The phones are active, knock yourself out."

"OK, I'll wait for you in the car."

He says as he goes down the boarding plank.

"Is your SEAL training still good in case the Ruskies come after us?"

"You don't have to worry about the Russians. We have created a very good cover with a genuine paper trail, in case they come poking around; but that is just as a precaution. However, in response to your question, yes, I can still kick some ass."

When I get into the vehicle, the Mexican questions me.

"Is the Master Chief, all right with the story you gave him?"

"He wants to be called Skipper. And you know that was not a story. Everything I told him is true."

"Except you left some details out."

"Need to know basis. He doesn't need to know about the device itself. I already told him the 'who' and the 'where' we're generating the cash flow from. I had to let him know it was a legit cash flow."

"Is he worried about the Ruskies?"

"He's more worried for you. He's a former Master Chief of the US Navy and, as far as he knows, I was Navy and we both can handle ourselves if it comes to that."

"Mierda! I can throw a punch, if that's what is needed."

"Our cover is our main protection. You just make sure we keep that very secure. For everything else, we're full partners, three ways split. You can trust Skipper, completely, in everything other than the details we just discussed."

"I already trust you, and if you say I must trust him, then I'll just have to trust the pinche gringo."

By now, we have arrived at the airport and he is ready to get out of the car.

"OK, you have a good flight."

THE ADDITIONAL TANKS, the retractable hydrofoil and the fiber optic tether spool are installed and all the other repairs and modifications are completed, the boat has been launched, **it floats**, just as Skipper said it would. The hull modifications both forward and aft are secured and dry.

"What now?"

"Now we do a shakedown run, so we can test all the equipment, and when everything checks out we go on to Panamá. Is anyone making the arrangements for the Canal crossing?"

"Capi's making the arrangements, and he said he will have everything setup so that we can go across the Canal by the time we get back from Taboga. The boat has to be within Panamanian waters and less than one day away from the Miraflores locks before they'll even schedule us to cross."

"What about the submersible? Are we testing it also?"

"That will have to wait until we reach Taboga, because we can't test it underway. We would need to be anchored, or in rotation mode. Besides, we need to have the fiber optic tether installed so we can test the sonar modifications at the same time we test the submersible operation."

"What's the timetable?"

"There's really no big hurry. The treasure is certainly not going anywhere. No one else is looking for it and we have to make sure all the equipment is working 100% before we go across the Canal. Once we reach the Caribbean we have to be in active search mode, from the time we get out of the Gatún locks."

"Now, Skipper it is time you train us in the handling of the boat. It's only the three of us and this is a big boat."

"You're both doing fine pulling the lines and following all my orders."

"Yes, and we're clear that you're in command of the boat. You **are** the skipper. What I'm talking about is how to drive and navigate the boat. We can't afford to stop while you rest, and you'll need to rest. One of us will have to be able to take a shift at the helm, while you rest, or eat, or go to the head, or in the worst case scenario, of an incapacitating injury."

"All right, all right, I see your point. I read you loud and clear."

"You, my friend, will give us a crash course in sonar and radar operations, including the deployment and retrieval of the submersible, for the same reasons. Each of us should be able to do any of the others' tasks at any time, so that we don't need to stop for any other reason than refueling and replenishing supplies. Skipper how long will it take to get to Panamá City?"

"Wait a minute. What are **your** tasks?"

"Yeah, what do we need to learn from you?"

Secure operations are not the exclusive domain of governments. Private companies also must keep their operations secured and protected from competitors. During this trip, security is required for the operation, because if another salvage company finds out what our target is, or they discover where it's located before a legal claim can be established, everything will be lost. The rule for underwater salvage is first come first served. More to the point, first claimant is the owner.

"I'm in charge of security, inventory and weapons. I'll be giving you instructions in weapons and explosive usage."

"Explosives you said?"

"As well as cleaning, disassembling, loading and firing the weapons. I'll also teach you everything you need to know about the NAV computer."

"The what chingado computer?"

"The NAV computer system"

"What is that used for?"

"It's a tactical computer used to determine how much fuel, water, food, bullets, etc. we've got left at any given time."

"Hah! Like an inventory system."

"Actually, it's more than that. You'll be able to assess how much longer we can be underway, before we need to go back to port. Depending on our position, which we should all be able to read once Skipper teaches us. Yes, I said explosives. You never know what you'll need out there, and as far as I know there aren't any hardware stores in the middle of the sea. What we bring with us is what we will have available to do the job."

"OK, OK, you've made your point, loud and clear. If we navigate only in regular sweep mode, cruising like we'll be doing during the search, it could take us more than a week. We can decide how long we want to make the trip, and continue whenever we're comfortable both the shakedown and the training are complete."

"I agree, Skipper, now tell us which one's the throttle and what are all those dials and shiny lights for?"

THE SHAKEDOWN GOES without any major glitches during the first three days. Then we get hit with a cascade of problems. First a fuel line failed because the line filter was clogged and one of the engines has stalled. The Mexican went down to the engine room and is able to replace the filter, but he then realizes we do not have any more replacements units.

During the process he also realizes that the main fuel tank is contaminated with water and rust, which caused the filter to clog in the first place, and that could have caused, eventually, the failure of the filter in the other fuel line. If the first filter had not failed so quickly, both engines would have failed. The new fuel tanks are both clean so after he replaced the filter, he switches to the new fuel tanks, and the engine is successfully restarted. The boat has to return to Armuelles for cleaning and repairing the main fuel tank.

"WE'VE GOT TO MAKE sure we bring all the spare parts we could need with us. Skipper, do you have any idea why the water separator in that tank didn't work?"

"Yes, it is my bad. When we decided to add the other tanks, the repair crew skipped the maintenance on the main tank, and I failed to verify if that part of the work had been performed."

"That's why we're doing a shakedown. Make a note, another point we have to consider from now on, we're **all** responsible for verifying any repair and restocking, double and triple checks on everything. We're all human, and prone to mistakes if one of us misses something, another should catch it. With any luck, it will be very difficult that the three of us miss something in concert."

WHEN THE REPAIRS are completed, the boat goes out again and this time the rest of the shakedown trip goes smoothly. A sweep pattern is plotted on the navigation chart and we rehearse with both the electronic navigation equipment and visual navigation aids for comparison and for practice, in case the electronics fail. I also deploy one of the GPS markers.

The Mexican and I had designed those. He helped me by incorporating a GPS transponder chip with the encrypted beacon signal and combining a buoy, which would all respond only to our own sonar equipment. Markers are needed in case a target is identified and for any reason we have to leave the area before the submersible could be deployed for scanning.

Skipper interrupts my thoughts.

"I feel comfortable with the performance of the equipment. How about you guys?"

"I think we need to practice one more thing, Skipper, and it's something I really expect not to need at all, but I rather be safe than sorry."

"Are you talking about the Russians again?"

"No, Skipper, not the Russians, but any other threat that would require we switch from normal run to jet propulsion, and at the same time deploy weapons for protection."

"Pendejos piratas?"

"You never know. The point is, that if we have to get the hell out of Dodge in a hurry, we should all know what to do in an emergency."

"As always you're one step ahead of me. I knew all that special training you got had to payoff somehow."

"What the fuck is Skipper talking about?"

Shit, here we go again. The secrets we must keep. He asks me in a very low voice so Skipper cannot hear.

"I thought you said he didn't know you were CIA."

I hate having to keep secrets from the two of them but it's for their protection, and mine, for our common protection.

"He's joking, he's always on my case because I tried to become a Seabee and failed."

I look at Skipper and he immediately realized he almost gave away my SEAL background and forms an apology.

"That's right, Mexicano, he learned a lot but not enough to become a Seabee. He became another type of Navy animal"

Not even stopping to take another breath, he went on trying to cover the mistake.

"How about if we do a dry run in slow motion and then we do it again as if someone was shooting at us."

"That is an excellent idea. Do we deploy weapons first, or do we switch propulsion systems first?"

The Mexican is so exited with the expectation of shooting the weapons that he immediately switches to macho, big guns mode.

"I'd suggest that as long as we all know what each of us is supposed to do, we do it together in the dry run, and then we each do our own task at the same time during the live run."

"Let's do the propulsion switch first, so you two get the hang of it. These throttle controls are the same for both propulsion systems. However, you have to remember, when you're switching back to regular propulsion, you will need to cut the throttle back to idle before engaging the shafts."

"Skipper, I can modify the mechanism to automatically cut the throttle before the shafts are connected."

"You know, if I didn't know better, I would think this guy was trying to steal my job. That is a very good idea! Can you help make the modifications in the circuits?"

"Seguro buey, we can do it while the fiber optic is loaded, and test the switch on the way to Taboga."

"Agreed. OK, like I said the throttle controls are the same and the propulsion transfer controls are right below the throttles. All that is needed is to throw the switch and the hydraulic systems will simultaneously conceal the propulsion shafts and the rudders in the aft hull and push the hydrofoil out of the forward hull. At speed of 7 to 20 knots, depending on how rough the sea is, the change may be unnoticeable. If the switch is performed at any speed above 20 knots the change in thrust will be evident almost instantly, because of the reduced drag, and the boat will begin to accelerate reaching the maximum speed in less than 20 seconds, regardless of the conditions of the sea, thanks to the hydrofoil config. Shall we test it gentlemen?"

"Go ahead Skipper, do the switch."

"I already did, you did not notice it. Now, grab on to something!"

The surge in speed is surprising. Even Skipper looses his footing. In a few seconds, the feeling is as if the boat is flying above the water. It almost is. The hydrofoil has the effect of lifting the main hull out of the water, except the portion of the aft hull where the intake and water jets are. The only portions of the hull touching the surface of the water were the aft portions, providing the propulsion, and the small cross section of the hydrofoil, which provides the lift.

A mixed chorus of amazement made us sound like kids seeing tits for the first time.

"Shit."

"Damn."

"Cojones."

"What about the fuel consumption?"

"It's more efficient running the jets?"

"The only reason to run the propellers during regular operations is the additional control with the tunnel drives at the lower speeds. The jets offer great maneuverability at speeds higher than 25 knots, but below seven knots, or for docking and running a grid pattern during the scanning operations, it's more efficient to use the propellers. With the gear reduction boxes the turbines run at almost the same speed when we're doing 20 knots with props or 30 knots with jets."

"Is it my turn now?"

"Show us where your toys are."

"Guys, I just realized that with this kind of surge in speed, it's going to be next to impossible to deploy the weapons after we accelerate. I think we should deploy the guns and conceal them, locked and ready in place once we're out to sea. If we need them, all we have to do is point and shoot.

"We can place one aft and one forward, in opposite corners for best overall coverage."

"Skipper, I suggest we prepare fixed mounts on the rail. I can take care of that out here."

"Sure I'll help you. Let's take a look at the toys and learn how to use them. I have not fired a 50 since I was in the service."

"Shit, Skipper, they are not 50s."

"That's OK, what did you bring, M2's?"

"They are not shitty M2's either. I got a couple of Electric Gatling guns, with the armor piercing rounds, they are more accurate."

Skipper's jaw drops on the deck, but the Mexican didn't have any idea of what was going on, except that whatever it was definitely blew Skipper out of the water.

When Skipper finally pulls up his jaw, he asks;

"What's the firing rate?"

"They are the slower, older model, only 2,000 rounds per minute, but I was able to get the 10,000 round supply drums. I was hoping you would be able to modify the trigger mechanism to limit the burst to maybe 20 or 25 rounds per pull. That way we don't empty the drums so fast."

Shaking his head at me he says,

"Sure let take a look at them."

The Mexican decided not to ask any questions and just listen. He is probably thinking; the two Ex Navy gringos are talking shop as if we're deciding what kind of meat to buy for the barbecue and this is totally out of his expertise.

"I assume one of you'll tell we what I need to do, once you decide it's time to start shooting."

"First, I'm sure Skipper prefers that we don't need to use them at all and so do I. But, like I said before, and I'll now repeat, I prefer to be ready than to be sorry, if the need arrises. Once we have the weapons setup you'll see that with these babies, it's like using a fucking PC, all you have to do is point and click."

"You mean just like if I was using the mouse on a computer? Won't there be someone shooting back at us if we're using these?"

"There is a very good probability someone is trying to shoot at you, but if you start shooting first and with good aim, they will be minced meat ready for shark meals before they can shoot back at us."

COIBA ISLAND IS RIGHT off the coast of the peninsula that is formed by the District of Santiago, southwest of Panamá City, the Island is a National Park. Southwest of Coiba lies Jicarón Island, much smaller and it's also a National Park. Jicarón is uninhabited and rarely visited because the only access to disembark on the island is on the western side, the side away from the mainland. If there are no boats anchored, then there are no visitors. The perfect place to work on the modification and weapons' installation on the rails, plus do some target practice, without being noticed.

"Is there any way we can monitor the radar without having to be in front of the screen on watch. This is draining my eyes, but I don't want any surprise visitors. Today is Saturday and it's the day most people take their boats out."

"Sure, let me ask Skipper if this system has an audio jack that I can hook it up to the deck speakers. That way, you can come out on deck with us. We can use the extra hands. Those pinche drums are larger than I thought and we're having trouble fixing them to the railing."

"Can't we just strap them down to the deck?"

"Hey, Skipper, I think we can promote this guy to engineer too. How did he flunk-out as a Seabee? Did he fuck some pendejo admiral's wife?"

"I think we have some Kevlar straps below."

Skipper and the Mexican look at each other, one of them probably wondering why he is surprised an Ex-SEAL would be so prepared and the other wondering why he is surprised an Ex-CIA field operative would be so prepared, but they are both recognizing neither should share his thoughts with the other.

"What? Shit yeah! I always have Kevlar straps they're like condoms you shouldn't leave home without them. You never know when you are going to need really quick to tie down ammo drums. By the way guys, I've decide we need to deploy the guns after we leave port because there's no way we would be able to set this shit doing 30 knots."

"We're so glad you see it that way. We were wondering, but neither of us had figured out how to bring it up with you."

"You fucking clowns! We're equal partners. That means if you're going to french kiss then, we'll fucking kiss three ways all the time, on equal basis."

"And one more thing, I've also decided that a big part of the cost of the modifications has been due to the changes we suggested, so we're all sharing all cost, the whole shit. You don't owe us shit. The split will be clean three ways. Which brings me back to what I was going to say, if anyone needs to say anything going forward you just go right ahead and say it. Don't fuck around. We'll all listen to each other. That's why we need to learn what each other does, so we can all substitute for each other, so we can make on the spot decisions, think and act alike because we all know what needs to be done. Like fucking Musketeers. One for all..."

"And all for one! But shit, you may not be the Skipper of the boat, but as far as I'm concerned you're the Big Kahuna for this mission."

"Orale, mosqueteros, I totally agree."

"And, you my friend, you have proven to be almost as good as a Seabee. You are a genius mechanic and most importantly a fucking expert in electronics. The enhancements you have made to my radar, radio and sonar are beyond anything I could have imagined."

"I suggest that we stop kissing each other's asses, and get on with our business. You are Skipper, I'm Chief and you're Sparks. From now on those are our war names and, gentlemen, we've got to get ready for war."

"Agreed. Let's finish tying these babies down so we can do some target practice."

"It's getting dark we should wait until morning to do the target practice."

"These drums are standard issue aren't they?"

"Yes, that's exactly why we should wait till morning."

"What are you two talking about now?"

"Chief here is worried the glow from the tracers would give us up, so we'll do target practice when there's daylight and the glow from the tracers won't be seen from far away."

"Skipper, you want me to run one of the engines to recharge the batteries? The engines have been off since we dropped anchor and we've been running the all the electronics, plus the electric tools, and we're going to continue using plenty of illumination to complete these installations."

"Check the gauges first. How much juice are we drawing?"

"It's only showing 13 amps but that's awful low for the electronics and all the lights we're running."

"Not when the illumination is all LED. I had it all retrofitted and rewired in dry dock. Why do you think it took me so long and cost so much?"

"Wait a minute, the main bank shows more than 950 amps we should be at least 25% less by now with the electric tools running this afternoon thru the power inverter. What kind of batteries did you put into this boat?"

"It's not the batteries is the solar panels."

"What solar panels? Where?"

Sparks and I raise our eyes to look for an array of solar panels but can't find any.

"Look closely at all the siding around the superstructure of the bridge."

"Now it's my turn to be ignorant. What are you two talking about? Are we going to run out of power or not?"

"Chief, Skipper has turned this pinche crummy looking outer shell into a cutting edge electronics platform and a mean lean fast machine. We're so fucking fast, we could escape from someone trying to pursue us even before they'd seen us, because our radar is better, or we could catch up with most targets even at their highest speed before the target even knew we were in pursuit of them because those solar panels act as radar deflectors, the way they are placed around the superstructure of the bridge."

"Skipper, is there anything we should know before going on?"

I ask turning to him.

"It's like this; before you came along with your proposal, I had decided to take a stab at modifying this boat to try to sell it to the US Coast Guard for surveillance in the Caribbean. I couldn't do anymore diving, not even for diving instructions, my other passion besides building bridges in the middle of the jungle."

"With or without the pinche Swiss Army knives?"

Sparks asks making a mocking face at Skipper.

"Anyway, you know what I mean, my technical expertise is the only thing I have left that I could make money on, since I cannot continue diving. I could not trust any stranger to partner up on salvage operations or diving instruction."

"Orale! You're trusting me! I'm a stranger to you."

"You were a stranger to me before I met you, but you came together with this guy, and I know him from way back, and believe me, I know that if he trusts you, I can trust you, even if you're Pancho Villa, and I think you know that much too."

IT IS A SPARKLING Sunday morning, there are no clouds. After breakfast on deck, outside behind the bridge, the anchors are lifted and the boat goes out to deeper waters. Without dropping anchor, the first target is deployed. Altogether, the targets will be six weather balloons, three filled with air so they float on the water; the other three filled with helium, all tethered to fishing lines so they can be retrieved after the target practice. Bullets will sink to the bottom of the sea, but weather balloons have a nasty habit of floating until someone finds them, or until they reach the coast. Either way, they raise questions and mark a trail you don't want to leave behind.

"Skipper, you want to go first, so that Sparks has a chance to watch and doesn't find any surprises?"

"Sure, Chief, but I'd suggest we start pulling, so we lower the flying targets these rounds are going to go very far, if we shoot so high in the air."

"I hear you, Skipper, but we'll keep an eye on the radar in case anyone approaches from the direction we're shooting. I want to make sure we can shoot at a plane or a chopper, if any should show up. Shooting at a low flying target would be about the same as shooting at a target on the surface."

"Sparks, you watch the tracers and see how Skipper uses them to follow the target by the second or third burst you should be able to hit the target, remember every burst is 25 rounds so after 4 bursts you have fired 1% of the total rounds available in the drum."

"How many drums do we have on board?"

"Only four, one on the gun and one backup for each gun."

"OK, got it. We only have 10,000, or rather 20,000, no wait that would be a total of 40,000 rounds for practice and protection."

"Negative! We can reload the drums when we exhaust them. But that's a bitch to do."

"You have more rounds on board? How many more? How did you bring 'em on board without us noticing?"

"I'll be dammed! You are a scary son of a bitch! Sparks, he did not bring the munitions aboard, you did!"

"What? Who? When? I did not!"

"Yes, you did, when you loaded the ballast down to the keel compartments."

"Skipper, you said that those were fucking ballast load!"

"My friend, anything that weights the bottom of the boat is, like you say, fucking ballast load."

"Chief, what else do we have down there, next to the keel?"

"Ah, don't worry Skipper. The C4 is very stable, and I made sure it was packed insulated, so there is no risk of electrical detonation. Besides, if something else causes that C4 to detonate, we would have been dead long before that happened! Hey, you don't need to shit in your pants! I'm just jerking you around."

AFTER SKIPPER completes his practice, the spent targets are retrieved and a next set of targets is deployed. Sparks is such a fast learner he hits the air target with his second burst and the water target with the first burst. I hit both targets with the first burst.

"Skipper, can we put another kind of target in the water and run the boat with the jets at maximum speed? I'd like to simulate a high speed chase, even though it would not be the same as shooting forward, it should give us the feeling good enough. What do you think?"

"We can wrap a couple of pots or pans in a bundle with Kevlar straps. If Pancho Villa here is able to hit that bouncing ball while we're running at 30 knots and we loose the target, it will sink. I don't think any of us will be able to hit anything while running at 30 knots, but it will be good practice."

AS IT TURNED OUT I'm not able to hit the target directly even after six bursts. But considering how close the bullets were hitting in the water around a target of that size, I would have done enough damage to a larger target the size of a boat. Skipper is also very close with only four bursts.

"I don't want to waste more rounds. That way Pancho Villa can shoot up to eight bursts if he needs to, and we keep the usage at an even six bursts per shooter."

"Shit, thanks for your vote of confidence, Skipper. Since I'll have more chances than you guys, please run it at maximum speed. That way we will really get a feeling of what we're up against."

"I will, but you better grab on to your cojones."

"OK, I'm ready. Punch it!"

THE BOAT'S MAXIMUM speed under jet power with the hydrofoil extended is clocked at 55 knots, more than Skipper or Sparks had expected. We have never pushed it to its limits before, and we are all pleasantly surprised. The faster the boat goes, the steadier the ride becomes, due to the hydrofoil lift efficiency increasing at higher speeds. Sparks decides to try an idea he had when he watched Skipper shooting. Skipper had swept the gun from side to side therefore crossing the target's path going up and down. Skipper never hit the target itself but was very close on every burst, close enough to cause severe damage to a larger target.

"Fuck! That is a hit. How did you come up with that idea?"

"I saw Skipper moving the gun from side to side, crossing the target's trajectory as it jumped up and down, and I thought, if I try moving the gun slightly up and down I might catch it on the bounce."

"If we have to do this for real, Pancho Villa is operating the forward gun."

ONE POT IS LOST, the armor piercing round turned the pot into a strainer. Sure, only pieces larger than a baseball would be stopped by that strainer, but it is a great conversation piece in the galley. The official explanation to outsiders is that the plasma solder misfired next to the pot. No one will ever ask why the pot was next to where the plasma solder was being used.

Surely no one will ever be told we were doing target practice with armor piercing rounds

UNDER THE WATER THE FIRST TIME

THE MARINA AND RESORT at *Fuerte Amador* is located at the far end of the Causeway. The Causeway is the protection to the entrance of the Panamá Canal on the Pacific Ocean. It was built with the dirt dug from the Culebra Cut and it joins three islands off the entrance to the Canal on the Pacific. When the latest excavations were made to widen the Culebra Cut the additional dirt was used to widen the causeway and the surface area around the islands. Now, the road is wider and there are several commercial developments on the Causeway. To Panamanians, it's simply known as Amador. The view from Amador at night is outstanding, with the city skyline and *Las Americas* bridge both illuminated.

"It's great you are here already. Fortunately, we do not have to spend too much time in this luxury marina. Everybody is looking at us as if we were going to scratch their yachts."

"Don't worry, Master Chief, they're just jealous because your boat is bigger. Yours doesn't require a registration with numbers, for larger boats only the name of the vessel they just hate not having the best."

"Yes, but why do you mention that? Did you have any trouble scheduling us for the Canal crossing."

"Yes, you're correct, Sir."

"Skipper, what's going on?"

"Aw, fuck, probably nothing. But when I acquired the boat, its name was *El Pescador,* the Panamanian vessels' registry allows a buyer to register a newly acquired vessel with a different name and I changed it to *Seeker,* but I have not received the paperwork yet, and we won't be able to cross until we straighten that shit out."

"Not to worry gentlemen! Got a friend at the Canal's Administration office and he alerted me to the problem before the request was derailed."

"What problem?"

"The original paperwork was sent to the dry dock in Puerto Armuelles, but apparently since they had started to work on the vessel under the old name, they filed the paperwork and forgot to tell you when they released it from dry dock."

"The name change was approved?"

"The dry dock operators have requested from the registry that the owner be given a chance to correct the oversight of making the name change on a timely basis. My friend who works at the Canal's Administration office reminded everyone involved that the rules require delivery of the notification to the vessel's registered owner, in addition, to the custodial."

"You mean the dry dock operator in this case!"

"Yes, and since the custodial is responsible for a vessel to navigate under the correct name, according to the registration, it seems nobody wanted to create problems for the vessel **or** to loose their respective licenses and jobs."

"Capi, how much time do we have to make the change?"

"We have to make the name change in Taboga. The correct name has to be shown on the bow and stern by the time you go into Panamá Port."

"We'll need to go into port for that. We don't have the paint or the stencils."

"No, Skipper, you can't dock in any port with the wrong name on the vessel. I already bought the marine paint and the stencils. All we have to do is make the change while we're anchored in Taboga. While we're anchored **away** from the dock."

Sparks and I were standing on deck with our mouths opened not knowing what to say. Everything Capi was saying sounded very serious and at the same time it seemed that all was under control.

"Capi, is that why you asked us to pick you up at the marina in Amador? To avoid us going into Panamá Port?"

I ask him.

"In part, but mainly I was trying to avoid you having to use your radio with the wrong call sign when you approached the port. The registry database is already updated, and you coming into port calling out you were *El Pescador* would have caused all kinds of embarrassments for many people."

"Why didn't you alert us not to use the radio?"

"I couldn't. I was calling you from the Registry's office where I was picking your registry papers. I couldn't say anything about the wrong name on the vessel in front of the people at the registry. Luckily, I caught you before you were closer to port. How the hell did you get here so fast anyway?"

"Skipper, do you think we can give Capi and his family a **smoother** ride?"

"Let me get a bit farther from Amador and we'll show him."

"Show me what'?"

"Capi, what would you say if I told you we can be in Taboga within twenty minutes?"

"I would say that you don't know what it's to ride a boat in choppy seas and that there are no roads out here."

Right after Capi finished saying that, the switch occurred and the smooth ride and acceleration made him change his mind. Skipper only pushed up to the point where the hydrofoil lifted the hull completely out and made the ride steady, about 32 knots. Twenty minutes later Seeker, formerly *El Pescador,* was dropping anchor off Taboga Island.

"If you guys don't strike it rich where you are going, we can set up rides to Taboga 10 times per day and make more money each weekend than the other operators make in one month."

"Skipper? It's your boat, your call. You want to make this run from now on? Or, try out what we proposed first, and then come back here and try what Capi suggests?"

Sparks eyes almost popped out of their sockets when he heard the question and he lost his breath, at least until he heard Skipper laughing out loud and saying he has always wanted to drive a boat thru the Canal crossing.

"Chief, you had me going there for a minute!"

"Don't sweat it, I was just yanking your chain."

"Skipper, I suggest you point the stern away from land and drop the aft anchor so we can work on the name change without attracting too much attention."

Capi adds.

"Do that and I'll go into the water with my family to make it look like business as usual while you guys work on the name change."

CAPI HAS PROVIDED THE marine paint and the stencils needed to paint the new name, Sparks rigs hanging chairs and the electric tools and the air compressor to remove the old name and paint the new one in minutes. Then each of us take position, two on the bow and one stern. Within minutes the old name has been scraped off the boat and the stencils with the correct name are fixed in place. After the paint is applied the job is completed so quickly that to any observer it would have looked as cleanup maintenance on the boat.

"ARE YOU SURE, HONEY?"

"Yes, I must've dropped it because I had it on when I came into the water and now I don't have it."

"Skipper, do you have a mask aboard? My wife dropped her necklace."

"A mask will do your no good. It's too deep here not even diving equipment will help."

"Skipper, that would be a good target for the REMSO!"

"Without the fiber optic tether how are you going to do that?"

"The depth finder is registering only 30 phantoms under the keel. With regular shielded cable there is no degradation at less than 330 feet, which would be over 50 fantoms."

"Electric cable will not be strong enough for hoisting the REMSO."

"We can use rope as tether and plastic tie wraps to keep the cable and the rope together."

"Sparks, you go ahead with the wiring and I'll ask Chief to help me rig the rope into the spool to hoist the REMSO."

"Capi, don't worry. We have something that may help us to find the necklace."

Skipper is trying to reassure Capi.

"Are you sure Skipper?"

Capi is very worried.

"Skipper has not seen this in action yet, Capi, but trust me. If the REMSO is within 30 feet of that necklace, I can find and retrieve it with the robotic arm."

Says Sparks to Capi.

"I hope you can retrieve it."

"Can you describe the necklace to me?"

Sparks asks.

"It's an expensive necklace. I don't even know why she didn't take it off."

"I was looking for a more detailed description."

"Here, look at this picture, I just took it before she went into the water."

"Great! What is it, gold and diamonds?"

"Exactly! Like I said, very expensive."

"Ready with the connections, we can launch when you are ready."

"Skipper, you operate the hoist so I can run the wires on the pulley and fix the tie wraps as we deploy."

IT TAKES THE REMSO roughly three minutes to dive down to within ten feet off the bottom. With the use of the internal GPS the REMSO is capable of following a programmed search pattern against the boat's GPS fix, even if the boat was moving the two GPS's system are capable of coordinating a search pattern. For this search the boat needs to maintain its position because the necklace has fallen off when Capi's wife was right next to the boat on the port side. The search pattern was started under the stern towards the bow and then moving slowly towards the port side.

"Chief, come take a look at this!"

Sparks sounds surprised and exited at the same time.

"Is that what I think it's? Why the dots?"

Now I'm the one who is surprised.

"I'm not sure until we bring it up but my gut's telling me the device is able to distinguish between the gold **and** the diamonds."

"Did you record the search data?"

"Never stopped. I set it up on auto record after you convinced us the guns should be deployed when we leave port."

"OK, we will look at the data when we're crossing, I hear it will take us a least ten to twelve hours to go across. For now we go top side and share with our guests the happiness of recovering the necklace. Grab it and bring it up."

"I'm ahead of you, already bringing the REMSO up."

Sparks says to me and then he calls out to Skipper.

"You may start retrieving the REMSO the package is in the bag."

"Did you get it?"

Capi asks.

"Unless someone else has dropped another gold necklace with diamonds in this place, I think we recovered yours."

THE REMSO IS HOISTED out of the water, secured in its cradle and connected to recharge the batteries. We remove the stencils, raise the anchors and Seeker is underway in a few minutes. First, we drop Capi and his family off at Amador and then Seeker continues into the port for the fitting of the fiber optic cable.

Thanks to the name change blunder at the dry dock in Puerto Armuelles, the Canal administration authorized passage without delay whenever Seeker was ready to go. **No waiting time**, the Panamanian registry office wanted Seeker out of territorial waters as soon as possible, trying to avoid the embarrassment which would be triggered if the information about this blunder became known.

For the first time in several days, Seeker's crew will be able to get a full night sleep, docked at port drawing power from the dockside instead of running the engines. The air conditioner is enjoyed without the noise from the turbines.

The next morning, the fiber optic arrives at dockside and the spool is loaded. Once the rest of the supplies are loaded and the refueling is completed, Seeker radios in a request for scheduling the crossing and it's authorized immediately.

"It feels good to be treated as royalty for a change. Only cruise liners get this kind of treatment and they have to pay extra for it."

"Yeah but I can't shake the feeling that this was not caused by an honest mistake."

I say but I'm really thinking out loud.

"You're just paranoid. ***Everyone*** is just trying to cover their asses and it turns out to be a coincidence in our favor. If you ask me this is a sign of good fortune at the beginning of our voyage."

"I sincerely hope you are right, but I don't believe in luck, and I don't believe in coincidences."

OVER THE WATER AGAIN

THE CANAL CROSSING GOES smoothly except for the fact that we are required to allow a safety inspection after coming out of the Gatun Locks, before departure from Colón. Departure safety inspections are not routinely performed. They are requested at random, but Seeker is a Panamanian vessel and we cannot ignore a request for inspection within Panamanian waters, even if it's carried out by the US Coast Guard assisting the Panamanian government.

"Thank you, Commander we will make sure we comply with the regulations and keep one life jacket per person, available topside at all times from now on, I understand the logic of the regulation."

"Skipper, the crew should also consider wearing the life jackets when you're working out on deck while underway. That's not required by regulations but it's a good safety practice, Sir. We always wear our jackets when we're on duty. Permission to disembark, Skipper."

"Permission granted, Commander."

After the USCG officers leave Sparks asks.

"Do they always video tape the safety inspections, Chief?"

"It's SOP since 9-11 Sparks. They do it as an excuse to take our pictures and run face recognition software for ID purposes. They don't have the authority to request ID's from the crew of any vessel unless we attempt to disembark or they find anything suspicious onboard."

"Will that be any problem. I'm not a US citizen like you and Skipper."

"Do you have any kind of criminal record in Mexico, or any other place?"

"Not that I know of."

"Then you don't have to worry."

After the boat is ready Skipper calls on the radio.

"This is Seeker, to Port Authority of Colón. We just completed departure safety inspection and request clearance for departure, over."

The response on the radio comes back immediately.

"This is Port Authority of Colón, Seeker, you are cleared for departure. Thank you for your cooperation. Over and out."

"OK, guys, pull and secure the lines. We're cleared for departure."

"Aye aye, Skipper."

THE WEATHER IS CLEAR and the sea is calm. Maybe Skipper is right. The beginning of this voyage is looking good after all.

"Sparks, please tell me when we're clear of Panamanian waters and clear of surface contacts within 8,000 yards."

"Thinking of engaging the jets, Skipper?"

"Yeah, why not? That way we can recoup the time we lost on the safety inspection and be in Cartagena before dark."

"Why go into Cartagena at all? We can continue directly to Aruba, one shot we have enough fuel."

"Sparks, you should know by now, Chief is always insisting we protect the cover. Right?"

"Yes, Skipper, but I don't understand what does that have to do with going into Cartagena, when we're capable of reaching Aruba without refueling."

"This boat can reach Aruba from Colón nonstop with the modifications we have, but a normal boat of this class could not make it without refueling at least once. Do you want to announce to **Everyone** that this boat is capable of such a long trip at high speeds?"

"Say no more, Skipper, when you're right you're right, Sir."

"Skipper, we just cleared Panamanian territorial waters, but there're still about 60 surface contacts within 8 k's."

"Not surprised. We're in the main traffic lane of the Caribbean coming in and out of the Canal. Let's call it at 5 k's. No one will notice us speeding unless they were tracking us. Anyway, I don't plan to exceed 25 knots. At that speed, we should reach Cartagena within 12 hours. It'll still be before dark"

"Understood."

"We won't deploy the guns. We'll just keep the hand guns available and the rifle locker open. Also the suggestion the Commander gave us about always wearing the jacket while on duty..."

"What about it?"

"We're going to follow it, starting now! The reason the US Coast Guard wears those jackets is because they double up as flack jackets and flotation devices, they're made of Kevlar."

"Don't tell me our jackets are..."

"Why are you surprised? Come on, guys, I hope we don't need them, but I prefer to have them. Standard US Coast Guard approved jackets!"

"You think that Commander took note of that?"

"He should have. I think he made the point to see what our reaction would be. Remember we were on candid camera."

"Skipper, no contacts within 5 k's, but there's one contact just outside 7 k's that if I didn't know better, I would think, they were tracking us."

"We'll know if they're tracking once we speed up. Gentlemen, just in case let's put on the jackets **now** and do a weapons check, please. Sparks, how high can this radar look up in the air?"

"With this equipment, we can track from the surface to maybe 50,000 feet up, unless it's a B2 stealth bomber, or an A117, we should be able to track it."

"Check towards the Northeast look for a stationery contact about 15,000 feet above."

"Can you give me a more specific bearing?"

"Sure, look it up in the charts, the Southwest tip of Puerto Rico. The Federal Government operates an over the horizon radar mounted on an aerostat. It floats at 15,000. If it's floating today, it's tracking us."

"Negative. But the surface contact is definitely tracking us, Skipper, when you engaged the jets and accelerated, the contact matched our speed and course."

"Any other contacts above? Maybe something flying in a search patterns above us?"

"Negative, Chief only birds up there. What are you looking for?"

"Can they track us at that distance with radar?"

"Sure, a luxury yacht easily has sophisticated navigational equipment and, with powerful engines, could easily match our current speed. You're definitely paranoid."

"Yeah, but even paranoids are followed sometimes! Keep watching and let's see if they follow us into Cartagena. Skipper, can we make it look as if we're going to San Andrés and then divert to Cartagena?"

We sure can. I was avoiding San Andrés to maintain our speed. But we can pull back to 18 knots and watch to see if they match our speed and course."

"Anyone want a peanut butter sandwich?"

"Chief, I can cook something. You don't have to show-off your culinary skills."

"No, mister, you have to watch that contact on the radar closely, and the peanut butter is for killing the appetite not for showing off my kitchen skills. That I'll accomplish tonight, when I prepare my world renown pasta primavera in olive oil."

"He's right, Sparks. You best keep watching the scope and read me any changes when I change speed or course."

"Aye aye, Skipper."

"Here, have your sandwiches now, so you'll have an appetite when we dock in Cartagena."

"Sparks, I'll lower our speed to 15 knots now. Keep and eye on the contact."

"Also, check again for contacts above us."

"Negative on contacts above, other than birds. But they're matching our speed and continue on same heading, 50 degrees."

"Skipper, do you still think I'm being paranoid?"

"Chief, the driver may be just following us thinking why bother plotting if I can follow the trail or..."

I cut him off.

"Or, maybe, the US Coast Guard decided to follow us. They have the sophisticated radars and fast boats, like those new 45 footers with jets."

"I don't think those have the range, but you could be right."

"Skipper, I don't know if I'm right or not, but I don't like to have a tail. Let's change course to Cartagena right now and increase our speed to see what they do."

"OK, Chief, let's do it your way. Sparks keep a close eye on them, and call their every move."

"Aye aye, Skipper."

"Changing course to 120 degrees towards Cartagena and making my speed 35 knots."

"Contact is not matching, they're maintaining heading 50 degrees but are increasing speed to 22 knots."

"Follow the contact until you loose it."

"Aye aye Chief, no change in contact speed or heading."

"Chief, you still think it was the Coast Guard?"

"I don't know Skipper, but it's too much of a coincidence after that departure safety inspection. Something doesn't add up here."

"One thing we can be sure. It's not the Ruskies!"

"Maybe not the Ruskies, but if it's not the Coast Guard either, then who?"

"Cartel, maybe?"

"If they somehow found out about the modifications we've made, they could be after the boat. That is something to consider. We have been so worried about keeping our cover for the sake of the Russians, that we may have inadvertently attracted the Cartel's attention."

"I would prefer it was the pinche Coast Guard following us. Better some gringo cabrones to these Colombian mother fuckers. Right?"

Says Sparks.

"We're 20 miles off Cartagena. I'm switching back to standard propulsion. Let's go into port and have the pasta, and a good nights rest. Tomorrow we'll replenish all our supplies to the hilt. When we go out, we'll wear our jackets have our weapons available at all times, and deploy the guns as soon as we're in international waters. From now on, we must be on alert for any craft approaching us until we're certain of their identity and purpose."

THE DOCKING AT Cartagena's port is uneventful. Seeker is assigned space at the fisherman's marina, next to a cargo terminal where the boat has access to refueling facilities, dockside warehouses and electrical power from the dock which avoids the need of running the engines overnight. Weapons are kept handy and the electronics are kept active just as a precaution. Shortly after dawn, Seeker obtains clearance for departure after settling with the marina for the supplies, the fuel and the electrical juice.

If you're trying to avoid detection from prowlers, you lay low, try to blend in, don't make any special request, and pay cash. But if you want to leave a clear trail so you can verify if someone is following you, then you make excessive requests that a normal salvage boat would not make, like high speed internet connections, large amounts of stores to clearly indicate that you want to have supplies for a long trip, in general run up a bill.

Then you try to pay with a card that you know will be declined, so you have to use a fancy corporate credit card and *Everyone* around you notices. That way you leave the paper trail you want to leave **and** your crew mates have a chance to observe who remained attentive during the incident and who just didn't care.

It's called observing the observer and it's a very useful surveillance technique, when you need to discover who's tracking you, or when you aren't sure if anyone may be trying to follow you.

"Did you see anything?"

"I didn't but maybe Skipper was able to see better from the boat."

"Let's go."

"Permission to come aboard, Skipper."

"Permission granted."

"Anything?"

"There was one guy behind you. I think he was out of Sparks field of view. As soon as your card was declined he pulled his cel phone and made a call, and he didn't end the call until you guys came out of the office with the clearance paperwork."

"OK, that makes it official. I'm now paranoid. Gentlemen, I suggest we go **now.** Out at sea we have a better chance to see any threats approaching. We need to clear this up once and for all before we start the search in Aruba. Right now, there're too many eyes on us for whatever reasons."

"Agreed. Let's get the fuck out of here as soon as possible."

THERE IS NO DEPARTURE safety inspection coming out of Cartagena and once Seeker is in international waters we put the boat on fixed rotation mode, around it central axis, while we deploy the forward and aft guns.

"Sparks! What the fuck happened to the radar audio signal?"

"Why?"

"Look at 9 o'clock from the center line. A mast on the horizon! Go, check it out, go, go, go!"

"Mierda!"

"Skipper help me hold this drum in place"

"We both push the drum together."

"OK thanks"

Skipper keeps the drum in place while I finish strapping the drum.

"Now go, go, cover the other gun with the canvas and I'll finish this one."

"Contact, bearing 359 degrees. They are coming straight to us. They're making almost 30 knots! Holly chingada! That's a fast cabrón for its size! Sorry, guys, I left the headphones hooked in. Won't happen again."

"Let's hope you have a fucking second chance."

"Hold on, guys, I've switched to jet and we're going to blast out of here!"

"Sparks, I want constant reads of what this motherfucker is doing until I tell you to stop."

"Contact, bearing 359 degrees. Still coming at us straight. They are making almost 30 knots!"

"Full throttle now! We should be doing above 45 knots in less than a minute."

"Contact, bearing 355 degrees. Still coming at us making 29 to 30 knots!"

"Our course is 90 degrees; speed is 38 knots and climbing."

"Contact, bearing 350 degrees. Still coming at us making 30 knots!"

All of a sudden we hear over the radio

"This is the US Coast Guard, Seeker please heave to! Over"

"Skipper! It's the Coast Guard! They are hailing us!"

Again over the radio

"This is the US Coast Guard, Seeker please heave to! Over"

"They don't have jurisdiction over a foreign vessel in international waters!"

Says Skipper. As the owner of the boat, he's very jealous of an interception. However, this could get ugly fast, and we do not have anything to hide.

"Skipper, that is why they are saying **PLEASE** instead of firing warning shoots across our bow."

"Let's hear them out."

Disgusted as Skipper is he knows it's the right thing to do.

"Give me that fucking mike!"

Very pissed over the radio

"This is Seeker, Coast Guard please state your intentions. Over"

Over the radio

"This is the US Coast Guard, Seeker we're requesting permission to board for a safety inspection! Over"

Skipper turns the mike off and says to Sparks and me

"Another fucking safety inspection, my ass, they can go fuck themselves this time."

Over the radio and now clearly loosing his patience and clearly showing in his tone of voice.

"This is Seeker, Coast Guard. You don't have jurisdiction while we're on international waters. Over"

There is silence for about a whole minute. In the mean time both boat maintained course and speed.

Then comes a **different** voice over the radio, a voice I recognize immediately. It's my CIA handler.

"This is the US Coast Guard, Seeker, or do we need to address *El Pescador*? We're requesting permission to board! Over"

I put my hand on Skipper's shoulder and say.

"Wait Skipper don't answer!"

"What is this? Why is the Coast Guard calling out our old name?"

Skipper asks again with the mike off addressing only us.

"Give me the mike, Skipper!"

He is trying to contact me. Why the hell now? And here? I grab the mike and answer over the radio.

"This is Seeker, Coast Guard, we will comply with your heave to request, and we also grant you permission to board. Over and out"

Skipper jumps at my throat.

"Chief, what the fuck are you doing?"

Sparks is also surprised but doesn't say anything. He is just shaking his head. He probably already realized it has something to do with the CIA.

"I need you both to trust me now, more than ever! I **know** that last voice. They only want to talk to me. We're going to let them board us. I'll go to the Coast Guard boat with our registry papers and passports. You'll surrender your handguns when they board us. I'll get this straightened out and we can be on our way in a short while. Trust me!"

They both answer one after the other, but their voices sound like children who have just been scolded by their father.

"Aye aye, Chief. I trust you."

"Aye aye, Chief. I trust you too."

Skipper is probably thinking this has something to do with my black ops stuff from when I was SEAL. Sparks is probably thinking it has to do with CIA business and he is most certainly correct. Seeker heaves to, as the USCG is requesting. We are side by side and 5 armed US Coast Guard officers board Seeker. I go aboard the US Coast Guard vessel. As soon as I'm in private with my handler, I demand an explanation.

"What the fuck's going on? The CIA better have a dammed good reason to send you here and blow my cover. Are you reactivating me?"

"What in hell are you talking about? I'm not here to contact you. I just learned this morning that you're involved in this because you were spotted aboard Seeker."

"Then why the fuck were you tracking us out of Colón yesterday morning?"

"We just came out of Gitmo this morning. What the hell are you talking about? What are you doing aboard that boat? Why did you pick up passengers off the marina in Amador, went to Taboga, changed the name of the boat, and how the hell did you arrange to cross the Canal on a priority basis?"

"You've been tracking us since we arrived in Amador?"

"More accurately, since you left Armuelles. We know the Cartel paid for your boat's modifications and arranged for the dry dock to let you sail under the old name,"

That triggered all kinds of alarms everywhere in my head.

"I'm giving you the opportunity to come clean with me. Tell me who the hell are you working for."

"You got it all wrong! That problem with the vessel's name was a blunder at the dry dock. It was cleared. That's why they let us correct it in

Taboga before entering the Port of Panamá, to avoid the embarrassment. I paid for all the work at the dry dock. That is my partner and I paid the bill at the dry dock. Skipper's an Ex-Navy guy, a former Seabee, and my other partner, Sparks, is a Mexican citizen, an electronic genius. I've been working with him for a long time. We're clean, I'm telling you. Your Intel is all fucked up!"

"I know very well who Skipper is. But that Mexican has Russian ties!"

"Yes! No! I know! That's how I met him. My last job before I was let go. Remember the Arab-Russian deal which was never classified. I checked him up and down, inside-out, backward and forward, before I made contact with him. I verified and double checked. **He's totally clean.**"

"For the record, you were never let go; you were outsourced. You're still active and that's why I'm cutting you some slack here."

"Listen, this doesn't add up. We're **not** working for any Cartel. **We're clean.**"

"We traced Cartel's money to the dry dock."

"Not in payment for the modifications we made to the boat. My partner and I footed that bill. You can verify the bank transfers we made. We paid for everything. We paid for fucking everything, not a cent less. This doesn't add up. You said the Coast Guard was not following us out of Colón?"

"No, the last contact with Seeker before now, was the departure safety inspection in Colón, which I ordered to get facial id's on the crew, and that's how I spotted you, when the photos were delivered to me this morning."

"This is not a Coast Guard vessel. Is it?"

"It is and then again it isn't. We're part of an anti drug Task Force. DEA, CIA and Coast Guard. Most of the Latin American signers to the Treaty have allowed the US Coast Guard to patrol their waters and granted us jurisdiction. So DEA and CIA tag along and give logistics and technical support. CIA is point because we have the Intel assets. I'm in charge of the Task Force. How the hell did you get the money to pay for all the modifications to that boat?"

"THE MEXICAN AND I have been partners for a long time now. The guy was trained by a Russian engineer during the Arab-Russian deal, locating and mapping oil deposits."

"Yes, I remember. That went nowhere!"

"The former analyst working that case out of Langley contacted me to track down the Russians, because he's now working for an…"

He starts talking in the middle of what I'm saying, completing my sentence as if all of a sudden he knows what I'm trying to tell him.

"An Alaskan oil company and they needed help locating and mapping the oil deposits in Alaska."

He does know what I was just about to say.

"How do you know that?"

But I'm glad you do know, because then you know I'm telling you the truth.

"Because he called me and asked for my help in contacting you. I gave him the lead after I verified the info wasn't classified, so you wouldn't get burned by helping him out. Now I remember reading in the file about the Mexican. Yeah, that's right. He's that the same guy that almost died in an accident. No wonder he popped up as having Russian ties."

"The one and only, and he's a fucking genius in sonar and electronics in general. We struck a royalty deal with the Alaskan Oil Company for the mapping of the oil deposits. That's how we're bankrolling this operation now."

Finally, everything is falling into place. Or, is it? I'm still wondering who was tracking us out of Colón.

Lowering his tone of voice, even changing his whole demeanor towards me.

"What exactly are you doing now?"

"First, are we clear with this bullshit about the Cartel?"

His voice now sounding totally calmed and relaxed, as if having unloaded a heavy burden.

"Yes! As far as you guys, I'm convinced you're not involved with the Cartel. But the Cartel paid for something, and if you say you spotted a tail out of Colón, that was probably the Cartel following you. You're involved in this whether you like it or not. You have to tell me what you're doing, so that I can help you. Why the fancy modifications to the boat?"

"I'll tell everything to you but you have to believe me, all we want to do is get on with our plans."

"I'm not so sure you can get on with your plans."

"What? You're going to stop us? Under whose fucking authority?"

"Mister, I can order you active, if I decide I need you to work for the Task Force on this mission. I'm the Head of the Task Force. As a matter of fact I'm inclined to make that determination"

"You better have a damn good reason. Because, if you do, you will blow my fucking cover. In addition, you'll have an operative working for you, very reluctantly, but no boat. The boat is not mine. Skipper is the owner."

"Then we'll confiscate the boat and use the boat for the mission."

"Good luck with that! After we tie you up in court with a cease and desist claim and present the proof that we paid for the dry dock and not the Cartel. I'll make sure the case is all over the news, so that the Cartel knows they should stay clear of the boat. The Cartels will know, the US government is trying to use it as bait. Yeah, that one works for me. Let's go with it, that way the Cartels will stay away from us and we can go on with our lives, exploring for treasures without anyone bothering us no more."

"Have you considered, that your families could be in danger? The Cartel probably has targeted them, if they are after the boat!"

Oh shit! Skipper's daughter and Sparks' mother. I totally lost sight of them because of the argument with him.

"Are you saying you know they are in danger? Or are you're just trying to use that possibility to persuade me to cooperate? Because, if it is the later, I don't welcome the CIA using my family ties to coerce me."

"What family ties? You are an orphan. You have no family."

"These two, now, are my family! Are they in any fucking danger, or not?"

"I don't know if they are or not. However, if you agree to help us, we can take steps to protect them immediately. Our Intel is that the Cartels are interested in the boat. They we're planning to buy the boat in an auction, after it was confiscated because of the name change blunder. I don't know if they had a plan 'B' for coercing you if that didn't work. Remember I only found out you were involved a few hours ago."

"You better not be fucking with me on this. You need us, because of the Cartel's interest in our boat. Right?"

"Well, yes, that's part of it. We shouldn't loose precious time. Tell me where the families are so we can make the arrangements to protect them."

"Not so fast! We can deal with the Cartel if they approach us."

"You'll be exposing your families!"

"You'll get farther along with me if you stop threatening me with that!"
He is right! I am gambling with our lives.

"If you want our help it has to be a two way street. We're not going to risk our lives and expose our families, for the CIA, dealing with the drug Cartels, just for nothing. The CIA must meet my terms. Or, you can start looking for another boat that the Cartel is already targeting. One that is operated, by people you can trust."

I have no fucking idea if Sparks can warn his mother, but Skipper's daughter is on her way to Antarctica on a six months assignment, she'll be safe.

"What's with the 'we' stuff? I am only talking about you."

"I already told you. I'm not the owner of the boat. Skipper is the owner you'll have to convince him about lending his boat to the CIA. The Mexican and I have a ton of money invested in the boat for this venture, but it is his boat. You're asking us to just fucking give it all up and risk our lives playing Cops against the Cartels! It's going to cost you."

Come on you need the boat. I can't let you realize you're succeeding in twisting my arm into accepting. I also need the CIA's help to protect my family.

"What the fuck are you proposing?"

LATER WHEN I COME back onboard Seeker, the US Coast Guard boarding party immediately returns our weapons and leaves.

Over the radio

"This is the US Coast Guard, Seeker, thank you for your cooperation with the inspection and we hope you can fix your radar with the spare parts we gave you. Sorry for the inconveniences we may have caused you, over."

Sparks and Skipper are both looking at me I can feel their eyes pointed at me like laser beams, as I respond to the Coast Guard over the radio.

"This is Seeker, Coast Guard, you are welcome and thank you for the spare parts. Over and out."

I turn the mike off and Sparks asks.

"What spare parts?"

I hand Sparks the box telling him.

"Here, the Coast Guard radio man said you would know what to do with this."

His face shows his disbelief. He has never had one of those to play with.

"Chief! Do you know what this is?"

"It's an encryptor, they set it up for the Coast Guard frequency plus point 683 megahertz. You'll switch to using the encryptor if the Coast Guard calls out to Mr. John Rogers over an open frequency. They'll give you a new code name every time we use the encryptor."

I'm trying to be nonchalant. Skipper has not said a word since I came back aboard Seeker. Until now that he chooses to ask.

"Chief, what heading shall I take?"

I try to sound as if everything in the world was OK, unsuccessfully I know.

"Aruba, Skipper."

I have made a deal with the Devil, that will probably puts all of us in harm's way.

"Heading 098 degrees, speed 12 knots."

"We're still going to Aruba, just in a different role. Guys, I have something to tell you."

I hope that what I chose was the best of the alternatives.

"What different role? Are we going to be spooks for the CIA now?"

Skipper's voice sounds full of sarcasm. Then as Sparks begins to shoot his questions, I realize why.

"Or, are we going diving with special SEAL equipment?"

Whoa, these two have been talking about things they should not be telling each other.

"You guys broke the rule!"

I say looking at Sparks.

"Calm down Chief! Technically, no one has broken the rule, if each of us knew the secret already!"

Skipper is trying, but not succeeding, to convince me that an exception can be made.

"How did you know I used to be CIA if he didn't tell you? And, how did he find out I was a SEAL if you didn't tell him?"

I'm angry and my tone of voice is clear evidence of my anger, not because they broke the rule but because of the consequences that it may trigger.

"I recognized the person who ***interviewed*** you aboard the Coast Guard boat when I saw him. He was the guy who recruited you for the CIA. I remembered he came to me with a Marine Colonel's phony ID and asked me to see your SEAL file. I never forget a face, specially one who lies to me. I told him he better look after you very well because you were very close to me."

What? Skipper has known all of the time I was working for the CIA?

"How the fuck could you tell his ID was phony?"

"Oh!,the ID was good. That is why I knew it was CIA business. I served with the Colonel whose name he was using! When I saw the guy on the Coast Guard boat after you agreed to let them board us, I realized it had to be Company business. When you said they just wanted to talk to you I knew you were a Company guy."

I wonder who else knows? My cover is blown!

"I just figured it out by myself. When we were taking the SCUBA diving lessons, you kept making suggestions to the instructor and he was thankful to you, meaning he took all your suggestions as valid. You told me you were CIA, I figured you were probably recruited from some special branch within the Military. It doesn't take a rocket scientist to figure. Expert diver, CIA must be SEAL trained."

"So much for air tight covers! Mine could be compromised."

Here I was, all the time I have been working undercover, comfortable that my cover was airtight and these two guys, one of whom I only met less than two years ago, and the other who had not seen me in several years, they have my deepest secrets figured out and they tell me so, as if they are telling me I'm wearing a crooked tie.

"No, way your cover is compromised! I knew you were SEAL because I trained you as a Master Diver, and the only reason I learned you are still working with CIA is because of your recruiter showed up here now."

He does have a point. Besides, even if Skipper had learned it before, he would not have told anyone.

"Handler"

"What?"

"He's my handler now."

I know he is going to jump now. Everybody fasten your seat belts. We're starting the roller coaster now!

"**Is now** your handler? Like in **present tense**. So this was not a fucking chance meeting. He was making official contact with you, cabrón? You're still active CIA! En la chinga madre CIA."

The first to react is Sparks and I can handle his anger, no sweat.

"Yes, and no, technically I'm still CIA, but I'm outsourced. It's like an independent contractor, more like a CI, a Confidential Informant. Only, it is not so simple. It was a chance meeting. He was giving me the opportunity to come clean, because the CIA thought we were working for a Drug Cartel."

"Drug Cartel?"

The look of tension on his face takes me by surprise. It is as if he has remembered something horrible.

THEN IT'S Skipper's turn.

"Chief, I said I trusted you and I want to keep trusting you. But, what the fuck have we gotten ourselves into?"

"It seems the Cartel learned about the modifications the you made to the boat. The Cartel paid the dry dock to fumble the name change so the boat would be confiscated when we arrived at Panamá Port. The Cartel would have picked it up at public auction. We all know how that plan ended, thanks to Capi's contact in the Canal's Administration office."

"Why's the CIA involved in all this shit?"

"It's not only the CIA. This is a Task Force, that includes DEA, Coast Guard **and** the CIA. Anyway, they are watching the Cartel's money movements and they're also keeping an eye on the Vessel Registry Office, because their Intel is that the Cartel is trying to acquire large fast boats for the drug runs. The Task Force tracked money from the Cartel paid to the dry dock and they took it to be for the boat's modifications. When we got away with doing the name change in Taboga and then crossing the Canal with VIP scheduling, the Task Force was sure we were delivering the boat to the Cartel."

"That explains the departure safety inspection in Colón."

"My handler ordered the inspection. He's now heading the Task Force. They're stationed out of Gitmo. He wanted faces and that's how he found out I was involved. I was able to clear everything with him, and in addition, made a deal which will allow us to extract the gold when we find it."

"What the fuck? We won't look for the gold now? No way we have way too much invested on this. You're asking us to follow you unconditionally? Then you go and bend over for the CIA to fuck you and us in the ass just like that! Increible este gringo pendejo, I can't believe this! What are we? CIA spooks?"

Sparks disgust is evident in his voice but I know it will not last.

"Sparks, the CIA will help us to get the gold but first we have to do this. By the way, when we dock in Aruba, the Custom officers are going to detain us for a chat. We're going to be interviewed by US Embassy officials, who will swear you in as a US Citizen and swear you both as CIA contractors."

A pair of jaws dropped on the deck.

"Just like that? No background checks? No security clearance evaluations?"

"Believe me, right now he's ordering that all of our banking records be scrutinized to verify we really paid for the boat fixes. Skipper's service record is being requested and the file on the Russian Arab deal is also being pulled. Everything will be verified by the time we arrive at dockside in Aruba."

"Why the Arab Russian deal file?"

"That will be the starting point in your case, he remembered I had reported a Mexican assistant who was involved in an accident."

"Orale! I'm going to become a pinche US Citizen? When I started working with you I never thought, I would get to earn so much money as we have and now, I'll have a chance to pay back those mother fuckers."

"Sparks, what are you talking about?"

"Never mind, I'm just saying, I hate the Drug Cartels, almost as much as I hate the KGB."

"You better be very clear you hate them and not be a sleeper KGB agent. Because, if you're a KGB sleeper, then you'll be shoot in the head the minute you walk thru the door, instead of becoming a citizen and a CIA contractor."

"Jeez Skipper you don't need to scare him!"

"I'm not scared I understand this is very serious business. Chief you once told me you believed that I agreed with the Professor about his dislike of the KGB and I do as much as I dislike Drug Cartels. Let me put it this way, I'm proud to be working with you guys. If we're going against the Cartels I'm good."

"How long until we get to Aruba?"

"It'll take us, maybe another ten or twelve hours. Will that be enough time for them to check us out?"

"Plenty this has become top priority for the Task Force."

"You need to tell us about the mission."

"First I'll explain the deal I made, then the mission."

"The CIA will provide us with all the necessary resources for the extraction of the gold, when we find it."

"Wait a minute! How long did you sign us for? The CIA is not going to provide that without something **big** in exchange. Does this guy have the authority to commit CIA resources like that?"

"He does, if he is committing to a CI contingent deal, under Law any Federal Agent has the authority to grant a CI a deal for 20% of the recovered value of assets seized."

"We're giving the CIA 80% of the catch!"

"Calm down Skipper this may still be a very substantial deal for us. Chief how much gold are we talking about?"

"According to the records I have been able to find so far, the Nazis were able to smuggle approximately 100 tons of gold but it was in several shipments to different destinations. I believe the main destination with 20 maybe 30 tons, was Brazil or Argentina and this particular ship was headed originally to Argentina but was forced to go to Aruba, the nearest Dutch Port, in order to avoid a storm. According to the records in the Dock's registry office of Aruba, the Captain of the ship decided to anchor off the northern coast instead of docking because he had sick and wounded and the doctors had recommended the patients should not risk contact with potentially dangerous insects on the Island."

"That was definitely a made up excuse for keeping the ship in deep water."

"Precisely!"

"How come no one else has figured this out before you?"

"I believe the US Government has already figured it out. That is why when we get to Aruba, we'll be notified that our proposal was accepted."

"Are you saying that there is no deal in place yet?"

"Yes, there is, but our clearance has to be approved first."

"Boy 80% of the cut is gone!"

"Skipper do you have any idea how much money it's the 20% even if it's only 20 tons?"

"How much?"

"Based on the current market price of gold it would be a little over $56 million."

"That is not so bad, $18 million for each of us."

"No Skipper, $56 million is for each of us, that's the 20%."

Skipper's eyes popped out and he fell on his captain's chair.

"You sure about that?"

"Check my math Skipper. It's roughly $1325.00 per ounce, 20 tons of gold would be a total value of $848 million."

"Gentlemen, please consider we will not have to deal with the Government of Aruba, we will not have to bankroll the operation, the CIA will cover all the expenses and the payoff will be tax free because this would be a covert operation."

"We won't even have to fund our own operation?"

"We're about to become officially CIA covert contractors, supplied by the CIA and based by the CIA. Skipper, the boat will continue to be yours to keep but the technology and specifications are going to become CIA property in exchange for a license fee of 10% of cost to built, for the designer. When any new boats are commissioned using your designs you will be paid the 10% fee."

"If we pull this rabbit out of the hat, that royalty will be part of our deal we split it three ways, after all your funding made it possible, hell, the hydrofoil was Sparks idea."

"How is the CIA going to supply and base us without blowing our cover?"

"Ah! That's the best part, immediately after we're signed up, we will be based out of a former US Coast Guard platform located southwest of Puerto Rico. That platform was used for monitoring Cartel drug runs before the aerostat was put in service. All of the Cartels know about it and they avoid as if it was a black hole in deep space. It has been out of service until recently, but it can be reactivated and resupplied covertly by cargo

VSTOL's. It's ours, starting when we leave Aruba and the Task Force will coordinate for the resupply out of Gitmo."

"If it's anything like the one off the coast of North Carolina which was decommissioned and converted to a Hotel some time ago we will have a luxury place for ourselves."

"I was told it has a larger platform because they use to fly hellos' out of it to track contacts and they had four hellos' on station. They should be able to land at least two MV-22's at the same time. Any questions gentlemen?"

"When do we start looking for the gold?"

"We do that after helping with cracking the Cartel operation, because if we don't, would have to keep watching over our shoulders for someone to try come and grab the boat while we're looking for the gold. The plan is, we pose as bait if you will. The Cartel will come to us to offer us a deal to take part in running drugs for them and we go in and **crack** them."

"Just like that? Without any shoots being fired or anything. Do you really think the Cartel is going to offer us a deal when they were setting us up to grab the boat with the scheme about the name change."

"Once we had all the pieces together on what happened we realized they don't want to grab the boat by force because they need it operational. There is an undercover asset deep inside this Cartel and the Intel being provided verifies the plan was to have you loose the boat when it was seized, then pick it up in the public auction and then go back to you and offer you to operate it for them."

"How in hell would they achieve that?"

"We're not sure but your daughter is already under US Marshall protection and your mother's farm is under surveillance by an ops team until we're satisfied the Cartel is not going after her and we can extract her."

"What? When were you going to tell us this?"

"Skipper, I'm telling you now this was going to happen even if we never got involved with the CIA. The Cartel was already tracking us out of Colon. We found out by chance when the Task Force intercepted us."

"Shit man, you are talking about my daughter. What is she being told?"

"The story is that you have become a government witness against one of the Cartels and you had to go into WITSEC, for her own protection and yours she is being placed under WITSEC too until you testify and then you will reunite with her. Skipper, I had to act quickly to keep her safe! The encryptor may be used to talk to her as soon as she is safely relocated and also to contact us covertly off course."

"What about my mother?"

"In your mother's case it's not as easy. For one she is not a US Citizen yet! And she is located in a foreign country where we don't have jurisdiction neither do we know how deep the Cartel's reach is with the authorities in Oaxaca, Mexico. However, as soon as you are sworn in as a US Citizen you can claim her she will be pulled in. Do you think she would be OK with leaving the farm?"

"She is an old woman, maybe she would like to retire and rent or sell the farm. But how do I contact her to let her know what's going on?"

"That's another reason why I requested the encryptor for so you could let her know that she can trust the people we're sending to help her."

"You already talked to my daughter?"

"I had to Skipper I didn't want her to be scared when the US Marshals intercepted her."

"How did you explain that it was you and not me calling her?"

"Skipper, you know that she knows I was SEAL you guys cared for me after I came back from Panamá when I was injured during the op, I told her I was sending the US Marshals because I was working the op when you witnessed the crime and she trusted me. I didn't lie to her."

"Are you sure she is safe?"

"Skipper, not even the CIA can get to them while they are in WITSEC. The only way you are going to talk to her is thru a delayed line she is not going to be allowed to tell you where she is, if she does the call will be dropped."

"OK Chief, we need to get these fuckers fast."

"Chief, I don't know if my mother will know what to do and even if she makes a decision. What do I to tell her?"

"I have an idea about that, just explain that some friends of yours are going to contact her and give her a code a word a name or something that she will understand is a message that you can't tell her over the phone, what is important is that she understands when someone makes contact using the code word she can trust that person. Also she can trust they will help her make the arrangements for anything she decides. They will take care of all the details and at the same time keep her safe."

"Can we call Mr. John Rogers now or do we have to wait?"

"Mr. Rogers will call us when Skipper's daughter is safely relocated."

"Can't I use my sat phone to call my mother? The sat phones are encrypted."

"Yeah, I didn't think about that. We can use those to contact the Task Force too."

"We will clear that with the Task Force when we arrive to Aruba."

"We better put away the guns, we're almost entering the territorial waters of Aruba."

"Sparks, please, first do the honors and request docking instructions."

"Aye aye Skipper!"

Over the radio

"This is Seeker, to Port Authority of Oranjestad, we're requesting instructions for docking, over."

Over the radio

"This is Port Authority of Oranjestad, please proceed directly to dock at Customs House. Over and out."

Customs officers assist with the mooring lines at dockside and board Seeker after the boat is secured. We're asked to disembark and are escorted to an office inside the building. Skipper is the last one to disembark and he recognizes the officers boarding Seeker are the same US Coast Guard officers who boarded earlier this morning, only this time they are wearing the uniforms of the Customs office of Aruba. Seeker will be safe under their watch.

"How did you guys get here before we did? You couldn't have outrun us we didn't see you go by."

Sparks is surprised.

"Were you watching the radar all the way in?"

"Not all the time but we would have seen you."

"One word. Helo'."

"You mean hello?"

"No, he means helicopter. Even if we had been on the look out for ships we would not have noticed an aircraft unless we were watching the radar."

"OK, your stories check out. Langley approved everything and we got fresh Intel the Cartel was watching your daughter but the WITSEC had already intercepted her. MI6 is helping on this and they inserted an agent in the trip to Antarctica. Your daughter is now a British woman, the paper trail for her is clean because all the verification at the Station in Antarctica are handled by the British Government. Your daughter was scheduled to be stationed for six months, we should be able to wrap this sooner otherwise that MI6 agent is going to have to endure another tour of duty in the South pole, at least she is also a geologist like your daughter and she will be busy there."

"You are sure she will not be recognized?"

"Don't worry Skipper she is the spiting image of your daughter, she could be her twin sister, that British woman is now your daughter according to all passport and other ID's. MI6 has proven to be very thorough in this kind of insertions and they are doing this internally in their own system, hell for all practical purposes the US Government now believes the MI6 agent is your daughter. The British agent filling in for her has been read on the mission she knows the whole drill. As for your mother, no one has approached her at the farm, yet, but we must bring her in quickly to be able to put her into WITSEC."

"We have encrypted sat phones I can call her right now, Chief suggested I give her a code word for your people to use when they approach her, that way she will know she can trust them."

"That's a good idea except that you don't want to say the code word in case the Cartel is already listening in on her line. We know they haven't approached her but we don't know if they have her under surveillance."

"Is there anything you can tell her **without** telling her you are giving a code. You don't want to say anything during the conversation that would alert the Cartel if they are listening."

"How about if I ask her to go into town to see my girlfriend and give her a message for me?"

"What good will that be? How do you tell your girlfriend to tell her anything? Besides it would mean involving another person, that is not safe."

"I **don't** have a girlfriend and my mother knows that, she will understand I'm trying to send her information, you provide a female agent and tell her to give my mother the code. My mother will know she can trust the woman."

"Chief, have you been training this guy on how to run covert ops?"

"Sir, you can't run a multimillion dollar business without a little security. How do you think we stay ahead of our competition?"

"OK, you can make the call and give me the code word."

On the encrypted phone.

"Bendición mama, (in Spanish) *yes all is good mom but I need to ask you a favor, I need you to give a message to my girlfriend mom, please tell her to come with you to meet me in Aruba I'll make arrangements for a private plane to bring you over you need to meet her at the cafe next door to the check cashing office in town, yes mom the cafe where she works. Yes, mom she is off work today but she will be there today to collect her pay you have to meet her there at 4:00 PM. Thanks mom I love you.*"

"Are you sure she understood?"

"We won't know until she shows at the cafe. The code you have to give to your agent is Mrs. Elena Maria Chavez."

"Who is that your grand mother?"

"Off course not, the Cartel could find that out easily. That was my father's first girlfriend before he married my mother. When my mother hears that name she will know the person she is meeting was sent by me."

"OK, Sparks your mother will be in the US by this evening under WITSEC's protection. Now I need you to raise your right hand and take the citizenship oath in front of the Embassy officer. Then both of you will take the oath as contractors. Chief is your Mission Chief, I don't think I need to remind you that you must trust him. When we're finished here you two can go back to the boat and your Mission Chief will brief you aboard."

"No sir, this is **my team** and the way we work is as a *TEAM* on everything. This guys have proven to me over and over that they can contribute to the mission in a variety of ways if they have first hand access to the Intel. They stay for the mission brief, **my *TEAM* my rules**."

"All right I'll agree to do it your way."

"While we're on this subject, when you make the checks for the CI cuts you make three checks equal amounts one for each of us. You may go ahead with the mission brief now."

Eyebrows are raised by the head of the Task Force, Skipper and Sparks and the briefing starts.

"Our Intel says the Cartel will try to contact you here in Aruba later today to ask you to work for them. But because they do not have in place the leverage against you to force you to sell the boat they are planning on asking nicely, whatever that means. We believe that the Cartel is planning to get the boat later when they have acquired the leverage. Which they won't off course."

"How are you going to play it out when my mother and my girlfriend never show up in Aruba?"

"The Private plane is going to crash while landing in Aruba to provide the Cartel an excuse to use that as leverage to force you to accept working until they can get their hands on Skipper's daughter."

"They will know they did not cause the crash."

"Sure but they will also think **you** don't know that. Aruba Customs will not release Seeker until after the crash to give the Cartel a chance to contact you. The boat's name change will be the issue until Panamá confirms the updated info on the vessel's registration. Any questions?"

"Are you going to restock and refuel us here?"

"Being done as we speak. Including more munitions for your hand guns and rifles. How were you guys planning of defending yourselves with just a few clips?"

"What? None of your officers noticed the two mini guns we have on the rail, when we were boarded this morning?"

"Mini guns? Where? No, we were focused on the crew when we boarded. The Coast Guard boys came back saying that you surrendered your weapons the moment they boarded and you never left the bridge."

"OK, we appreciate the additional ammo, but we have two rail mounted mini guns one forward on the starboard side and one aft on the port side with 10,000 rounds in the drums."

He is looking out the window trying to locate the guns on the boat.

"Where are those guns, I don't see them?"

"We don't deploy them until we're over international waters and when deployed, we keep them covered. They look like small cranes maybe that's why your officers didn't spot them."

"How did you put that one past the dry dock in Armuelles?"

"We didn't, we installed the guns ourselves out at sea. Sir, I already told you, our team has an electronics genius, that's me, and a former Seabee, you know one of those guys who can build bridges in the middle of a jungle with nothing but the trees around and their Swiss Army knives."

"You keep forgetting I told you, we were never issued the dammed Swiss Army knives!"

Skipper clarifies one more time.

"Yeah well let's hope it doesn't come to you needing to use the guns. According to the Intel we have the Cartel is now planning on using fast large boats to run the drugs after a handoff on international waters from a smaller short range boat."

"Like the Cigarettes with triple high performance engines?"

"Yes, they intend to use the smaller fast boats to deliver a load once they are on international waters, to the larger boat, which has a longer range. The larger boat runs the drugs to another location just outside US territorial waters and another handoff is made again to a smaller fast boat which brings the drugs to Florida, Luisiana, Texas or Mississippi. The destinations will probably be into coastal areas uninhabited where there are no resorts just the mangroves and the alligators or crocodiles I can never tell the difference between those animals."

"The Cartel will probably approach you here in Oranjestad, sometime later today after you have been released. They will try to persuade you to work for them."

"What makes you so sure it will happen today?"

"Were you able to set eyes on the contact which was tracking you out of Colon?"

"No, we were monitoring it on radar too far to see it."

"What kind of radar do you guys have?"

"A modified version of the crap you have on the USCG boat you were riding!"

"Anyway, I pulled the imagery of your exit from Colon and we were able to identify the contact which was following you. You said it broke off the pursuit when you changed course towards Cartagena and they went on to San Andres correct?"

"Yeah."

"Please come to the window again. See that luxury yacht coming into port? It departed from San Andres after picking up the person who we believe is the person in charge of the distribution operations for one of the Colombian Cartels. Our Intel says several Cartels are combining their resources, they are trying to improve the distribution channel by means of compartmentalization. The instructions for the next drop would be handed together with the shipment at the handoff. Only the coordinator and the assets delivering and receiving the handoff will have the information about where the shipment is going next."

"That means that unless there is someone inside the distribution chain we will not be able intercept."

"And, worse, if we do intercept they will know who was the leak."

"That is a though one to crack, if they are successful setting it up."

"Sparks, if you had one of those gadgets for causing radio transmission jamming, how far could you jam?"

Skipper's eyes are glowing because he had an idea.

"Depending on the equipment you want to jam, for cel phones maybe one to three miles but once a cel is out on international waters it becomes academic because it's just too far from the land towers, for the boat's radio we could jam from as far as 10 to 15 miles. However, remember jamming is only good in the direction we're coming from, the opposite direction would be clear of the jamming."

"What about if there was another jammer coming from the opposite direction?"

I ask to help with Skipper's idea.

"That would be more effective but the best would be a three prong approach with an overlapping pattern, that way the target would be totally isolated."

"Chief, I tip my hat to your team, you were right in requesting them to be present during the mission brief. I can provide two drones airborne with coordinated multi spectrum jamming equipment ready to start jamming at the command from Seeker."

"Can you make those stealth drones?"

"**They are stealth drones** or did your radar see the drone which took the imagery of the Yacht and you coming out of Colon?"

"Shit! Sparks you told me our radar could track any air contact short of a B2 bomber."

"Chief, if this man could track one our drones which are a fraction of the size of a B2 bomber, I would be sending him to work with our tech division instead of risking him out here on the field so don't blame him. Besides, he probably did see the drone but since they do not fly a fixed pattern they are easily dismissed as birds."

"How the hell do they maintain a fix on the target being followed?"

I ask trying to understand how Sparks was fooled.

"Maybe Sparks can explain after everything he has heard!"

"The only way I can think of is that they are using invisible laser targeting for the cameras like those used for targeting."

"It more like in addition too. The respective targeting systems for the cameras **and** weapons each provides redundancy to the other. For the controller or pilot if you will, who is flying the drone it's transparent both systems are engaged during the mission."

"Are the drones armed?"

"Sure in case air support is required."

"Who has authority to shoot?"

I ask. *It is good to know there is air cover available, but it is even better to understand what the rules of engagement are.*

"In the Task Force, I have the ultimate authority but for the individual mission, the chief of the mission has the authority to request cover fire, the pilot is patched in on all radio transmission if he hears the distress code he knows he is authorized to engage when he has acquired a target. You will have a big gun at your disposal if we cannot reach you in time. Now listen, the Cartel's yacht is about to dock here, when they walk in to clear Customs you are going to be in lockup over there yelling and screaming for us to contact directly the Panamanian Vessel Registry."

AS THE DOOR TO THE lockup is being closed behind us, two well dressed Hispanic males and an attractive female walk into the office. The lockup is conveniently located next to the entrance of the facility so that detainees can be secured immediately upon entering. There is no way the new guests are going miss the show.

"Now you listen to me! We have been detained here for several hours and you have done nothing to confirm our registration is in order."

Skipper takes command of the situation and he is the first to complain.

"Gentlemen, we have already made the formal request thru proper channels, we just have to wait for their response."

I am surprised to know my handler can imitate a Dutch accent so well, if I didn't know him I would be fooled to think he is Dutch, and his looks help him at that too.

"Don't you **gentlemen** us when you have kept us locked in here like we were common criminals. Dammit just call the Panamanian registry directly they are open until 4:30 P.M. The telephone numbers are listed on the registration papers. **PLEASE!**"

I add to stress the point, just so that they become aware of the complete situation.

"OK, OK, enough! We will make the call when we finish processing the yacht which just arrived."

Now let's see what their reaction is. One of the Hispanic males who just entered is the first to speak.

"No officer please, if I was in their position I would really appreciate that you helped the guests in the order they arrived. Please make the call and release these men promptly I'm sure their predicament is just an error that may be clarified with that call."

Wow that was unexpected he wants to see how this develops risking to spend more time with the authorities, or is he just ballsy.

"If you insist, we certainly do not want to detain them more than it's absolutely necessary. Please sit down and we will be right with you."

Task Force is picking up the telephone, he is making the call now we're giving the full show and they have front row seats.

"Hallo, may I speak to an English speaking official?…Oh you do, thank you very much. I'm calling from the Customs Office in Oranjestad, Aruba, we have intercepted a Vessel running under the name of Seeker but according to the database records the only Vessel matching the description and dimensions should be running under the name of *El Pescador,* however, the operators claim the name change was authorized recently. Would you be so kind as to verify? Yes, thank you I'll hold."

No reactions to the names of the vessel, no surprises there, these are the guys who planned to take over Seeker.

Task Force starts shuffling papers on his desk and motions one of the Hispanic males to approach the desk, leaving all the paperwork for Seeker clearly visible. I also notice the Hispanic male is focused on the paperwork and the female is using her cel phone to take pictures of the documents laying on the desk when Task Force has turned away from the desk to look for some forms to give them.

"Kindly fill these forms while I finish with the call that way we will not keep you longer than is necessary, we really appreciate your cooperation and patience."

"Sure no problem I know the procedures may I have a pen."

This man must be the Boss he is very cool and calm, almost like a trained agent, the woman must be very close to him.

"Yes, Sir here you may keep it too is a souvenir from the Tourist Bureau they want us to distribute them."

Sure, sure, that was a plant if I have ever seen one.

"Thank you."

"These are beautiful may I have one too?"

Good she took another pen, let's see if they are so careless as to keeping them aboard the yacht.

Task Force is on the phone again.

"Hallo, yes, yes, yes. Ah so I see. The boat was recently acquired. How come they have traversed all the way out to Aruba before the updated database has been distributed? Oh I see. Well, thank you very much if you would please FAX the certification over so we will have all our paperwork in order before the update is received. We appreciate your cooperation."

Hanging the phone and jumping to open the door to the lockup was almost simultaneous actions. Task Force returns the registration documents and provides all the entry clearance documents without a single word being spoken. Skipper just wears his long hard face as he receives all the documents, without saying a word either. I ask.

"Are there any mooring facilities outside the port we could use? I understand there is no dock space available because of the Carnival. May we have permission to moor outside the port over the wreckage?"

"I'm sorry Sir but I'm afraid that will not be possible because it's a special weekend there will be many tour boats going out to the wreckage area. We cannot allow you to moor there until next week."

"Captain, I'm sure we can obtain permission from the Officials at our Marina to allow you to dock parallel to our yacht and share our power connections."

The Cartel is initiating the contact right in front of the authorities, really bold or really desperate. *The train is leaving the station there is no backing out now.*

"Thank you very much but I'm only the First Officer not the Captain."

I turn to Skipper and lay it on him to answer.

"Skipper did you hear the offer?"

I need to let him know who is in command of Seeker although he probably already knows. Or, does he? I need to get a felling for how good his Intel is.

"I sure did and I appreciate it very much it's better to sleep in port, less movement and no noise from the engines if we can hitch power from dockside. Are you sure the Marina will allow a boat like Seeker among all the luxury crafts?"

Skipper is giving him a way out.

"Yes, our Captain has friends at the Marina it **will** be arranged!"

"We will follow you to your dock. That is if we're free to go."

Skipper is enjoying this too much he is challenging Task force.

"Officer?"

"Yes, Captain, Seeker and its crew are free to go, I need to apologize for the inconveniences caused by the blunder with the paperwork."

"Will we have to go thru this procedure every time we come into port? We're planning to spend several weeks around these waters exploring the wreckages in the area and…"

Before Skipper was able to complete his inquiry, Task Force interrupted him, I wonder why.

"No, If you are going to be exploring within a radius of 200 miles north of Aruba we can give a special permit for the next four months which will give Seeker free passage in and out of all Ports in Aruba. You will need to renew it if you will be longer that four months."

Whoa! Making up things like this is dangerous, now look who is ballsy, these two just overstepped in the act.

"That will work! What do we need to do for obtaining the special permit?"

"You will need to provide authenticated copies of your passports and your fingerprints plus fill out some forms, we can process it now so you do not have to come back."

I hope Task Force knows what he is doing because this could back fire if the Cartel finds out It's a fake permit.

"We will do it tomorrow because we need to follow these gentlemen to their Marina but thanks anyway."

OK Skipper came to his senses now we have a way out of this, it was just a teaser.

"Captain, please complete you paperwork for the permit I'll leave our crew man here with you to direct you to the Marina and clear the way for you."

Crap now we have to work magic to show the permit. The Cartel is not going to let go the opportunity to have access to a boat with free passage in and out of the ports in Aruba. Seeker has become the flagship of the Cartel's flotilla in a moments notice and our lives could be safe for the time being because our credentials and fingerprints are tied to the Special Permit if we can make it legit with the authorities of Aruba.

"Chief you are going to have to cook your pasta primavera tonight to thank these people for their hospitality. Where are you from?"

"Various parts of Latin America. How about you?"

We're Americans, I mean US citizens, my family was Irish, Sparks here, his family is from Mexico and Chief's family is Italian. You can say we're from various parts too!"

"Our crew member will wait for you outside and board Seeker with you when you are ready to depart he will direct you to our dock in the Marina. We look forward to enjoying your pasta."

Saying that he takes the girl's arm and walks out of the office. *Is she his significant other? They act as if they are a couple.*

THE PRIVATE PLANE does not crash, it hasn't even departed from Oaxaca. The departure from Oaxaca was delayed the moment the Cartel decided to initiate the contact at the Customs Office. *Now a decision has to be made about what to do with Spark's mother and girlfriend. That decision according to mission protocol rests on my shoulders.*

"Chief how do you want to play it? I'm sure WITSEC prefers the plane crash, it makes their job easier but I don't mean to put any pressure on you."

Sure you don't but the pressure is still there, every time a life or death decision has to be made there is always pressure. If the wrong decision is made it could easily cost the mission or worst the life of one or more persons.

"Can we delay the decision until tomorrow, I'm sure tonight they are going to grill us with questions because their Intel can only be telling them at best the locations of the targets. They may have eyes on their victims but they don't have access to them yet."

"I agree with Chief they will not play the strong hand with us yet. We have bought additional time with all that racket you came up with for the passports and the fingerprints."

I wonder if Sparks is agreeing with me because he trusts me or because he cannot understand the possible repercussions of making the wrong decision.

"It was Skipper who opened that door."

"What?"

"You can't blame me if I have been to Aruba before."

All eyes turned to Skipper and I ask.

"Do you mean to tell me there is actually a Special Permit for passage?"

"Yes, there is for exploration vessels. Didn't you ever read our registry papers? After so many times you have handled them, Seeker is an exploration vessel."

Skipper never ceases to surprise me, I'm so glad he is watching my back.

"You have until noon tomorrow, otherwise it becomes suspicious to hold the departure from Oaxaca for too long. we don't know if the Cartel has heard the conversation."

"Then we need to confirm if the conversation was heard or not. We need your assets in Oaxaca to put in overtime and get solid Intel on whether the Cartel heard the conversation with Spark's mother or not."

A LAND LINE IS known in telco jargon as a POTS (Plain Old Telephone Line) and it can be bugged very easily but only at one of the physical connection points between the telephone company central office and the demarcation point at the customer's facilities. Otherwise, the line is clean, that is the beauty of old analog lines, as insecure as they are, they are simple to verify if they are clean.

One of the field tech attached to the ops team in Oaxaca is an old school guy and he is able to verify the line was clean end to end in less that two hours after the request from Task Force is received.

There is no way the Cartel could have heard the conversation. Once the female agent presented her credentials to Spark's mother, the mother put herself in the team's hands without questions. The mother was very happy her son is now working with the people fighting who she despises, the drug Cartels.

The ops team inserted an agent in the mother's place, a look alike, at the farm and Sparks' mother was flown into WITSEC hands that evening. Before the pasta is served in the yacht both Sparks' mother and Skipper's daughter are secured under WITSEC protection.

ON THE RADIO Skipper arranges our departure.

"This is Seeker, to Port Authority, requesting permission to clear the dock at Customs House. Over"

Radio response is heard immediately.

"This is Port Authority, Seeker you are clear for departure. Over and out."

The Hispanic guest aboard Seeker was ordered to help us, he is carrying a gun with silencer, he must be a bodyguard, *I wonder if he is the Boss' or the girl's bodyguard.*

"Captain the Marina is about one and a half miles west of here past the airport you may reach it via the inland water way or if you prefer we can go out of the port."

"It's getting dark I'll use the inland waterway, there is more traffic control inside. If you don't mind I also prefer to be addressed as Skipper."

"Off course, Skipper. I apologize."

The man is educated also.

"Radio contact with the Marina is on VHS Channel 19."

"Sparks please setup our guest with the radio on Channel 19 so we can get docking instructions."

Skipper motions Sparks to make the Radio call.

"This is Seeker, Marina at Oranjestad please come in. Over"

"This is the Marina at Oranjestad, Seeker please go ahead. Over"

"This is Seeker please standby for a request by one of your members. Over"

"This is the Marina at Oranjestad, Seeker your entrance has already been cleared you may proceed to docking side by side to *El Real* docked at slip number 81 parallel, it will be on your port side when you enter the Marina. We suggest you rotate before docking due to your LOA it will make departure easier for you. Over"

"This is Seeker, copy that we're grateful for your suggestion. Over and out."

Skipper looks at me sideways when he heard the suggestion from the marina. *The look indicates to me Skipper recognizes that the Cartel most probably had just about every bit of information they need to know about Seeker, except maybe the size and color of the underwear we're wearing today.*

THE DINNER GOES WELL, a lot better than I expected after all the up sell Skipper made about my culinary abilities. The Cartel's representative is curious about our family ties, he asks me first. I explain I have no living relatives. Skipper explains he has a daughter whom he does not see too often because of his work away from home at sea most of the time. Sparks explains he only has his mother.

"My father's death was very hard on my mother, I think she wants to move to the US with a new friend she has but I don't even know when and where she will move to, or if she has moved already. I'm going to have to wait for her to get in touch with me to find out where she lives now, so I can go visit her when we finish this exploration."

"I wish my daughter would contact me before she travels."

That is better Skipper short and concise Sparks has to learn to keep it short when you elaborate you risk disclosing details you don't want or should not either way it's trouble.

"Chief, I can't believe you have no relatives at all."

"The closest I have to a relative is this old man."

Reaching out to place my hand on Skipper's shoulder.

"That is why I stick with him. Did you know he is a former Seabee? He worked some of the repairs on the boat himself."

Skipper looks at me sideways and I know that look, he is complaining I have disclosed his credentials, he does not understand I'm probing how good their Intel is.

"Would it be OK if we went aboard your boat, you have more open deck than we do and we can enjoy some cigars."

This is awkward but it will be more awkward if we don't allow it.

"Sure why not?"

After we're aboard Seeker.

"Gentlemen I asked you to join us tonight because I work with a group of people who are interested in acquiring Seeker for a project."

The man does not waste any time to start talking business.

"What kind of project would that be? This is an exploration vessel."

"Skipper, we're very well acquainted with the modifications you made to your boat and the capabilities the boat has, its speed and its range. It fits our needs perfectly even if you did not have the special passage permit you obtained today."

"The boat is not for sale. Anyway you wouldn't be willing to pay what it's worth to us, we put a big chunk of cash into it making all the modifications."

"However, if you would let me finish please. Now that you have the special permit we may be able to offer you a different arrangement instead of buying the boat we would buy your services."

"What services are you talking about?"

The Cartel probably wants to discuss the proposal aboard Seeker to be away from the dockside so no one can hear the conversation. The first thing they did when they boarded Seeker was to perform a bug sweep to assure the boss there are no electronic listening devices in place.

"We run a transportation business but let's say for purposes of this conversation, that the merchandise we transport is very difficult to clear thru Customs. To avoid interception we're establishing a new procedure which allows us to change on a moments notice the intermediate and final destinations for a particular shipment. However, the new procedure has proven to be confusing to our own people in the distribution chain and disruptions in the final delivery is bad for the business. Our partners have requested we fix or eliminate the problems to be able to maintain the flow of the merchandise otherwise they want to close the distribution channel. We need fast reliable transportation to achieve our goals."

"We're all grown ups here you are talking about running illegal dru…"

Skipper, please if you annoy him, we don't get the info.

"Please don't use derogatory terms Skipper."

"OK, sorry the point I was trying to make is that if it's new procedures you are trying to implement, why would you bring in strangers to run it? Unless you are trying to avoid loosing trusted personnel when something goes wrong and you just kill the outsiders?"

"Precisely the opposite, our personnel is not used to thinking on their feet, they are just used to be pointed in a direction and pushing the pedal to the metal as you gringos say. We're proposing the other Cartels to establish a procedure that will minimize the interception of the merchandise. To achieve that goal our Cartel is willing to risk loosing some merchandise in test runs if that is what it takes. The **Strangers** will act as **Trainers** and I'll guaranty you will not be blamed for any lost merchandise during training."

Are you serious? The Cartel is going to place a shipment of drugs in the hands of strangers, without leverage! My ass.

"If you want our help, you have to assign one or two men to come aboard with us on Seeker so that your people will not shoot us at first sight."

I'm not agreeing I merely want to see what is your reaction to my counterproposal.

"That is impossible. It would require the finger printing of our personnel by the Authorities of Aruba they would run them thru Interpol, before the paperwork was completed you would be arrested and your boat would be seized. We know you and Skipper are Ex-Navy and he is a respected business man from Panamá. None of you have ever had ties to any drug business."

OK, now we're getting somewhere he is disclosing his Intel and it is pretty accurate not too difficult to obtain but fast and good.

"What makes you think we will get involved with the Cartel now?"

Show me your cards.

"I have three reasons for you; first, you are listening my proposal; second the money in our business is good and you could repay your bank loans for the boat's repairs faster than by exploring wreckages."

Not bad those are legit. What else?

"What would be the third reason?"

"The third is that even if you have no idea of where your loved ones are, we do."

Oh shit! Could it be possible that the Cartel has someone inside WITSEC? Is he just bluffing? Our faces turn pale including mine. At least that reaction was not faked, it might have been worst if we remain calm, this is the normal reaction for the situation. I'll not be able to alert Task Force, nothing can be done but to go ahead and play along until the situation is sorted.

THE NEXT MORNING we are invited back to the yacht for breakfast and to receive the instructions for the first shipment. The instructions are simple just a set of coordinates, we're ordered to wait for the fast boat at the given coordinates and receive the handoff, which will consist of the merchandise, the new set of coordinates and the ETA required. According to the procedure, Seeker will not know where the delivery will be until we receive the info at the exchange and only two other persons will also know, our employer and the captain of the receiving boat.

As we're preparing to release the mooring lines we're given one final instruction.

"Skipper, I believe you have encrypted sat phones, three of them, please hand them over. We will keep them onboard *El Real.* We will be monitoring your radio transmissions in case you need to contact us."

Without the sat phones we're unable to contact the Task Force, if Seeker initiates a call for Mr. John Rogers it will be heard by the Cartel. We have to go on as if nothing happened. Skipper is ready to request departure on the radio.

"This is Seeker, to Marina at Oranjestad please come in, over."

"This is the Marina at Oranjestad, Go ahead Seeker, over."

"This is Seeker, we're ready for departure from the Marina at Oranjestad, we're requesting permission to clear the dock, over."

"This is the Marina at Oranjestad, you are cleared for departure Seeker, over and out."

Another voice is heard on the radio immediately after the clearance for departure.

"This US Coast Guard to All Stations in the waters north of Aruba, we are requesting help in the search and rescue of Mr. John Rogers who went overboard last night from a private yacht, coordinates unknown, any vessel which can help please respond, over."

OLD SCHOOL TECH IS less detectable than sophisticated wireless electronic listening devices. A loudspeaker may be turned into a microphone by merely reversing some wires and it will still continues to act as a loudspeaker if the wires are rigged correctly. Seeker had speakers almost everywhere so that Skipper's orders are heard on the deck even underway and during bad weather.

We were not aware, until now, that the US Coast Guard boys who had spent their time aboard, while dressed as Customs Officials from Aruba, had rewired all the speakers and connecting them to a second encryptor.

"Calm down Sparks! Every thing is under control you can tell Skipper also his daughter is safe everything is in place. The Cartel guy **was bluffing**. We heard everything he said last night over the speakers on the deck also this morning. I personally contacted WITSEC and the US Marshal in charge of your mother's relocation is a woman who protects her witnesses like a female bear protects her cubs. She used to be a Secret Service agent she has top clearance and you can tell Skipper she is also in charge of his daughter, they are together."

"We heard Task Force thank you for that."

"It has played out in our favor because the Cartel believes they have cornered you. Before we move any further, we need to establish new communication protocols since you don't have the sat phones. We cannot be throwing people overboard every time we need to contact you. Now we have ears on board. If you need to warn us you will use the phrase *Peanut Butter* if you are in distress you will use *Peter Bravo*. If the Task Force needs to warn you, we will use the name *Karen Thomas* for imminent danger for abort the code will be Kilo Tango."

"I suggest we intercept this first assignment. They are testing the procedure and if we break it from inception they may be forced to abort using it. We can jam the radio as planned when the small boat approaches us, we grab the crew and the merchandise then we sink the boat and ship the crew and the merchandise to Gitmo."

Either we stop it at inception or we don't have any means of knowing where it will go.

"Sounds like a plan. The next code name will be Mrs. Rose Alberts. But remember anything you have to tell us we can hear you always over the second encryptor."

Yeah thanks for telling us now had we known last night we would have been able to sleep.

"Ask the guys who wired the speakers if the wiring for the speakers can be rigged into the second encryptor? That would give us full time two way comm over the second encryptor."

Sparks always with his great ideas.

"I'll check and let you know. You need to provide me with the coordinates and ETA for the first contact."

"The coordinates are 13 degrees north 70 degrees west it's about 50 nautical miles north northwest of Aruba. The ETA is noon which is perfect, the sun will be in their eyes if they look up for aircrafts. We're planning to arrive around 11:00 AM. Over and Out"

THE MINI GUNS NEED to be deployed, Sparks has to connect the jammer and we all have to unwind from the pre mission tension and the tasteless prior evening thinking a daughter / fiancé and a mother could be in harm's way. *I can't stop thinking about what will happen when Skipper finds out about our engagement before I have the chance of telling him, I'll need WITSEC protection from Skipper's rage.*

After we deploy the mini guns we leave them uncovered, Sparks must go to the bridge to work on the jammer and Skipper has to engage the jet propulsion. Seeker should arrive at the coordinates within 90 minutes. Then Skipper will switch to normal propulsion and start fixed position rotation to maintain position at the designated coordinates.

"All the radar and sonar contacts we're tracking are from normal traffic. Nothing is coming at us and no contacts within 20 miles except a couple of birds flying a random pattern."

"Would you be able to tell they are the drones if you didn't know?"

"No way their pattern is truly random they must be on some kind of auto pilot mode while they track. I imagine if they have to fire the pilot takes over."

"Not if they are shooting laser guided missiles, the pilot just has to designate the target and he can shoot in any direction, the missile will know where to go once the target's designation info is transferred at the moment it's launched. Those drones operate truly shoot and forget, so that they can return to base right after deploying the weapons and they are extremely accurate. They could shoot at a boat parked next to us and we just have to take cover from the shrapnel."

"Let's hope it does not come to that."

"Contact bearing 180 degrees 10,000 yards coming at us at 25 knots. Do we start jamming?"

"No don't start jamming until we have eyes on them. Keep calling position and speed. At that speed it could be any other leisure boat we can't risk alerting the wrong people with the jammer."

"Contact bearing 180 degrees 8,000 yards coming at us they increased their speed to 35 knots."

"When can I see them?"

"Not before they are at less than 1,500 yards they are probably running very low in the water."

"I can point Seeker to them and heave to in their direction, that will cut the distance between them and us faster."

"Do it!"

"Changing course to 180 degrees at 8 knots!"

"Contact bearing 180 degrees 3,000 yards still coming at us at 35 knots."

"Chief it has to be them. I'm going start the jammer."

"No, Sparks wait! There are too many persons aboard. I can't see who is aboard that boat but my gut tells we should have some peanut butter sandwiches."

I hope Task Force hears via the second encryptor and orders everybody to hold positions. We need the drones to zoom in their cameras but avoid detection, the cameras may be able to confirm a head count. If I'm right and there are four persons onboard that is too many there should only be two or three at the most. The Cartel will not risk disclosing the info on a drug run in the hands of so many people.

"Contact bearing 180 degrees 1,000 yards still coming at us at 35 knots."

"Shit! **Peter Bravo**, the Cartel Boss is here, he probably is going to ride with us he is checking on us personally. Probably because they are unable to make good on their threat."

A FEW MINUTES LATER the smaller boat is alongside Seeker and the cargo together with the Cartel Boss are transferred. There are no words exchanged just a sealed envelope is handed over to me. We stow the merchandise in the concealed cargo hold. He is just watching.

"Release and secure the lines."

"Aye aye Skipper, lines are secured."

"You want to come to the bridge with us."

"I don't want to disrupt your operation I'm here merely as an observer."

"I'm not asking, I'm telling you because when Skipper gets underway if you are not holding on to something you will go into the water. **Please** follow me to the bridge now!"

The Cartel Boss Is seated next to Skipper and Sparks takes his position at the radar.

"Contact bearing 180 degrees 3,000 yards heading 180 degrees straight away from us at 35 knots. No other contacts within 10,000 yards, Skipper you can punch it!"

"Setting course to 000 degrees, speed 35 knots."

"Chief **kindly** open the sealed envelope and find out our destination so that we may plot an accurate course and speed for the next rendezvous."

"Skipper from your tone of voice, I detect you are not too comfortable with our arrangement or my presence aboard you boat."

"Mr. I do not enjoy being threatened or having my family threatened. You are dammed right I'm not comfortable with our arrangement but as for your visit I do not mind."

Nicely played Skipper, or is he really mad at the bastard?

"Skipper I can assure you there is no harm coming to your family as long as the cargo is delivered properly."

"Sure I understand that. But, if one of your employees messes up a transfer and a delivery is not completed you are going to blame us for it and then its bye bye to my daughter or Sparks' mother."

"Skipper, you daughter is in Antarctica Station and she will be there for six months. We cannot reach her, you don't have to worry."

Wow! Now that is good Intel. I got to tell Task Force, no, no, there is no need he has already heard.

"What about my mother?"

"We will not harm her either because if we did you would not want to work for us."

"So you are saying we have a Mexican standoff! No pun intended."

"No gentlemen we have a business arrangement with benefits for both parties if you allow me to explain."

Benefit yes please explain our benefit I'm dying to hear your logic.

"I need your boat and your expertise to setup our new distribution system, you need the money to pay your loans on the modifications,"

Again more good Intel, faulty but good, it's what we planted.

"We will pay well for your service and you can use the money to repay for the loans otherwise we both loose the boat to the bank and surely you also want mama and daughter to continue in good health. I'm sure we can finish our business arrangement before the six months are up and then we will buy your design at a fair price and we part our ways without harming anyone."

The Cartel has accurate but incomplete Intel, which means their source probably only has knowledge of the location but not eyes on Sparks' mother. As for Skipper's daughter, admittedly they do not have access to her, just knowledge of where she is located. It all seemed to confirm what the Boss was saying, for them it's strictly business, like real corporate business not the drug murdering business.

This Cartel is radically modifying their strategy. To make the business more profitable, they are consolidating the distribution channel and they are bringing in professional managers to run it, with minimal coercion and good monetary incentives. Not too different from the way a legit corporate business operates. You had to be aware of all the damage, death and corruption caused by their business, otherwise, you could think you were in business with a smart enterprise making a sound business decision.

The Cartel's new distribution strategy would be unbeatable without having Seeker inside. Even with Seeker on the inside disrupting the new system is going to be extremely challenging for the Task Force.

UNDER THE WATER AGAIN

"SKIPPER THE NEW COORDINATES are 27 degrees north 87 degrees west, ETA is set for noon three days from now. That will be 72 hours from now."

"Sparks, please plot a course on the Nav computer to those coordinates at a speed of 45 knots."

"Skipper, we will reach those coordinates in 31 hours, approximately 7:00 AM day after tomorrow. You need to make your course 300 degrees now!"

"We will have about 40 hours to spare. Maybe we should stop in Jamaica or Belize to refuel and have some drinks with the local señoritas!"

"Are you crazy! You can't stop in any of those ports carrying the merchandise. Besides, we have made arrangements for you to refuel in Havana on the way back."

You did not expect Seeker would be this fast huh? Now you have to make a decision.

"Relax, Boss we won't need to refuel, the Nav computer is indicating we have enough fuel for a round trip back to Aruba as long as we do not exceed 50 knots. You need to tell us what we do with the spare 40 hours?"

"Boy, I'm really glad you are here after all, because otherwise we would have to figure what to do without being able to call you for instructions."

Skipper is rubbing it in and pressuring you until you crack or yield.

"Can you really sustain 45 knots for 30 hours?"

"Yes, and more if needed but 45 knots is the best cruising speed to maintain a balance between ride comfort and fuel efficiency. We can go into Havana on the way up if you want, that way we kill some of the time there."

"No, we cannot, they agreed to the refueling but the merchandise cannot be aboard the boat when we go into Havana. The Cuban authorities need to maintain plausible deniability."

"Can't you contact your people and change the ETA for the rendezvous?"

"It would be too risky to do that over the radio."

"What is more dangerous, spending 40 hours more on the trip with the cargo on board or changing the ETA?"

"Reduce your speed to half."

He is grasping at straws, almost ready to consider my plan.

"You really want to feel the ride doing 25 knots? OK, you are the Boss."

"Reducing speed to 25 knots, Sparks please recompute the Nav specs."

"Aye aye Skipper, I will update the Nav calculations."

Here we go, Seeker starts bouncing up and down like a basketball, the dammed waves are going to break us apart, oh shit that was a hard landing and a loud noise.

"Skipper, at a speed of 25 knots we'll arrive approximately 9:00 AM three days from now but we'll need to refuel on the way back the rate of fuel consumption increases by 33% at this speed."

Skipper decides to try to reconcile with the Boss, between bounces from one wave to another.

"Listen I think we started on the wrong foot. I'm going to forget for a minute that we're running drugs or that you have threaten us. Let me tell you this, if you really want to improve your profit margin every expense counts and one-third more fuel at today's prices is a big chunk plus this ride is worst than taking a ride on a road full of pot holes."

"OK, you are right increase your speed again. I'll think of a way to move the ETA."

"Maybe you won't need to change the ETA. Sparks are you able to modify the frequency on the marker buoys?"

Now is my turn to put the pressure on you!

"Yeah! Sure I can program them to any frequency."

"Boss, do you know if the sonars in your boats are specific or variable frequency?"

"We use variable to minimize the possibility of detection why? What are you planning?"

"I'll tell you when I confirm some more data hold on. Skipper can you tell me from the charts the depth at the destination coordinates?"

Sweat it out you bastard I'm cooking this one in low flame to make you suffer.

"I'll have to pull the charts give me a minute, I stowed them since we're using the NAV computer."

"Do you know the frequency for the sonar on the boat doing the pick up?"

"Yes, I have it in my smart phone. What is it that you are planning? I'm not following you."

"Chief, the charts indicate a depth of 50 phantoms."

"OK, it should work that is more than 200 feet so it would be below the thermal layer and sonar detection would be difficult."

"**Now** can you explain what you are planning?"

You cannot hide your anxiety anymore you are ready to pop.

"One more question and I'll explain. What are the instructions for the boat if we're not at the coordinates on time?"

"When they arrive if you are not at the coordinates they are to wait for one hour monitoring their radar after that they call into my sat phone indicating *the egg did not hatch*, which is the code for no show."

"Are you able to call them now on your sat phone?"

"No, I left my sat phone aboard *El Real* together with your sat phones."

Now I understand your anxiety you really did not have anyway of doing this other than my suggestion and I thought I needed to corner you. You cornered yourself the minute you did not do your homework on Seeker's speed capabilities and miscalculated the ETA.

"You really don't trust us at all! Don't answer that! If I was in your position I would do the same. Are you able to give them additional instructions during that call?"

"I suppose I could. What kind of instructions?"

"Just saying ping with sonar…"

I look at Sparks

"How many pings are required for the activation?"

"Three pings in less than 5 seconds Chief."

"You would need to tell them to ping with the sonar rapidly, three times in a row. That'll cause the activation remotely on the buoy's mechanism and it will float to the surface, we'll write the rest of the instructions for the retrieval on the buoy itself."

"I do not follow. Are you proposing to drop the merchandise in 300 feet of water and then leave with the hope that my people will be able to find the buoy understand the instructions and retrieve the merchandise?"

Exactly, take it or leave it. If you have a better idea let's hear it now. Otherwise go for it.

"Yes, that is exactly what I'm proposing. It's clean, the boats will never be together near US territorial waters, we don't even have to stop to make the drop and when your people retrieve the merchandise you can give new instructions for the final delivery if you need to."

"Can you guaranty it will work?"

I can guaranty we're going to bust your shipment, that is what I can guaranty.

"There are no guaranties in life but I'll bet you that if it don't work I'll be eating only **Peanut Butter** sandwiches for the rest of my life."

Task Force better be listening this conversation I'm clearly giving the code and it should be recognized as a change in plan, I'm requesting to let this first shipment go through. It may be a bold move but I know it will work. Task Force should give me some leeway I'm after all the mission Chief I'm running the op from within the lion's mouth so I'm not able to lay all the cards on the table until we can talk later. By now he is probably on a separate encrypted channel giving instructions to all stations, to hold actions and not to intercept until further notice only surveillance of targets.

"Skipper we need to get to the drop coordinates and back to the Marina in Aruba by the time the pick up boat reaches the coordinates, so that the Boss can take the call and give the instructions. Can we make it?"

I know Seeker can do it I just want to make the point for the Boss.

"I'm pretty sure we can but have Sparks run it on the NAV computer just in case we need to do any speed adjustments. Make sure you take into account we will slow down to say 7 knots for about 3 minutes while we drop the cargo and reverse course."

"Aye aye Skipper, I am running the calculations."

"You better like peanut butter in case this fails."

"Don't you worry Boss I've loved peanut butter my whole life."

That response is to make it crystal clear to the Head of the Task Force that I have a plan in place going beyond the drop coordinates. DEA State side should be alerted that the merchandise is going thru but also ordered not to intercept just follow with surveillance if located. Seeker's crew and cover must be protected at all costs.

"Skipper if we increase the speed to 48 knots we would be back in Aruba by 11:00 AM or one hour before the ETA."

"Give the sonar's frequency to Sparks so he can program the buoy. And Sparks when you finish programing the buoy, I need your help with the aft gun drum. I'll be below deck packing the merchandise, Boss if you want to make yourself useful you can help me packing."

"Tell me what you need."

"We're going to pack the shipment into canvas bags and secure them so that nothing is lost during the drop or the retrieval, I just need you to help me handing over the merchandise so that I can pack it very tight we need to minimize the air pockets inside the bags so it will be less buoyant and will stop producing bubbles in less time."

"Why are you doing this?"

Short answer, because I want to destroy your new distribution channel.

"What do you mean?"

"Why the change of heart? Why are you making sure our operation is successful?"

Because I need to gain your trust.

"I don't like to be threatened either. Even if you don't have any family member to hold against me those two persons above are more than my friends they are like my family and I don't want to see them hurt. I'll make sure your system works **and fast** so that you pay us and we part our ways the sooner the better."

"Does it not bother you that you are helping to distribute drugs?"

Sure it does that is why I'm trying to stop you.

"It does as much as the fact that it's going to occur even if we're not involved, because I know as well as you know, that if we don't do it you'll get someone else to do it. In the end it will continue one way or another. I'm not as naive as you may think, if we don't cooperate you'll find a way to come after us or my friends' families. But I believe that if we're able to set up the distribution channel for you in a way that it cannot be intercept over water, you'l be compelled to keep us and our families alive in case you need us again."

We're infiltrating a Criminal organization the best way to gain the confidence of the target and remain alive is by playing along or more accurately making it look like we're playing along. The Cartel is so desperate to make this new distribution system work that the best way to distract them is to make it work. The Cartel knows that it is a fact of life that merchandise is lost during transport on land all the time and they accept it.

"As long as the merchandise remains secured from interceptions over water you'll be deemed to have fulfilled your part of the bargain. You would never be held accountable for merchandise lost after the arrival on land because it would be already in the hands of the consignee and out of your responsibility."

"I'm very glad to hear you say that, I believe you operate on the principle of keeping your word and I'll hold you to it."

"Good we understand each other. You also have my word that if this solution fails, your price will not be blood I'll only hold you to your word about the peanut butter for the first failure. Let's finish packing the merchandise."

"Chief I finished programing the buoy. What do you need me to help with?"

"We got to finish packing the merchandise and get it ready for the drop."

"You are aware we need to weight those bags otherwise they won't sink."

"Are you asking or stating?"

"Both!"

"Sure I'm aware Sparks that is why you are going to help me on deck with the ammunition drums. When we're done packaging we're preparing the ballast."

"I took the liberty of indicating in simple wording how to retrieve the merchandise by pulling the line in until the end of the rope reaches the surface and then pull the rope. Boss do you need to add any other instruction?"

"No, I think what you wrote is very clear you have done a very thorough job and I sincerely hope Chief can continue to enjoy the pasta he cooks. I'll be on the bridge with Skipper."

"You sure you want to be alone with Skipper?"

"I'm sure, I believe Skipper understands same as Chief by now, surely he heard everything I told Chief over the intercom. I'm not so naive either Chief."

When I hear him say that I switch the intercom off. He does not know but I wanted him to know Skipper was listening.

After the boss left Sparks asked,

"What was that all about? The pasta and the understanding the intercom?"

"He made it clear that as long as the merchandise is not intercepted on the water we won't be held accountable for any interceptions which occurs on land because the merchandise will already be in the hands of the consignee."

I made sure he noticed I switched the intercom on, so Skipper could listen on the bridge. I know he is outside listening to what I am saying to Sparks, I want him to hear it too. I motion to Sparks to refrain from talking until we're sure he is gone.

Sparks verifies he has climbed to the bridge before asking

"How are we going to stop the shipments then?"

"You have already taken care of that Sparks!"

"What? How? When?"

"Come on Sparks help me move the munitions drum to the aft gun. We have to remove the one installed and take out some of the rounds to use them as ballast."

"Why don't we just take them out of this drum?"

"Because **this** drum doesn't have any spent rounds. We're going to remove the spent rounds from our target practice. We'll use the empty cartridges as ballast and replace the empty cartridges with live rounds but the process is too time consuming. I don't want to be caught with my pants down with a gun unable to fire if it's needed. We'll replace the drum and bring the other drum below deck to replace the rounds. The whole process is probably going to take us five to six hours. Let's switch the drums and get something to eat before we get started once we start working on the drum down here I don't want to stop until we're done."

THE PROCESS IS INDEED time consuming but I figure the practice will be useful for both Sparks and me because eventually we might have to reload a drum under pressure. A drum dispenses rounds from a continuous chain which can be opened, same as any bicycle chain, at any of the links. To replace a drum you first remove the chain from the gun by opening the chain at the last link before entering the gun and run the gun in safety mode so the chain is ejected. Then you insert the you insert the chain from the new drum and run the gun in safety mode until the end of the chain comes out and close the chain.

After the drum with the spent rounds is brought below deck the spent cartridges are removed one by one and dropped into another bag. Each spent cartridge is replaced on the chain by a live round inserted into the position. There are a total of 825 spent cartridges but we only need 200 cartridges which will provide enough weight. Two hundred cartridges are a few pounds short of 300 pounds which would be sufficient to weight down all the merchandise. Skipper prepares a special marine knot which will release the merchandise bags when the line is pulled up leaving the bag with the cartridges on the bottom of the sea.

"Thanks for helping with replacing the rounds Boss."

"Don't mention. I realized it was taking too much too long and I wouldn't want the first drop to fail."

"Neither do we. Believe me!"

"We're approaching the coordinates get ready to make the drop when I reduce the speed and when the merchandise sinks I'll reverse the course."

"Aye aye Skipper."

"Come back into the bridge after you make the drop. I don't want you falling into the water when I accelerate."

"Aye aye Skipper."

"Boss if you have any seconds thoughts this is your last opportunity. Talk now or forever be silent."

"No, you may go ahead I'm confident this will work as long as we get back to Aruba on time. I guess I need to order 300 pounds of lead for every trip from now on, so that you don't have to use anymore spent rounds. By the way who did you shoot at with 800 plus rounds?"

"That was just target practice. It would be useless to have the guns if we cannot hit anything with them!"

The part of the plan you don't know is that the buoy also has a GPS marker which will be turned on remotely with an encrypted signal bounced off a GPS satellite after the drugs are in transit. Task Force will alert DEA agents so they will locate the vehicle break a tail light, turn off the GPS signal.

We'll probably let the merchandise be intercepted later by some LEO because of the broken tail light.

BACK OVER THE WATER AND THEN UNDER THE WATER AGAIN

"HOW DO YOU LIKE your new home? Did all the supplies arrive?"

"It's great we just need housekeeping service and we would have it all."

"The last trip bringing in supplies will also bring a support crew who will stand watch when you are on the road and run security for you, I'm sure they'll also keep the place clean for you and maybe even a hot pot of coffee waiting for you when you arrive the next time."

"Thanks for that, it sure is good to have a place to come back to where we can unwind."

"How did you persuade him to keep the buoy all the way with the merchandise?"

"Skipper's argument reminded him about cost control and Sparks explained the buoys are a proprietary design, plus a replacement CO cartridge only costs $1.50 so it would be better to recycle. But, what really persuaded him was that Skipper suggested he should use it as a showcase for the other Cartels so he ordered everybody down the line kept the buoy together with the merchandise and return it to Aruba after the merchandise arrives to its final destination. Unfortunately, we cannot use the same trick for the next time. I don't think he'll be too happy when he watches the bust on CNN. I'm still waiting for him to blame the buoy after he sees the busted tail light."

"Don't worry I have it covered. I have requested access to the Brilliance Marker."

"Did they finally get that project working?"

"Yes, they did! Until now it was restricted for use on the currency distributed in Iraq and Afghanistan but since we're not going to use it on currency it was authorized for our project. It will work perfectly for us too."

"What is the Brilliance Marker?"

"It's a dust, if you will, that sticks to any material and emits a passive electronic signal only traceable by our satellites it's undetectable by any other means. It's so accurate we'll be able to tell where each package of the merchandise is at all times. At least until the packaging is remove assuming they destroy the packaging. We'll have the capability of deciding when and where to bust causing the most disruptions to their operations."

"You don't want to do that!"

"What? Sure we do! What are you saying?"

"No, what I mean is that with that kind of capability it would be best to use it against themselves. Provoking turf wars by making a Cartel feel threatened by another Cartel because they think they shipment info is being leaked. You have to remember, this guy has set himself up by deciding the problem will never be the transportation over water. He'll be absolutely convinced that the problem is something else on land. Since nothing exist it will send them on a wild goose chase among themselves. How many people on our side know we're going to use the Brilliance Marker?"

"The four of us, the techs in Langley and the people operating the tracking satellites no one else knows. We can restrict the info so the rest will just receive actionable Intel about the location of the drugs when we decide where to strike."

"I heard there is a liquid version being developed which once applied to someones hands for example it could transfer and never fade. Did they finish that yet?"

"Chief I don't know that! How the hell do you know about that?"

"Need to know only and I guess when I was told you didn't need to know."

"I do know now!"

"That may be the case but it would be illegal for me to tell you and besides it's best you ask upstairs and get fresh info from the horse's mouth. If it's ready and we can put that stuff on the people who have initial contact with the merchandise we would mark everything from the source even after we're no longer working for the Cartel."

"You are right it would be equivalent to planting a virus in a computer which would corrupt any new file created. I'll ask and if the liquid version is operational and request it for our mission, this one is top priority the Commander in Chief, he has been briefed by the DCI in person and that was how the gold deal was approved."

"WOW! Double WOW!"

"We're sitting here listening to this conversation and I'm starting to fear that by the end of the conversation one of you two is going to realize we need to be eliminated because of what we just heard."

"Skipper under other circumstances you would be correct but under mission protocols anyone who is authorized to hear mission briefs is authorized to hear any classified info discussed. We decided already that you would always participate in the mission briefs so you are cleared. Having said that, I need to remind you that it would be considered treason if you discussed with anyone outside us four about anything you heard during a brief. Thank you for your concern Skipper."

"Thank you for the clarification."

"Let me get this straight, all we have to do is cover the merchandise with this dust and it will not be washed in the water or fade with the handling or anything."

"Correct."

"How about us? Will we be marked permanently?"

"Not with the dust version, the marking will fade from the skin in about a week with normal hygiene and if we use latex gloves when we're handling the dust we would not be marked. With the liquid version...well, we better wait for the Head of the Task Force to explain that to us after he learns about that."

"That means that everybody who handles the merchandise after we dust it, may be located during the next week or so by the satellite."

I look at Task Force and he looks at me with wide eyes. *What Sparks just concluded out loud opens a whole new set of possibilities, everybody in the distribution channel will become a potential target. If it was sanctioned any of those target could be easily eliminated or compromised.*

"I'll make sure to bring that possibility to the attention of the people upstairs when I ask for the info on the liquid, that should help expedite the approval for our request."

Being able to locate anyone implicated in the drug trafficking business gives an immense strategic advantage in the war against drugs. Knowing where a target is can be as important as knowing who the target is and who he has contact with, and finding his associates and or victims of coercion or extortion.

The Cartel is known to have many government officials in different countries working for them, some do it willingly for the money but the great majority are victims of coercion by means of threats against their lives or the lives of their loved ones.

If the Task Force has access to the identity and location of a victim maybe protection could be put in place shielding the victim from the coercion. With this new tool the protection could be as simple as running interference on the access to the victim, a trip out of town, a promotion or a new job assignment.

"Chief your sat phone is ringing I believe it's him."

"Hello. Yes, Boss...What?...We're out at sea looking for one of the wreckages...Sure when and where?...No Sir how would we know?...Yes it has but it was never activated it has to be hard wired to Sparks computer to make it active same as when he programmed the sonar's frequency. I'm sure the tech who took it apart for you is able to confirm what I'm telling you...Sure I'll wait."

I mute the sat phone and ask Sparks,

"Sparks are we sure DEA deactivated the GPS after locating the merchandise?"

"I couldn't tell I switched off all my equipment when he came aboard just in case they made another electronic sweep like they did at the Marina. But, Task Force must have been recording all the time."

Sparks answers pointing at Task Force.

I look at Task Force and ask him to check.

"Call and confirm those suckers at DEA turned it off after locating the..."

He comes back on the sat phone.

"He did, I told you...would you have let us make the drop if I had told you about the GPS capability?...of course not because there was and still is much distrust between us and maybe you will always distrust us, but when I told you I had decided to cooperate I meant it and I still do."

Sparks is giving me a thumbs up, meaning he has confirmed the GPS was turned off by DEA after locating the merchandise.

"I want an opportunity to prove to you the buoys are safe and it has nothing to do with the bust...Sure you did not say that but you and I both know, **that is** what you are thinking and until you are satisfied otherwise you will continue to look for the real cause of the bust. I personally believe in Ockham's razor, ***the simplest explanation is usually the correct one...*** ah you have heard about it good. Then you should give us a second chance and let us give you all the buoys we have. Sparks will show your tech how to program the correct frequency and make sure the GPS is turned off... because you'll give us the buoy to be used and the instructions for the final delivery will already be coded on the buoy we won't even know where the merchandise is going after we do the drop...yes, I know and the other Cartels should be able to trust your distribution system too!...OK, where are you and we'll go meet you, please make sure your tech is at the meeting so Sparks can train him...Let me ask him hold on."

I turn to Sparks

"Any special equipment needed to program the buoys?"

"No Chief any regular computer with at least one USB port. The instructions are entered from a command line prompt with access protected by password."

"Did you hear that?...I didn't understand either, I but as long as your tech did…he does?...Good. We should be there in about let me ask. Skipper how soon can we be at the Marina in Oranjestad?"

"There is too much traffic we won't be able to engage the jet propulsion I would say in about three hours at least."

"You heard? OK, see you then."

I close the call and Skipper jumps at me.

"**You are a scary cool son of a bitch!**. Remind me never to play poker with you."

"Skipper after a while it becomes second nature. Once I knew they had found the GPS chip there was no use in trying to deny it. Look at it as a reverse application of Ockham's razor. I can tell you, it has saved my skin in more than one occasion. Besides I play chess. Poker requires you have luck with the cards and I don't believe in luck, chess is pure strategy. You should try it sometime."

"You mean the simplest explanation is to admit the truth to the enemy?"

"Sure, what is more possible? That we would dare to use sophisticated electronic means which would have been detected when the merchandise was brought aboard the pick up boat. Because you know those guys probably ran a sweep on the package. Or, that some punk let himself be caught with the merchandise because he had a gun in plain sight when LEO's stopped him for the broken tail light. Hell from his point of view even if we were Law Enforcement it would have been too risky to use the GPS chip. He is still trying to decide **if** we're Law Enforcement undercover or not, but he will give us a second chance, because otherwise his only alternative is to kill us and that would also mean he would have had to delay the new distribution system until he has a new fast boat and crew in place, meaning he would have to admit to his Employer and the other Cartels he has failed. Believe me, he'll give us a second chance."

"What makes you think he won't kill us anyway when we board *El Real*?"

"Because you, Skipper, convinced him that maximizing the profits is important and the cost of giving us a second chance even if we fail, is minimal, three bullets one on each of our heads. In addition, Sparks here is going to teach his tech how to remove the GPS chips from the buoys so they have added security."

"How many buoys are we going to give them?"

"How many do we have on board?"

"Chief! We will need buoys for the exploration later and I would need to start from scratch all over to be able to…"

I cut off Sparks.

"OK, Sparks I hear you, leave a couple here at the base and we'll request Task Force to resupply us later."

I complete the statement looking at Task Force and he nods acknowledging the request.

"Why do we need to leave any here if Task Force can get more?"

"Because this is not standard issue CIA equipment these buoys were designed and assembled by Sparks and me. The CIA techs will need a sample to replicate without having to reinvent the wheel."

TWO HOURS LATER we're docking at the Marina next to *El Real*. After the lines are secured we bring 16 buoys to the yacht.

"You arrived early. How far were you?"

"We were about 75 miles north but when Sparks spotted a hole in traffic with the radar I was able to use the jets and make up time."

"Skipper I sense you more relaxed around me now. What has changed?"

"Sir, Chief brought to my attention that if we were not dead by now, it would mean that you were indeed going to give us another chance to prove our worth to you."

"Do you need to refuel? Or need any supplies?"

"Depends on where we're headed?"

"These are the new coordinates your ETA is in two hours."

"How are you going to get the buoy to the boat?"

"You will bring the buoy with you. The merchandise will be delivered to you already packed and weighted. All you need to do is attach the buoy and be on time at the drop coordinates. ETA is set for 50 hours from now but I'm sure Seeker is capable of beating that."

So you are testing Seeker the same trick will not work twice in a row and the Brilliance Marker is not available yet.

"Skipper can we make it to the coordinates on time?"

"No problem, what's bugging you?"

"You know what's bugging me, we should not let the drugs go thru but using even a similar trick will blow our cover."

WHILE SEEKER WAS at the base for refueling and resupply the USCG techs rewired the speakers following Sparks' suggestion to make available two way comm over the second encryptor. Only the Head of the Task Force has access to it so that the channel will not be opened by mistake and give away the cover. The clear code is that the **peanut butter would not** be served.

"Sparks it's your turn in the galley but please **don't** make any peanut butter sandwiches."

The Head of Task Force hears when I gave the clear code over the second encryptor,

"That's right Sparks we don't know yet if the Chief is going to have to eat that type of sandwiches for the rest of his life."

Everybody on the comm laughs.

"Seriously Chief you have to make a decision I'll back you up either way. You have to keep in mind the safety of your team."

"Task Force **the mission is to stop the drug traffic!**"

"Wrong Chief! **The mission is to disrupt the new distribution channel** after they trust it, **the purpose is to stop the drug traffic**."

"That's it! You are right!"

"Off course I'm right, I'm the Head of the Task Force."

"No, I mean that is what the Cartel guy is doing! He is focusing on the bigger purpose not on this trip. He told me that his Cartel was willing to loose some product to insure this distribution channel works safely. This is a smaller shipment. He decided not to remove the GPS marker from the buoy he gave us, even after Sparks explained to his tech how to remove it. Sparks do you think his tech would be able to track the GPS marker if we turned it on?"

"Most probably yes, he has everything he needs to track it because the GPS frequency is inscribed on the chips and we used off the shelf equipment all the chips on all of those buoys are the same frequency, yes I'm certain they could track this buoy if we turn on the GPS marker."

"That's it, he is setting a trap for us."

"What are you saying Chief?"

"I'm saying I'm willing to bet you that I'll eat those sandwiches for the rest of my life if they pick up this drop. They are not sending anyone to pick up they are going to let the merchandise sit on the sea floor and wait for us to turn on the GPS marker. He is trying to control all the possible variables. He is forcing the same situation as the first shipment. If we turn on the marker he'll know and we will become toast. Sparks do they have the frequency to turn on the signal themselves?"

"They don't need it, the signal's frequency for the turn on or turn off is randomly generated by the satellite system it's based on the MAC address for the chip, which he has recorded in his computer from when he connected via hard wire to change the sonar frequency and I'm absolutely sure their tech knows, all of this info because the information is available on the distributor's web page."

"Chief if you are wrong those drugs are going thru."

"Have the drones follow us to the drop and keep and keep eyes over the site. If they attempt to pick up the merchandise, then we decide what we do."

"Roger that Seeker. Drone control your heard the request from the Mission Chief, you have authority for air surveillance please provide constant watch until further notice but no interception is authorized, repeat no intervention of this shipment. Over and out."

WE GOT TO THE DROP coordinates after picking up the merchandise northwest of Aruba and return to Aruba for refueling and restocking. This time we avoid returning to base because there are too many eyes watching us. We have to allow the Cartel to feel comfortable and in control. Carnival week is over by the time Seeker returns to Aruba and we are able to find a slip in Oranjestad's water front, next to where the Cruise ships dock.

Discreet protection from a potential deadly attack is easily obtained from hiding in plain sight. If the Cartel decides to eliminate us and take control of the boat, the last thing they will provoke is a shootout at the waterfront. The publicity of such an action would make it very difficult to take control of Seeker. Besides the Cartel has our sat phone number's and they can easily request to meet anywhere out at sea and shoot us.

OVER THE WATER AND UNDER THE WATER AGAIN

GETTING REFUELED AT THE water front in Oranjestad is first come first served basis and when you are fourth in line behind three passenger cruise ships that means waiting for a long time. We decided to take turns going ashore to do some sight seeing while we waited and when it was my turn alone aboard Seeker I called the US Marshall and requested that a message be passed to Skipper's daughter. To my surprise Task Force had requested and obtained authorization for one delayed encrypted call from Seeker's crew to each of the WITSEC's guests.

"Is worst than that baby, he does not know yet that we're engaged and I'm more afraid of him finding out than I'm of failing the Cartel."

I almost dropped the sat phone overboard when I saw the shadow next to me on the deck as I turned around expecting to see Skipper I froze, it's not Skipper!

"Now I understand what you said about considering Skipper almost like your father. Does he know he is about to become your father in law, is that why he seems more relaxed now?"

"No, he does not know yet and I would like to keep it that way for the time being I don't want to add to the stress him again after he has relaxed like you say."

"Who is relaxed?"

"Skipper, when Chief said he was like your son he wasn't lying after all."

"What are you talking about? Off course not I have known this chump ever since he came out of high school I was his professor at the Naval Academy, he is like a son to me."

"And, do you know he will become your son in law too?"

Skipper looks at me in the eye and with all his cool he answered the question without any hesitation.

"Sure I know, my daughter doesn't keep any secrets from me. I was just making him sweat it out, since he has been waiting for the right time to tell me!"

The Boss turns to look at me his jaw is on the floor and I just raise my shoulders and drop them again while smiling a very nervous smile because I'm without words. I better let Skipper run with it, anyway I'm not thinking straight *I'm trying to decide if Skipper really knew or if he was being so cool he was fooling everybody including me.*

"I came to let you know the shipment arrived well and there has been no interception so we're good!"

"You mean we passed the test?"

"The test is never over but the other Cartels are becoming impatient and want to move ahead. The asshole who lost the first shipment because of the broken tail light was fired last night in jail."

"Fired?"

"You know, terminated, executed. The stupid bastard cost his employer some $8 million."

"When do we go again?"

"I'll let you know, keep your sat phones available. Skipper permission to disembark."

"Permission granted sir."

"Again congratulations on your engagement"

"Sure, thank you."

After the Cartel's representative left, Sparks asked us,

"Chief, Skipper, what just happened?"

"You mean here in Aruba or in the US? Because here the only thing that happened is that Chief just learned I can play chess as good as him! In the US some punk got killed for being in the wrong place at the wrong time. And, I believe, this Cartel guy was trying to bait us with that crap about the second shipment arrived without problems. What do you think Chief?"

My brain is still in neutral at the moment, I'm still trying to analyze the additional information about being baited by the Cartel.

"I think....that...you...are...right."

"About what? My abilities as a chess player? Or, that he was trying to bait us?"

"Both?"

"I for one think he fumbled because he was not able to read any reactions from us, you with your brain in neutral, Sparks with his stupid look on his face not knowing what the hell was going on and me with my expert chess player reaction calling his bluff. Oh, Chief get over it I'm happy for both of you even if neither of you had the decency of telling me. I remember her face full of anguish when you were home with us recuperating from your injuries. I knew she has been in love with you for a long time and I swear I could not be happier for both of you, she knows where your office is at you don't have to lie to her."

"Thanks Skipper I needed that kick on the head."

"Did Task Force hear what went on now?"

"Someone must have heard but not the Head of the Task Force he went to Langley to request the info and if possible the approval for the liquid in spray."

"Chief your sat phone is ringing."

That must be him, whoever is monitoring the second encryptor must have contacted him.

"I hear congratulations are in order for your engagement!"

"Don't mess with me, my head is still spinning"

I look at Skipper but still talking on the sat phone,

"I should have told him when I met with him in Armuelles after so long. Again, a lesson about not leaving things unsaid."

"I checked with drone control the merchandise is still sitting at the bottom of the Gulf of Mexico, he is trying to bait us. Skipper is right the fact that your brain went into neutral is the best thing that could have happened, the fact that there was no reaction at all could not have been staged. That threw him but he's one cool bastard, he was the one who ordered the hit on the guy who lost the first shipment. We have active surveillance on him. Remember the souvenir pens him and the girl took at the Custom house? At least one is still transmitting, we heard him ordering the hit."

"You too are bold, solid cojones man. If they find it during a sweep he will know who gave it to him. How come they have not detected it with the sweeps?"

"Apparently they don't sweep their own yacht regularly and anyway the markings on the outside disappeared one hour after I gave it to him, even if they found it's untraceable because it records the audio in a buffer and burst the digitized audio into the internet by way of cellular connections into proxy servers our friends at the Dutch Intelligence and Security Agency developed it, they gave them to me so we could plant it. I brought one to Langley and gave it to the tech division to see if they can copy it."

"Now that you mention about copying technology, we left two of the buoys at the base. Can you have the techs replicate about a dozen or so, we're going to need them later for the exploration."

Sparks is signaling, he has something else to request.

"Hold on there is one more thing."

I ask Sparks.

"What?"

"Ask him to tell the techs to substitute the GPS chips with programable frequency chips that way they will be more versatile."

I go back on the sat phone,

"Did you hear that?"

"Yes, I did I'll pass on the request but you do know that means the equipment becomes part of my toys."

"Sure but you must remember that we gave away for the mission 16 of our toys before they become classified. So please, figure a way of replacing those unclassified."

"Consider it done. Talk to you later."

"Always a pleasure, enjoy your trip back to Gitmo on the G5."

Skipper asks.

"What do we do now?"

"We wait for the refueling. We need to set watch schedules so we can each have some sleep."

"We should have gone to the Marina and refuel there."

"I prefer to be as far away as possible from that murdering bastard. I'll take the first watch you two go to sleep."

NO SHIPMENTS HAVE BEEN made during the last two days. According to the Intel obtained from the bug, the Cartel's tech is taking all the GPS chips out of the remaining buoys. That probably means that Seeker's probation is over and the Cartel has decided to move ahead using the buoys as we suggested. The only thing needed now is the Brilliance Maker dust to mark the merchandise.

"CONTACT BEARING 175 degrees moving away from us at 28 knots. No other contacts within 12,000 yards. We can jump to warp speed Skipper."

"Sparks activate the audible warning on the radar and go help Chief stow the merchandise."

"Aye aye Skipper."

"Sparks bring me the Brilliance Marker."

"Whoa! How are we going to apply the Brilliance Maker dust if they gave us the merchandise packed already? Is it packed like the last time?"

"Yes, we're going to have to be quick."

"No, I mean because of the locks on the bags."

"Sparks don't you know that the first things spooks learn is how to pick a lock?"

"Yeah Chief but these are locks with double combinations not with keys. They could have other tamper detection gadgets inside the bags. We didn't examine the bags last time because we were focused on the trap."

Damn, he is right!

"What is going on guys? What is Sparks talking about?"

"Sparks is right Skipper we never checked the bags the last time, shit we should have kept the eye on the ball!"

"Skipper could we stop at the base and still make it on time to the coordinates for the drop?"

"How much time do you need at the base?"

"About an hour maybe, we need to put the merchandise thru an X-ray machine. I need an ETA at the base so that Gitmo get the ball rolling on flying in the X-ray machine on time."

"Sparks, make the calculations based on 55 knots and hold on guys. Changing course to 44 degrees, speed 55 knots."

"Skipper if we spend an hour at the base at this speed we will be able to reach the coordinates with approximately 90 minutes to spare but we will need to refuel at base because the fuel consumption will go thru the roof on this run."

"Sparks, recalculate, if we go to the last drop and then spend two hours there before going to the new drop coordinates and use 48 knots for this calculation."

"Chief if we do that run we would have 6 hours to spare and the fuel consumption would allow us to return to base for refueling."

"What are you suggesting we do Chief?"

"We go to the last drop, retrieve the merchandise with REMSO open the packages and figure out what we're facing and how to defeat it."

"Hold on. Changing course to 300 degrees and reducing speed to 48 knots."

"Sparks please cancel the peanut butter for the X-ray machine!"

I say that to signal that we're not going to need the X-ray machine at the platform.

"Do we need to request drone surveillance on the drop site?"

"I believe Task Force ordered it to continue until further notice but we need to confirm it has not stopped."

I say that again for the benefit of Task Force.

WHEN WE ARRIVE AT the drop site the REMSO is deployed in a search pattern using one active sonar ping every 5 seconds to avoid an accidental activation of the buoy due to a frequency harmonic bounce. It takes the REMSO three hours to locate and retrieve the merchandise. The buoy is also retrieved and Sparks destroys it.

"We better record video, in case we need to bypass anything in the new package."

"OK let me set the boat to maintain position and I'll get the camera, Sparks is finishing stowing the REMSO. Do you need a knife or are you going to try to pick the locks?"

"Let's use the knife on the bottom if they did put any tamper detection gadget it would be for the front entrance not for the back door."

"What do you make of this?"

I recognize the contents of the bags and caution Sparks.

"Don't touch anything else those packs are not drugs, that's C4!"

"What do we do now?"

"Are we recording video?"

"Yes, never stopped."

"OK, I can disarm this but the problem is we still don't know if today's package is rigged."

"Then let's bypass it."

"How Sparks we haven't learned anything from this package?"

"Yes, we have, we learned that the son of a bitch was trying to kill whomever opened those bags."

"Listen guys I don't want to rush you but the clock is ticking and we still have to figure out how to paint the merchandise and it's a long drive to the other drop."

"You are a genius Skipper."

"I am? Yes, I am! But why?"

"That's what we will do, we'll paint the merchandise."

"Sparks can you rig the air compressor hose all the way from the engine room to the front locker where the mooring lines are stowed?"

Necessity is the mother of invention.

"What do you need on the hose?"

"What Skipper suggested, the paint gear we used for changing the boat's name."

"Yeah, that's right if it worked for that thick marine paint it should work for the Brilliance Marker dust."

"All we need to do is make a few random holes on each sack and shoot the marker in with the pressure hose we don't need Picasso to do the job any old Seabee will be good enough."

I say the last statement looking sideways at my father in law to be and he smiles back at me.

"If we're going to use that Brilliance stuff under pressure we better put on masks, the CIA hasn't mentioned anything about comprehensive medical insurance yet, I mean in case of severe respiratory diseases."

I look around double checking that we're not within the range of the speakers on deck which are rigged to listen.

"Skipper, they do have adequate coverage for accidents at work at least for high velocity lead poisoning I know that from personal experience."

I'm remembering the way I was taken care of when I was shot during the Panamá op.

"You have been injured more than once during a mission?"

"No, just the one time during the Panamá op."

"But you were still SEAL back then."

"Yes and no, I was still attached to the SEAL team but I was already working for the CIA, it was my first mission for CIA."

"Chief can you talk about this?"

"Yes, I can the mission was declassified when my SEAL cover was blown that is why I was taken out of the SEAL team but at least I was able to complete the extraction even though the subject ended up saving my life."

I say that because the only reason the mission was completed is that Capi patched me up and kept me alive until the Calvary arrived.

"You? You were the one who extracted Capi to Jamaica? No wonder he was so happy to meet me when he found out you and I were acquainted. Why was he extracted?"

"That part was classified! Need to know basis and I did not need to know, I never knew and he has never told me. If I had to guess, it must have something to do with his employment as an Air Traffic Controller before the invasion of Panamá."

"Does Capi know you are CIA?"

Sparks is trying to find out if the rule of secrets had been broken before.

"Not officially, but he knows I was SEAL working on a non SEAL op so technically my cover was blown, plus I had a hole on my back the size of a golf ball. Anyway my handler arranged that after I was released from the hospital I could go recuperate at Skipper's home. All these years, up to the morning when we were intercepted by the USCG coming out of Cartagena, I thought it was because he knew from my file that Skipper had been my diving instructor at SEAL school. That morning when Skipper told me he recognized the guy who recruited me and the warning you gave him, I realized he had placed me with the only family he knew I have."

"Don't get all mushy on us here!"

"I have worked with him all of my career at CIA, not even once has me mentioned anything."

"Maybe, but he cares, trusts and respects you very much!"

"I guess you are right. OK, enough mushy stuff let's paint the merchandise and hit the road we have a cargo to deliver."

SPARKS IS ABLE TO fit a needle adapter used for inflating balls into the nozzle of the compressed air paint gear. The puncture made on the bags is not noticeable afterwards because the fibers are never broken by the needle, only displaced. After the Brilliance Marker is sprayed all around the interior of each bag we stow all the gear and continue to the drop point.

"Skipper we're approaching the coordinates. According to the Nav GPS we're 1,000 yards from the drop."

"Slowing down to 7 knots go and make the drop so we can go back to the barn."

"Aye aye Skipper."

Skipper calls over the speakers and the urgency is evident in his tone,

"Sparks I need you at the radar, multiple contacts approaching!"

"I believe we completed the drop before you saw the radar contacts. Do you think they saw us?"

"Don't think so. They could not have, they are too far. Contact Alpha is 10,000 yards, bearing 070 degrees but it's coming at us at 40 knots. Contact Bravo is 9,500 yards, bearing 350 degrees, also coming at us at 40 knots. Contact Charlie is 8,500 yards, bearing 110 degrees, coming at us at 48 knots. Even contact Charlie is too far to be able to see us making the drop."

"Sparks, can you identify the contacts? Who are those guys?"

"I have no idea Chief. No way to tell from the radar."

"What do you want to do?"

"Let me think! Surely they are tracking us if we run we may raise suspicion. Continue calling the target's position."

"Why don't we ask for eyes on the sky aren't the drones watching?"

"The drones must have gone home for refueling after the pick up, the drones cannot track the Brilliance Maker they have most certainly switched to satellite surveillance by now."

I'm afraid we're alone on this one. We're going to have to shoot our way out if these are Pirates or another Cartel.

Over radio.

"This the US Coast Guard, Seeker heave to and prepare to be boarded! Over."

What is the Coast Guard doing intercepting us without coordinating with Task Force? That one, I did not expect!

"Skipper start stationary rotation and Sparks go and start to deploy the REMSO."

We have to protect our cover above everything!

"What? If we deploy the REMSO we'll loose it if we have to escape Chief."

I know that and we will not.

"We won't need to escape this is the Coast Guard remember. Give me the mike."

I don't have time to explain, they trust me and they act as I told them to.

"Aye aye, Chief"

I take the mike and over the radio I respond.

"This is Seeker we're a Panamanian vessel on international waters, Coast Guard please say again, over."

"This the US Coast Guard, Seeker heave to and prepare to be boarded! Over"

Whatever is going on these guys are on a mission, could it be the comm broke down and Task Force ordered the intercept, no he would have warned us over the open frequency using the codes.

"This is Seeker we're a Panamanian vessel on international waters, Coast Guard you do not have jurisdiction we're on an exploration mission on international waters, over."

BY NOW ALL THREE USCG boats are within 500 yards of Seeker pointing their guns at a position in front of Seekers bow. It is evident that something is wrong but we cannot broadcast over an open frequency our credentials. I decide to play along until Task Force is able to intervene. Otherwise we will have to explain our own way out.

Over the radio again

"This is the US Coast Guard, Seeker we have reason to believe you may be transporting illegal cargo and we intend to board you for inspection do not, I repeat, do not resist, or you will be fired upon, over."

Whoa, that was a clear warning if I have ever heard one.

"Chief, you sure these are the good guys? The sure don't sound friendly to me."

They don't sound friendly to me either. It doesn't make any sense. If it is not coming from Task Force this could get ugly and I don't intend to fire on our own guys to protect our cover.

"This is Seeker we're a Panamanian vessel on international waters, Coast Guard you do not have jurisdiction we're on an exploration mission on international waters, over."

"This is the US Coast Guard, Seeker we have search warrants issued by both the USDOJ and a Panamanian Magistrate authorizing us to intercept and arrest if necessary the crew of Seeker, we **do** have jurisdiction and **we will exercise force** if you continue to resist, over."

What? Arrest warrants from both Countries? This definitely did not go thru Task Force.

"Chief this is getting out of hand we have to identify ourselves!"

"No, it's too late. It was already too late when we picked up the cargo this time. The Cartel is setting us up again to see how we would get out of this situation and Task Force probably knows that would blow our cover, that is why the call has not been made."

Some how that bastard was able to push this thru past Task Force and he is testing us.

"I repeat, this is the US Coast Guard, Seeker, we have search warrants from the USDOJ and a Panamanian Magistrate authorizing us to intercept and arrest if necessary the crew of Seeker, we have jurisdiction and we will exercise force if you continue to resist, last warning, over."

This is it but I need to give Sparks and the Skipper a say in this.

"Guys we have two choices, we show our credentials and we end the mission here but we spend the rest or our lives looking over our shoulders even if we go into WITSEC or we muddle our own way out of this and show the Cartel we don't have a connection with Law Enforcement. I'm sure that by now Task Force is listening in and letting us decide otherwise he would have made the call already."

"Chief this is a no brainer, this son of a bitch has placed a bomb to kill us or other Law Enforcement officers just to make sure his business continues. I say we bring the war to his front door, we have to continue the mission."

Ok that's all I needed to hear.

"This is Seeker we will not resist Coast Guard, we will allow you to board. We're armed but we do not intend to resist, do not use force, over."

TWO OF THE COAST GUARD boats approach Seeker one on each side while the third boat maintains at a distance of 200 yards behind with all the 30MM guns pointing at Seeker's bridge. After Seeker has been boarded and its crew and visible weapons are secured, the third boat moves to a position in front of Seeker's bow and begins preparation to secure a tow line. The Coast Guard officers keep a close watch on all of us with guns pointing at us all the time.

"Commander we're US citizen and this boat is under Panamanian registry would you please explain what this is all about."

"No can do Sir. We have orders to intercept and bring your boat into the nearest USCG base to execute the inspection authorized by the warrants. We do not know what they are looking for sir, the warrants are sealed."

"Commander we have all the intention of cooperating but you come at us with force and without any provocation. Can't you at least lower your weapons now that you have us in restrains?"

"Sir, we were told to expect heavy resistance from Seeker we expected you too make a break for it and shoot your way out. We were briefed on your boat's specs we know that it's capable of accelerating to over 50 knots in less than one minute and we were told you were well armed. Why didn't you try to run? You have enough guns and ammo in here."

"Commander we have nothing to hide! By the way we also have guns on the rails forward and aft. Which we never intended to use against you, they are only for our defense."

Having said that, the Commander looked at one of the other officers and motioned with his head to go check the rails.

When the officer comes back after a couple of minutes he reports to the Commander.

"Commander each gun was covered and with the safety on, two mini guns with ammo drums attached Sir, big drums Sir, larger than the ones we use."

"Skipper, care to explain that kind of fire power."

"I'll take the dance card Skipper, if you don't mind. Commander I'm in charge of the exploration Skipper is just providing the boat and driving. We're exploring for sunken treasures in the hope of finding a big one. If someone drops on us while we have our equipment deployed underwater, we're unable to run away to safety, we would be forced to defend ourselves and Commander for the record we're US citizens and even if we're on a Panamanian vessel I believe we would still have the same rights."

"Yes, Sir you would!"

"Then I would like to have the opportunity to make a ship-to-shore call with your radio, ours doesn't have the capability."

"Sir, we only have available a sat phone."

"May I use it Commander?"

I can't call Task Force but I can call Capi and ask him for help without involving Task Force, Capi can get us a good lawyer.

Again the Commander looks at one of the other officers and motions with his head to go get the sat phone. When the sat phone is handed to the Commander he asks for the telephone number to dial.

"Sparks give him the number for Capi."

"Chief I have it recorded on the sat phone."

"Capi's number is area code 507 and the cel is 6671-6747 and don't look at me like that, I gave up using the stupid phone memories after I dropped my third phone overboard, now I memorize the telephone numbers."

Thank God for old school, when you least expect it saves the day. Always so reliable like if he was expecting my call on the sat phone.

"Capi is me. Yes, yes, but listen I need a favor from you…Cap will you please listen…who…ok I'll tell him but let me…OK, OK I'll tell him now."

Why is he so insistent, I turn to Skipper and deliver the message.

"A friend of yours Toni Forster called he is trying…to…reach…you."

Toni Foster, TF, Task Force why didn't I pick that up he was being so clear and insistent.

"No, no, Chief, you tell Capi **not** to get that guy involved in this situation he is only going to make things worst for us tell him to get us the lawyer."

I deserve a kick on my ass Skipper reacted faster than me, I'm so glad this man is part of my TEAM, part of my family. As covert operatives we only have ourselves we have to get used to being on our own without reliable support to maintain the cover from the enemy. However, when our cover is threatened by friendly Law Enforcement our only resources are our personal friends.

That is the reason why I decided to reach out to Capi for help in getting an attorney. However, Capi is clearly talking on behalf of Task Force I forgot that Task Force as my former handler was the case officer who debriefed Capi after the extract to Jamaica. Task Force knows he cannot interfere with the arrest and seizure of Seeker, it would be a clear sign for the Cartel that Seeker was undercover. *I hope Capi can get us a good attorney otherwise we're chopped liver and we'll be out of the game for a long time.*

"Capi Skipper says to keep that guy out of this...ok you heard him, good... but listen we need you to call Karen yes Karen Thomas kilo tango and tell her we're going to be at, wait a minute,"

I turn to ask the Commander

"Which base are we going to Commander?"

"Coast Guard Station Key West, Sir."

"Capi we're going to the Coast Guard Station in Key West please tell Karen to meet us there if she can and Capi we **need a good attorney** that is even more important than contacting Karen...OK we will thanks Capi."

"Thank you Commander."

"Sir, I'm sorry but we have to put the restraints on you again. We will transfer you to the boat on the port side these officers will remain onboard Seeker and it will be towed."

Oh, oh, people aboard unattended the **Device** *I look at Sparks in panic, but he is not looking at me he is in a blitz.*

"Gentlemen if you allow me to make a suggestion."

"Yes, Skipper what is it?"

I try again to attract Sparks attention when everybody is paying attention to what Skipper is saying.

"Commander if you are aware of Seeker's capabilities you know we can cover the shafts, propellers and rudders to eliminate drag that will make it easier on your engines. I can show your pilot what he needs to do if you want."

"Thank you Skipper for your cooperation. Please do."

Sparks is also attentive to Skipper, I hope he took care of it.

"Son, just flip that switch under the throttle control."

"Commander, do we need to run dark?"

"Yes, make sure there is no drain on the batteries the engines will remain shut."

Sparks explains.

"No need Commander we have solar panels providing recharge continually. You may run all the electrical you need to."

Now he is looking at me and giving me a wink with his eye, he did take care of it, he was just waiting to give an unequivocal signal I can trust him he is good I keep forgetting that is his baby as well as mine.

OUT OF THE WATER

TASK FORCE RECEIVED THE call from Capi immediately and later Task Force played back the recording he had of the conversation when we met in Key West.

"Captain make sure you tell me everything he said don't leave out anything please."

"OK, at first he did not let me talk until I mentioned the name of Toni Foster I had to tell him the message was for Skipper so that he would listen to me."

"Did he?"

"Yes, he did and after he repeated the name to Skipper apparently he realized what it was. When he heard himself saying it to Skipper, anyway Skipper was very quick to react and he said not to let you get involved and please, call me Capi."

"OK, Capi but no editing please I need to know the exact words spoken."

"OK, OK, exactly: **No, no, Chief tell Capi not to get that guy involved in this situation he is only going to make things worst for us tell him to get us a lawyer** I heard Skipper clearly and I told Chief he did not have to repeat it."

"Did they say anything else?"

"Just asked me to give a message to Karen Thomas to meet him at the Coast Guard base in Key West."

"He just used the name?"

"No he also stressed the spelling **kilo tango**."

"Thanks Capi. Did you get the lawyer?"

"Not yet I figured you would want to take care of that."

"No can do Capi. According to the message you just gave me I would burn them if I get the lawyer but Capi don't spare anything, get the best attorney money can buy, Chief has the money. If the attorney requires pay in advance, I know Chief can access his bank account in Panamá."

"OK I know the right lawyer."

Task Force turns of the recorder.

"I just wanted you to hear exactly what was said so that you have the same info I have."

"Thanks."

"After the meeting at Tocumen Airport with Capi I boarded a flight to Miami, rented a car and drove to Key West and I guess you have been here already for several hours."

"I have lost track of time being inside the brig."

"I can imagine. I'm wearing the US Coast Guard's Commander uniform and ID, I'm here as Task Force, officially I'm here to interrogate Seeker's crew. Unofficially I'm here to find out how the hell the warrants were issued without notifying the Task Force. The whole mess occurred just as the drone surveillance had stopped so we were blind when the three boats were dispatched from three different Coast Guard Stations to intercept Seeker. Everything occurred so fast that we found out listening to the radio transmission after it was too late to stop."

"I figure that much when they said they had the arrest warrants and would use force if we resisted"

"When the door opens whomever it's I'm going to start interrogating you."

"I know the drill."

Just in time the door opens and the game starts.

"Sir, I don't think you understand the gravity of your situation if we find an ounce, hell if our dogs sniff anything we're going to tear apart your boat and you are going to jail until we find who you are transporting the merchandise for."

"Commander, the only thing I'm saying to you before my attorney arrives is this Sir, we're going to sue the USCG and everybody else for false arrest and illegal seizure of property."

"Good luck with that, sir."

With those words Task Force exits from the interrogation room. Later he also plays back the recording of his conversations with the Station Chief, *Task Force has learned that showing the cards to the whole team was a good idea in case someone else picked up something missed by others.*

"Lieutenant, I need to talk to the Station Chief."

"Sir, aye aye, Sir, follow me this way, his office is right outside the lock up."

"Thank you. Show me the way."

"Station Chief, the Commander requested to see you."

"Send him right in."

"Thanks for receiving me, Station Chief."

"No problem Commander I was told to cooperate with you in every possible way I can. What can we do for you? Are the detainees talking?"

"They lawyered up. They claim they are just doing underwater exploration and they have nothing to do with drug trafficking for the Cartel."

"Yes, I read the after action report. Have you seen it Commander?"

"No why?"

"It says they surrendered without offering any resistance and they even notified the Commander in charge of the boarding party about the two mini guns they had on the rail. According to the Commander who arrested them, they were very polite and cooperative they just objected to being boarded in international waters. What do you make of this?"

"I don't make anything yet, I'm here to follow the evidence, we'll have to wait for the dogs to do their job and process the boat is CGIS here yet?"

"They are stretched thin, top command requested DEA to assist but then your Task Force gig came up and they told us to hand it over to you. How do you want to proceed?"

"I'll make a few calls and see who can help us the fastest NCIS or FBI. May I see the warrant I know that's the first thing their attorney will ask to see it when he walks thru the door."

"I'm sorry Commander we don't have it. We just received orders for the intercept and the seizure. My understanding is that the warrant is sealed."

"Who would have it? We're going to need it."

"I would suggest you call DOJ."

"OK, Thank you Station Chief you have been very kind in receiving me."

"Don't mention it."

"Commander, excuse me sir the Station Chief said to notify you directly when the attorney arrived Sir, he is here."

"Thank you Lieutenant, please show him to the interrogation room and let him know I'll meet him there later but we will give him time to talk to his clients alone."

"Sir, the attorney requested to talk to all the crew together."

"Sure why not we don't have anything on them yet and from the looks of it I don't think we will."

"Station Chief do you have a secure line here at the station?"

"Lieutenant, please show the Commander to the signal office and tell them I ordered to provide a secure line with privacy for the Commander."

"Aye aye, Station Chief, follow me Commander please."

THE ATTORNEY ARRIVES to meet with us.

"Chief, may I call you Chief the Captain said I should address you as Chief, Skipper and Sparks. May I ask why the anonymity?"

"Yes, you may ask. But first, tell me what else did Capi tell you."

"He said that your boat was illegally seized on international waters, that you needed legal representation and that money was not a problem then he rented a private plane in Albrook and flew me here personally he did not let me talk to my wife to tell her where I was going."

"How well do you know Capi?"

"We have known each other since before he started working as an Air Traffic controller I helped him contact the US State Department to make arrangements for his extraction to Jamaica. He told me I should explain that to you Chief. He also told me to tell you that I was the attorney who was present at his debriefing after the extract. I'm an attorney in Panamá, but I'm also admitted the Federal Bar, therefore, I'll be capable of representing you in front of both the US and the Panamanian Magistrates."

"OK, then we're covered. What is next?"

"I need to talk to whomever is in charge of this circus and request to see a copy of your arrest warrant to determine the strategy we will need."

Knocks on the door are heard.

"Yes, come in please."

Task Force is coming in so soon. I wonder why? He is talking to someone outside the room.

"Ensign, let me make myself clear go talk to the Chief of the Station if you need to confirm my orders, I want the recording turned off. Please let me know when you have complied with my orders."

What is he up to now? Addressing us in the room but motioning us to remain in silence, who is he asking to remain in silence?

"Good afternoon gentlemen, please remain seated."

Again knocks on the door are heard.

"Yes, come in please."

"Commander the recording equipment has been turned off and disconnected."

"Thank you very much, Station Chief."

Task Force closes the door.

"Doctor it's a pleasure to meet you again. I'm glad Capi was able to reach you it simplifies the matter immensely for our purpose."

Task Force has met our lawyer before now?

"Gentlemen your attorney is cleared in certain matters by the USDOJ so we're cleared to speak freely in front of him short of reading him into the mission, all the facts he may need to know to defend you, may be disclosed to him. Before you say anything I need to give some info which will probably put matters into perspective and give you a better grasp on how to proceed with your defense."

With that Task Force plays back the conversation with the Chief of the Station.

"Are you here as Task Force or what?"

"In this room now I'm here as Task Force this is why I played back the recording Doctor so that you are better aquatinted with the situation, as far as everybody out there knows, I'm trying to negotiate an immunity deal with you in exchange for your cooperation. But, you will not accept any deal since the dogs are not going to find any drugs. You never opened the merchandise aboard. Right?"

"Roger that the boat is clean unless the dogs can sniff the…"

I raise my hand stopping Skipper and Task Force realizes he was about to disclose the presence of the Marker.

"Got it. Don't worry Skipper no that is not detectable by the dogs."

"Sorry Doctor need to know on that one and it's not relevant to your defense."

"Understood, Commander."

Obviously this is not the Doctor's first rodeo and he is aware of the way the game is played.

"Why does he address you as Doctor?"

"In Panamá an attorney must have a Doctorate in Law before he can be admitted to the Bar."

"What about the C4 can the dogs sniff that?"

Sparks asks.

"It's all securely sealed the dogs won't sniff it."

"I'm not talking about your C4 Chief."

"OH shit! Skipper does your license cover that?"

I ask.

"What license? Covers what?"

Task Force asks.

"Explosives, C4 to be more specific."

"Why don't we ask your attorney? Guys believe me Capi got you the very best. Even if he wasn't cleared by DOJ. But if we find explosives onboard which are not covered under the salvage license. We're going to be forced to arrest you. On the other hand if the explosives are covered by the salvage license we would have to let you go but the boat would remain here until ATF gives DOJ the clearance. They told me that's standard procedure under the treaty when assets are seized."

"That is correct Commander. I suggest you clear the way with ATF and I make sure the salvage license includes explosives."

This Doctor is cool as a cucumber he appears to be a very calm and calculating man.

"Agreed. Now let me disclose to you how we got to where we're now. I called the DOJ with the excuse to request a copy of the sealed warrant and they gave me the run around until I was finally contacted with the Secretary himself. It turns out that WITSEC had classified everything to do with the name Seeker, I told you, that girl was like mama bear defending her cubs, when it came to the people she protects, anyway when the request for the warrant came thru from Panamá all the alarms went off and the warrant was sealed before the Task Force was notified, by then you had reached the target, so we pulled the surveillance according to our plan and we did not see the USCG boats coming at you. We were blindsided until we heard the USCG hailing Seeker and by then it was too late to do anything."

"Gentlemen I hope that whatever the Commander has said is useful for you, because for me it's completely useless information for deciding on a legal strategy."

"On the contrary Doctor it helps to make your decision also. Commander did they tell you who or why the warrant was requested?"

"No, the Panamanians would not disclose the information to the DOJ and under the treaty the cooperation has to reciprocate so the DOJ was compelled to put out the warrant also, without the information."

"I believe this worked out better for us. Because if Task Force had been given a heads up, you would have stopped it and we would be good as dead the moment we arrived in Aruba."

"Chief what are you saying?"

"Think about it guys, there was actionable Intel providing the time and place for an intercept. The USCG told us they were briefed on Seeker's capabilities and were told to expect heavy resistance from us. If we had not been so early doing the drop they would have intercepted us while carrying the merchandise and we would have only one of two choices, to shoot our way out to avoid the intervention, or identify ourselves."

That causes silence in the room as everybody is contemplating what I just explained.

"Chief is right! Only the Cartel Boss and us knew the coordinates for the drop the only source of the information would have to be him."

"What are we going to do now?"

"Nothing!"

For now, I don't get mad I get even.

"What? That son of a bitch tried to kill us twice in the same day!"

"No Skipper he was testing us and we have passed the test. Now we're in."

"How can you be so sure?"

"Because I would have done it the same, to test my asset. That is the way we're trained."

I address Task Force and ask him,

"Do you have background on this guy before he started with the Cartel?"

"What do you mean?"

"He is operating the way we would, if we were trying to verify an asset was not a double agent. Skipper told me the other day that he and I were playing poker but I told Skipper I was playing chess not poker because poker requires luck with the cards. Now I'm sure it's chess what we have been playing but up to now, we have been very lucky. This guy has been trained in covert and counter intelligence."

"I'll have to dig."

"The question stands. What are we going to do now?"

"The answer stands. We do nothing. Because if I'm correct, he is checking us, so we have to let it play out and let the chips fall where they may, hoping the Doctor here is as good as Capi and the Commander say, so that we can go to our graduation ceremony after passing the test. If I'm wrong and we walk, without walking the line he will eventually find out and we're dead. Which do you prefer?"

I want to get even and we need to stay in the game for that.

"Doctor the ball is in your court."

"I should go back to Panamá to make sure the salvage license is correct."

"Doctor, how did you get here so fast?"

"Capi flew us here in a private plane he is waiting at the airport? Commander, he said you are picking up the tab for that."

"Yes, I know don't worry."

Knock on the door again,

"Yes, come in."

"Commander the sweep on the boat was completed, nothing was found sir."

That took everybody in the room by surprise. The dogs did not sniff the C4. *Has there been any intervention or just pure luck again?*

Skipper started to laugh and said.

"It's amazing what a little grease can do! Do you have any idea what 200 pounds of C4 will do to any ship if exploded next to the keel? I remembered from Seabee training that if you cover plastic explosives with grease you protect it from accidental electrical detonation, but I didn't know it would also fool the dogs."

"What do we mark that as luck or expertise?"

I'm going to call it both, we are in luck that you have the expertise.

"Commander, may I take my clients with me back to Panamá? The sooner we appear before a Magistrate the sooner this matter will be cleared for them so that they can go on with the underwater exploration."

"Yes, yes, sure and I'll expedite the release of Seeker on this end plus have the USDOJ provide the results of the inspection to the Panamanian Government. Doctor will you be able to inquire who was the source of the information triggering the warrant after the matter is clarified?"

"I'll try but legally I would only be able to release the information to my clients."

"Good enough! Have a safe flight back to Panamá."

USCG OFFICERS ESCORT the four of us to the Key West Airport, Capi has the plane ready for departure when we arrive. We are back in Albrook three hours later and from the airport we go directly to the Doctor's office downtown to prepare all the required documents for updating the salvage license to include the explosives.

In the morning we will have to appear before the Magistrate to show the paperwork of the release after the Coast Guard inspection. The Doctor suggests we file a request to be released without bail until the documents from the USDOJ are received and processed. The Doctor explains to us that because we were all Panamanian residents and our boat was in the possession of the US government it would be easy for the Magistrate to determine we would not pose a flight risk.

"Now you go home. Rest there is nothing more to do until we appear before the Magistrate."

"Capi you have been very helpful with all that you've done for us but one last favor please. Can you drop us at the apartment in Punta del Este?"

"Sure can it's my way now. We moved close by last year, Skipper knows where."

"Chief I know you changed your mind and everything about the rental vs. ownership deal but would you mind if I rent tonight?"

Why does Sparks have to bring this up now?

"Rent what a movie?"

Shit, here we go!

"No, Skipper he is talking about *rental property* you know female company."

"Yeah, Chief explained it is better to rent than to own although he changed his mind about it. But I'm still looking for the right property to buy."

"Really? Chief said that to you? Was that before or after you decided to make a commitment to buy?"

"Skipper is not what you think, I was just trying to teach Sparks how important it's to protect the cover. You know as well as I do, that if you buy she has to know what you do or you have to continue for the rest of your life lying. I won't have that problem both her and my father in law know where my office is at."

He is enjoying making me sweat this one out.

"OK, but there will be no renting on my watch! Let me rephrase that, I don't think you should bring a stranger in the apartment at this stage of the game. But you can go to a local Gentlemen's Club to relax."

"Skipper is right Sparks besides we need to do a complete sweep of the apartment before I can call Task Force on the secure line. I need your help, can you postpone?"

"Sure Chief, you guys just put my head back on my shoulders. If I fuck tonight, we can all get fucked. We can't afford to take the eye off the ball even when we're on shore leave until this matter is concluded."

"Listen both of you. One of the things I'm going to ask Task Force is to request from WITSEC delayed contact with the family they owe us for exposing us."

"But you said you believed that it turned out to be better for us."

"I do believe that, but WITSEC doesn't have to know. Task Force should be able to use that as leverage."

In addition I want to test a theory I have about a possible mole in the DOJ.

WHEN WE WALKED into the apartment, before a single word was said, Sparks performed the security sweep. It was just a precaution but one that was needed, even if the building's security controlled the access, the apartment had been unattended for too long.

"Chief it's clean as a whistle, I'm going to crash see you tomorrow."

"OK Sparks good night"

"I'm beat too but if you think we'll be able to get the delay comm tonight I'll wait."

"No Skipper that takes time to setup and I need to discuss other matters with Task Force before going into that. I'll request the comm for tomorrow afternoon that way if she has seen anything in the news you can explain we're out of the woods after the hearing before the Panamanian Magistrate."

"OK good night"

"Good night"

I make the call on the secure line.

"Hello."

"Where are you?"

"We're at the apartment in Panamá."

"Did you sweep it?"

"Relax. That was the first thing we did the minute we walked in and Sparks declared it clean, he does as good a job as your techs or maybe even better, I've seen him using some kind of device he wired himself."

"Where's the apartment located?"

"I told you in Panamá. No way you get more, this is **my safe-house** need to know and the Company does not need to know. Besides if your techs came here it could blow our cover. Some of my neighbors are foreign government officials and their security could smell your techs miles away. Trust me, Sparks does a very thorough job."

"I might have to offer him a permanent position."

"When the mission is over you can ask him if you want but for now I need him and remember he is as wealthy as I'm, I wouldn't be surprised if he turned you down. Having said that, I can tell you on behalf of the whole crew that we all are willing to continue working as subcontractors under the same arrangement as now."

"That is good to hear."

"Then that is settled. Next item! Is the Brilliance Marker surveillance picking up the merchandise yet?"

"Nothing at the drop"

"What does Langley say? May have faded underwater?"

"No, once it is applied to non organic material it does not fade. Water fades it from skin after a week or so."

"Oh I see, then the pick up probably has not occurred yet because the Cartel has no way of knowing if the merchandise was intercepted or not and they would not dare do the pick up until they know the area isn't hot."

"How long before the water affects the marker?"

"The water will not affect on non organic material."

"It doesn't? I thought you said it fades in a week or so."

"Only on skin, organic material but that is the dust the liquid will not."

"Yeah but we used the dust not the liquid...wait a minute is this what you think or is this the current info?"

"This is the most current info I was read in on the specs, Langley approved we use it for the mission."

"They did? When can we have it?"

"It will be tested first on the subject."

"What kind of test?"

"I was not told. We don't need to know."

"We don't need to know? This is our mission if we don't need to know who does?"

"Take it easy Chief we have to trust the people upstairs too."

"OK, OK, so let me make sure I understand the specs, correct me if I'm wrong, the dust will stick to any non organic material permanently including natural fiber such as cotton or canvas, but it will stick only for about a week to ten days to organic material, such as skin or live plants."

"Affirmative."

"The liquid will be permanent on all materials."

"Affirmative."

"OK got it."

"Now surveillance control is confused by something that appeared which looks like a spider web or lines."

"What? Where?"

"In Key West at the Coast Guard Station"

Sure I know what it must be.

"I think I now what that would be, they must have switch the mooring lines to the lines from the boat."

"What are you talking about?"

"When the USCG towed Seeker they used their own lines to preserve evidence, and they tied Seeker to the dock with lines from the dock for the same reason. They must have switched the lines after the boat was cleared it is SOP for a boat to use its own lines when docking."

"Why are Seeker's lines marked?"

"Because we had to use compress air to inject the dust into the bags without opening the bags. We did it inside the locker below the bow where the lines are stowed."

"Compress air so you got that stuff all over you too?"

"What? No, we wore overalls masks and gloves and everything was disposed, except the lines. I hope the USCG personnel wore gloves when handling the lines otherwise they got Maker on their hands."

"Why didn't you just open the bags and applied the Marker as you were instructed?"

"Because the son of a bitch booby trapped the merchandise if we had opened the bags we would have been blown to bits. Where do you think we got the extra 200 pounds of C4? That is what we found on the shipment we picked up, he had it booby trapped. If anyone went looking for it, they would have been blown too. We worked below deck so you would not have heard any of that."

"Booby trapped?"

"Yes, when we opened the bags we picked up, we opened it from the bottom looking for tampering detection and what we found was the 200 pounds of C4 wired to the locks. No merchandise only the 200 pounds of C4. This brings me to the next item on the agenda."

"What is that?"

"I believe that this guy is operating just like we would except he does not have to be accountable to Langley and the rest of the freaking bureaucracy. He probably responds directly to the Cartel's top guy."

"OK, so what is your point?"

"My point is that not too many people on the Totem pole know the specs of what we're doing. I mean the specs of the new distribution system and if I'm right..."

"And, I believe you are..."

Good then you will probably be agreeable to my suggestion.

"If I'm right and we let him prove to the other Cartels the system is safe they will use the channel for more of the merchandise."

"Are you proposing we let the merchandise go thru?"

"Let me finish. Yes, but painted! Then DEA and LEO's can plan their parties or Task Force continues to coordinate to make it look random, you decide those details or maybe Langley I don't care. The point is that if they dismantle or reduce the traffic on their other distribution routes and then we close this channel they will be crippled real bad."

"I see what you say, yes."

"They will have to go back to reactivate the old routes and that takes time, some will have to start from zero others, maybe not so much but in general is going to cause disruption which in turn causes carelessness and that ends up in a general decrease in their business. Allowing us to put more resources towards completing the seizures."

"I like the idea but how do you propose we close the channel?"

"First, we need to confirm that he is the only one holding the keys to the distribution machine then…."

Then we eliminate the threat!

"You want me to request sanction?"

"Sanction for a **Kilo Alpha.**"

"A Kilo Alpha has to be sanctioned by the Commander in Chief."

"Yes, but to get the approval only the Head of CIA and the NSA are involved, no Senate Intelligence or anyone else. I'm telling you this guy has his finger inside many cooky jars he could see us coming if we're not careful."

"How would you do it?"

"We discuss that when the Kilo Alpha is approved."

"OK let me bring it upstairs. Fortunately after so many cages were rattled by WITSEC I have the Director's ear, he is taking personal interest on the Task Force but I'll have to show my face at Langley for a second time in the same month."

"That brings me to the last item on the agenda!"

"Oh, Oh, what is it now?"

"My partners would like to talk to their families. Can you request delayed comms for tomorrow around 1500 Zulu we should be back from the hearing before the Magistrate by then."

"That I'm sure I can, the Secretary of DOJ said to call him directly for anything I needed on this case, it seems the White House asked him to cooperate and coordinate with Task Force."

"There you go you see you already have one foot inside the door to make the request for the Kilo Alpha."

"Go to sleep Chief you need the rest."

"Good night"

"CHIEF WHAT IS a kilo alpha?"

I turn around surprised.

"Sparks I made you sleeping."

"I was but I had a night mare the weirdest thing about that C4 exploding in our face and it woke me up so I went to the bathroom and then to the kitchen and I heard the end of you conversation with Task Force. What is a kilo alpha? Don't evade the question."

"Go back to sleep and I'll tell you in the morning, I need to go to sleep too and when I explain it to you I'll need your full attention."

"OK, good night"

"Good night"

I might as well bring them in now because I want to be ready to execute the minute the Kilo Alpha is approved.

WATCHING THE SUNRISE and sunset from Panamá is a unique experience because it's the only place in the whole world where you can see the sunrise in the morning over the Pacific Ocean and the same day in the evening see the sunset over the Atlantic Ocean driving only 50 miles from one coast to the other.

The Isthmus of Panamá is shaped like a S laying on its side and Panamá City lies on the Pacific Coast facing to sea towards the East. The city of Colon lies on the Atlantic coast but it's facing towards the West.

The view of a sunrise from 45 stories above the street is astonishing when the weather is clear. We are all early risers and we are enjoying together the sunrise this morning having breakfast on the balcony facing the coast.

"I can see why you chose this penthouse there is no way anyone can see or hear us talking out here on the balcony, unless they were on a boat."

"I just want to be safe when I retire, I don't want to have to worry about security. The other two Penthouse apartments are also facing the ocean and both are available if you are interested."

"Are you serious? Who owns them? How come they haven't sold yet?"

"Don't know but I can inquire if you are interested. I would rather have people I know as neighbors. Skipper do you think she will like it here?"

"Hell I like it maybe after the gold thing I can go for the one next door."

"How about you Sparks? The parking space assigned for the opposite corner penthouse is right next to the one you are using now. It's closer to the elevator."

"Sold!"

"OK, I'll call that lady realtor who helped me find this one maybe she can help you guys."

"Who was that let me guess, Capi's cousin?"

"Yeah how did you know?"

"She helped me sell my first home here in the City before moving to Chiriquí."

"So you both know the realtor? I'll definitely call her before we leave so she can start moving the paperwork."

"Good!"

"Do me a favor Sparks when you talk to her, tell I want to start making inquiries on the one next door too."

"Will do Skipper. OK Chief no more delays. What is a kilo alpha?"

"You're requesting a kilo alpha?"

"Who are your trying to fool? Sparks already told you!"

I look at Sparks and he gives me a sad puppy look.

"It's just a proposal not a request, yet."

"Will someone explain to me what is a kilo alpha?"

Sparks is desperate to know.

"Kilo Alpha is a code for **Kill All** it has to be sanctioned otherwise we would be found guilty of murder if we were prosecuted."

"It's not murder if it's sanctioned?"

It still is murder always when you kill another human being.

"Not technically because it's carrying out the sentence determined by the National Government in the interest of National Security. The process involves presenting to the highest authority the arguments of threat to National Security and the proposed action to deter the threat. If the national authority approves the action, then it's sanctioned."

I'm trying to explain an absurdity. I had never even been involved in one before let alone suggesting it myself, strangely it's not revolting my stomach like it did the first time I ever heard of the term and it was explained to me.

"Sparks when a pilot shoots down an enemy plane or a sniper kills a target from 800 yards away or a soldier thrust a knife between an enemy's ribs all those actions are considered sanctioned. Because those actions occur during a war no one questions them as murder. However, a kill resulting from a covert operation has to be addressed in this way because we have to be accountable otherwise we're just like the Cartels killing indiscriminately any innocent person who happens to be in their way."

Skipper has explained it much better than I did.

"I know that was how my father died after I left for Cuba, he and my mother went to visit my grandmother in El Paso, Texas. When they returned across the border, they stopped to purchase gas for the truck. They were caught in the crossfire during a territorial dispute between two of the northern Mexican drug Cartels. My mother was saved because she was in the restroom, but dad was sitting in the truck waiting for her, and the dammed KGB did not allow me to go to his funeral because I was already working with the Professor for the fucking Russian Navy."

"I was a baby when my parents died, I never knew if it had anything to do with drugs or not but my grandfather who raised me was always steering me away from the drugs and pushing me to go into the Navy I always thought it was because my father used to be Navy too."

Sparks has a legitimate reason. Based on the same incident he despises both the Cartels and the KGB. I never had such good reasons I just got involved because I hated everybody and everything.

"Anyway I need you two to help me formulate a plan to have everything ready when the Kilo Alpha is approved."

"How can you be so sure the Kilo Alpha will be approved?"

"Because it is the only goal in chess! A Check Mate, first we made him trust and depend on the distribution channel by allowing the painted merchandise thru. Second we confirm the Boss is the only one controlling the info and contacts on the operation of the channel and how it works. Then we close the channel and with the Brilliance Marker in liquid form all the people who continue handling the merchandise are going to be marked even if the merchandise goes thru other channels. We'll cripple them."

"You sold it to me but I'm not the one who has to approve it."

"I know that but I firmly believe it will be approved and I want to be ready."

"What do you need from us?"

"I need you to put your heads together and work a plan to place the 600 pounds of C4 below *El Real's* keel. Skipper mentioned that C4 could do much damage close the keel of any ship. I checked and the damage would be devastating we just need to figure how and where to place the 600 pounds of C4 below that keel. Correct me if I'm wrong Skipper. The info I found is that a ship sinks because the water displacement capability is compromised not because they take in water. How fast the compromise occurs determines how fast the ship will sink if at all. The Titanic sank in less than three hours because the design allowed too many compartments to flood, after the impact with the iceberg caused the hull breach. However, if flooding is effectively contained and the water displacement capability is not compromised too fast, the vessel can remain afloat. Case in point, the attack on the USS Cole during refueling in Yemen. The hull breach caused by the explosives was so big, that a train locomotive could fit thru the hole with room to spare. However, the flooding was contained and the ship remained afloat. An explosion of 600 pounds of C4 under *El Real's* keel would cause devastating damage breaking the yacht in half and sinking it in minutes."

"You do not need to be corrected. If we can figure how to place correctly the 600 pounds of explosives, we can simulate a Whale's Fart. When are we doing this?"

"For now just the planning but I want to have alternatives ready before the Kilo Alpha is approved. Let's get ready to go meet the Doctor at his office and go to the hearing before the Magistrate."

THE DISCUSSION WAS concentrated on the facts around the interception and the arrest. The audio recording of the radio comm provided by the USCG was reviewed by the four of us and the Doctor asked for clarification on some points. Nothing was discussed about the mission, the attorney was very careful to request and discuss only the information pertinent for an effective legal representation.

When we came out of the hearing the Doctor was pleased

"I told you gentlemen, once all the evidence was presented before the Magistrate he had no other alternative but to grant the dismissal of charges."

"Doctor, does that mean they can travel out of Panamá?"

"Capi we didn't expect you to be here!"

"Yes, Capi they are free to travel but the boat will not be released before the end of this week. There is no use in traveling to Key West until all the paperwork is ready."

"They are not going to Key West Doctor. Guys we need to talk. Let's go to the Albrook Mall, there is a new restaurant inside the Mall, I have been looking forward to try."

What's this about Capi? Who contacted you?

"Doctor, thank you for everything but I hope we don't need your services any time soon."

"I understand Chief but I'm at your service, Sir. It has been a privilege to represent you in this matter."

On the road to Albrook I say.

"Capi I still get confused with the roads here but I think you took the road to Albrook Airport not the Mall."

"I received a call from Sparks' sat phone, asking if I knew you guys."

"What did you answer?"

"The truth, I said I had only met Sparks a few months ago but that I have known you and Skipper for many years now."

"Did they ask anything else?"

"Yes, that is the reason we're heading for the Airport. He asked me if I was certified to fly a G5, then he asked me to bring you to Aruba, he made arrangements for the jet and this morning he wired $10,000 to my account for my services. He said that if you trusted me to bring you the lawyer to Key West, he could trust me too."

"Good news and bad news! The good news is he is confident we're clean. The bad news is that he must have eyes everywhere. He knew Capi flew the Doctor to Key West and he also knew the Hearing before the Panamanian Magistrate was today."

"Chief that would not have been to difficult to follow I had to file a flight plan and the Hearing was **a matter of public record**. Nothing spooky all the info could have been obtained from Aruba over the phone or the internet."

"Even if you are right Capi, I don't want to expose you and your family any more than would be needed. Call Toni Foster and report the payment so that he knows you are keeping the cash to protect your cover and after you bring us back from Aruba no more contact with us or Toni Foster. You hear me?"

"I hear you."

Capi is not part of the operation, I cannot allow him to get hurt trying to save me again.

"One more thing, is $10,000 adequate as your fee for the round trip to Key West."

"You don't need to pay me!"

"Yes, we do, to protect your cover."

"Then I give you the friends and family discount. It would have been only $5,500."

"No Capi it has to be strictly business to protect you."

"Relax I was kidding the normal charge would be less for a prop instead of a jet they are much more simpler to fly. He paid the fair fee, strictly business."

"OK, we will wire you the money when we come back from Aruba."

THE G5 WAS FUELED and ready when we arrive at Albrook Airport, even the flight plan is ready. Capi only has to review and file it. We board and a female greets us. This is the same girl he had with him aboard the yacht and at the Customs House. What is she doing on the G5?

"Nice to meet you again. Are you going to serve us during the flight? Skipper, Sparks you remember her she was the steward who served us aboard the yacht!"

I have to alert them, we need to avoid any mission critical conversation, Capi realizes he should be there only as the driver, strictly business, he got the message too he stays inside his cabin the whole flight, over the plane's intercom

"Lady and Gentlemen, we're beginning our final approach please secure all service items and buckle your seat belts, thank you."

A BLACK LIMOUSINE IS waiting for us when the G5 parks in front of the terminal, the girl remains onboard the G5 together with Capi, we go to *El Real* on the limousine. As soon as we board the yacht departed.

"Chief, Skipper, Sparks, did you enjoy your flight?"

"Very good and the service was excellent."

"Ah yes, she is a very good steward that is why I sent her along."

What else is she for you? You acted like a couple at the Customs House and she was more of a hostess than a steward on the yacht.

"Where are we going?"

"To get some privacy for our meeting."

Not much was said after that.

ABOUT 15 MILES out thirty minutes later the anchor is dropped.

"Tell me where is the merchandise?"

"At the drop site unless you picked it up already!"

"We have not retrieved it. When you were released, I assumed you had been able to dump it before you were intercepted."

"We didn't dump it before we were intercepted but we made the drop at the coordinates indicated and two minutes later the USCG was on top of us from three different directions with their fast boats. They were too far to see us make the drop so we started fixed position rotation on top of the drop to give it time to reach the bottom. Anyway with the noise from the engines of the four boats there was no way any of the sonars would have detect it."

He is assessing what I just told him. Apparently, he is in the dark about what happened. Is it possible he did not cause this?

"Bold very bold and brave on your part. I was sure the merchandise had been lost when I heard you were intercepted."

He did not set us up there is another leak.

"OK, now I have a question for you. Where is the leak? Only your people and us knew the location and time of the drop. The USCG told us they had been briefed on Seeker's capabilities and expected us to present heavy resistance. Who the hell set us up and why?"

"Calm down! You don't think I would be so stupid as to throw you to the wolves with our own merchandise."

"I don't know whose merchandise it was and I don't care, all I care is to stay alive and out of trouble. So before we do another trip we need to know what happened. This one was very expensive between the lawyer and the flight and the USCG were as unpleasant as they could be."

He motions to one of the armed security with his head.

"Please meet one of my **former** partners."

Directing the attention with his hand to a person being dragged from below deck.

"What happened to him?"

Sparks was caught by surprise when he saw the bloody face.

"He hit his head several times against a baseball bat. Hey, careful I don't want blood on the deck, go ahead."

After the order was given the victim who was already bound and restrained, was tied to a bag full of lead and finally dumped overboard.

"He will not be able to stay for lunch. He has a previous commitment. He was the head of one of the other Cartels. A few of them had reservations about the system because I was not sharing the information with them and they were able to talk my employer into allowing him to follow this trip from start to end so that they would be more comfortable with the system. I shared the info with him right after you left, he said he wanted to measure the time it took for the whole transfer, he did not believe the capabilities shown on Seeker's specs."

"So he had access to…"

Before I was able to finish the question he interrupted me.

"Eyes only Chief, never went off the yacht or had them without my trusted female steward standing next to him."

That means that the info is still contained.

"To be brief when I got the news of the intercept, I called my employer and he called the other Cartel heads who had been involved in making the request for information and this morning he was delivered to us the way you saw him now before he stepped off the boat."

"Why are we here then?"

"They asked us to dispose of him but I thought you deserved an explanation and I wanted you to see I was not making up a story. We inquired who was the pilot who took your lawyer so quickly to Key West and when my tech saw the pilot's cel phone number on the flight plan papers he recognized it as one of the numbers on your sat phones. I believe you know the rest of the story."

"How can we be sure this won't happen again?"

"Believe me, the other Cartels are now convinced that the system works if the information is contained. Only my operational group on board *El Real,* you and the other two boats will know the information on each trip. We just need to train the other crews with a few more trips and then you are out."

"I hope this is not a notice of termination. We still owe a bundle to the bank."

Or an indication that we will be fed to the fish same as the departed guest.

"Don't worry if the loan is not paid off by the time we complete our arrangement we will pay off the rest. But remember we will need to substitute Seeker so you will continue to work for us for some time. We need to give the dry dock time to locate another vessel with double tunnel drive."

"I don't think they will. Not many were ever built but they could use any single tunnel boat and add two jets. That should work fine too."

Good play Skipper that is the game make him believe we're still cooperating with him.

"I'll make sure that information is relayed to them Skipper thank you."

WHEN WE WENT ashore at the Marina the Boss gave us back our sat phones before we boarded the limousine.

"I'm going to call Capi to give him a heads up for the departure. Also to ask him if he received the call from…"

I motion Sparks to stop talking.

"Give me the phone I'll call him."

At the same time I write on a piece of paper the word BUGGED!

"Capi we're on our way to the Airport can we be wheels up in less than 30 minutes?...great."

"He says we can be wheels up immediately after we board."

I warn them again we should not discuss anything about the mission by writing down on the paper NOTHING MISS CRIT!

"Chief I'm hungry do you think that beautiful steward will have some chow for us?"

"I for one lost my appetite after watching that fellow turned into pulp tossed overboard."

"That poor fellow almost had us killed I don't have any sympathy for him."

NOT ANOTHER WORD is spoken during the rest of the trip to the airport. The only communication is another message I write: STAY WITH THE PHONES WARNING CAPI.

Skipper and Sparks stay behind, with the three sat phones, offering a tip to the limo driver.

"No sir no need my fee including a generous tip for service has already been paid."

"Capi we're here. Where's the girl?"

"After you left, she went to the galley cooked some food then she went into the bathroom to change and when she came out, gave me this for you,"

Capi hands me a small spray bottle.

"She said more would be delivered to the...platform?...she said you would understand!

I must have the most stupid look ever on my face.

"What?"

Paint me stupid, stupid, stupid. She is the source of our Intel, that is why she took the second pen at the Customs House.

"OK Capi listen we might be bugged."

I try to warn Capi, but he interrupts with another punch from the girl.

"No, she said to tell you the plane was clean!"

"Not the plane, the sat phones Sparks has them outside, we need a noisy place on the plane to stash them out of the way until Sparks can check, otherwise we're not going to be able to talk on the way back and there is much to discuss."

And I need to finish processing all the info I just received.

"This is a G5 it should have an external cargo door just in front of the port engine that a very noisy place if there is one."

"OK get ready to depart I'll help Sparks with that."

"Limo gone?"

"Affirmative."

"Help me with this open this door Skipper."

Skipper smiles and corrects me.

"Hatch not door!"

I look at him trying to process what he just said and realize the correction,

"Whatever. Sparks bring the sat phones place in a bag or something, don't worry there is a net here.

"Close the door? I mean the hatch."

"Everybody climb aboard."

"Where is the girl?"

"Gone, she is not going back to Panamá."

"I was hoping to have dinner on the flight back I'm still hungry."

"Gee me too my appetite came back."

Says Skipper.

"Anything else she said Capi?"

"Yeah Chief, she said Sparks was cute."

Oh no, I need Sparks focussed and look at his face light before even hearing about dinner.

"She also left dinner for you in the galley, I already ate it's delicious. You are going to have to serve yourselves after take off, buckle up will you please."

"Incredible, beautiful, double agent and she cooks."

"What are you talking about?"

"Capi gave me this."

I hold up the spray bottle.

"She left it for me together with a message saying more will be delivered to the platform and the plane is clean!"

"She is a double working for Task Force?"

Sparks asks.

"I don't think Task Force knows about her but I'll ask. Dinner anyone?"

"Yes, I'll have some. Can we talk freely now?"

"Yes, Skipper, we can talk freely."

"I want to tell you an idea which occurred to me during the flight this morning. The REMSO has an effective range working on battery power alone, of four nautical miles. Correct?"

"Skipper remember the range is unlimited while tethered it has power from Seeker."

"I know but I'm saying without power from the tether, for what I'm proposing it would have to be untethered. We can program it to go under *El Real* and with the infrared cameras map the bottom of the hull so I can determine the best place to locate a shaped charge with the C4. We would be able to inflict the most damage to the vessel in a short time, if I can design a shaped charge to produce a large underwater bubble, it would be like a whale's fart hit it. Sparks you are going to have to come up with and idea for a remote detonator and Chief the C4 is going to have to be installed manually. That is my plan any comments?"

"I have one comment. WOW!"

My father in law to be is truly brilliant.

"Double WOW! Skipper that is brilliant simple but effective we can put it into action immediately when we get Seeker back to Aruba."

"Hold it not so fast. Don't we have to get green light from Task Force and wait for the kilo alpha authorization?"

Don't spoil it Skipper.

"Not for this we're not going to act. We're just preparing an alternative. Sparks can you design a remote detonator with ample range?"

"How ample?"

"I don't know what is the most you can give me? How about something out of this world?"

"I'll have to give it some thought."

"OK you have until I dive to install the C4."

"Chief you sound like you want to have this guy dead tomorrow."

"No, not tomorrow but the same day, if possible the same minute, the kilo alpha is authorized. You heard it from the horse's mouth today, him and the operational group aboard *El Real* are the only people who hold the info before each drop shipment."

"Chief the girl is aboard *El Real*. Do we burn her or do we kill her?"

The question hit me on the head like a 20 pound hammer. I'm so angry at the Cartel Boss I am loosing my perspective. Collateral damage sometimes is the price to pay when executing an assassination, even if it's sanctioned. However, the main purpose of the process is to force everyone involved to plan and execute the sanctioned action in the most effective way with the least collateral damage possible.

"We will make sure she is not aboard before we press the button. I'll make sure don't worry my head came out of my ass again."

"Ah! I see. That is why you words sounded so muffled at the end because your head was in your ass."

Says Skipper teasing me.

"Shit!"

"You are smelling it now?"

"No, I just realized the sat phone, my sat phone I mean."

The sat phone had the number I dialed to call Skipper's daughter.

"Chief I'll make sure they are clean when we get back to Panamá. If they are not clean we decide what to do with them, even if they are bugged we're probably safe if we have them turned off."

"Not worried about that Sparks I'm sure you will keep us safe from the bug with the equipment you have. What I just realized is the WITSEC number for…"

Sparks interrupts me in mid sentence. Skipper's eyes widen.

"Not to worry either Chief, Mama Bear has you covered, if anyone calls my mother out of schedule for an authorized delayed comm call, the call is routed to the agent impersonating her at the farm. I'm sure the British agent in Antarctica Station would be the one who answered if they called her."

We all relax.

"OK that is it I'm going to sleep the rest of the flight, please wake me up before we land."

THE REST OF THE week was spent unwinding and planning while waiting for the paperwork to come thru authorizing Seeker's release from Federal custody.

Sparks was able to confirm the sat phones were indeed bugged but ineffective if they are turned off and safe to have them with us because there was no location chip only a secondary signal emitter to send the audio to another sat phone. In essence whenever a call was made or received by any of the three sat phones it would also ring in, most probably the Boss' sat phone.

FINALLY THE PAPER WORK comes thru notifying Seeker has been released and we can go back to Key West.

"Sparks call Capi and ask him to rent the turbo prop to go to Key West the Doctor just sent me an email notifying the documents are ready we can go to get Seeker."

"You want to let the Cartel know we're going to pick up Seeker?"

"No Sparks the Cartel probably has the information already, maybe even before the Doctor was notified. I want to see if the Cartel will provide the G5 and pay for it."

WHEN WE ARRIVE AT Albrook Airport, Capi is coming out of the flight operations office and informs us the plane is being fueled.

"We're in luck. I called to rent the turbo prop but the Albrook flight operations office indicated it was not available but they were making the G5 available without charge."

"Really? I guess we owe you another $4,500."

I smile and look at Sparks and he lowers his head admitting defeat but also with a smile on his face.

"No Chief I also received a call from your friend, he asked me to tell you he was covering the trip and he also asked me how much was the cost of the first trip and asked how much did the lawyer charge?"

"What did you tell him?"

"I told him the cost of the trip but told him to ask you about the lawyer."

Capi's phone rings

"That's him it must be for you."

Capi hands me the phone.

"Hello...yes he just informed me thank you. Sure it's much more comfortable, we appreciate it and more important it's faster...Let me ask him hold on."

I refer the question to Skipper.

"How long will it take us to get to Aruba from Key West?"

"I'm going to guess 36 to 48 hours after departing from Key West. But I would need to see a nav chart to plot a course accurately."

"Give us time to get onboard Seeker and I'll call you from the sat phone when we're underway to give you an accurate ETA...I guess so let me ask him."

I address Skipper again.

"Do we still have the coordinates where we made the drop in the NAV computer?"

"We should, I don't think the USCG would have erased anything but it's the same ones he gave us, we made the drop at the correct coordinates."

"Did you hear him?...What?...No way we can't do that...Why were they killed too?"

I can't believe these people, they just kill anyone who messes up, I can't believe we're still alive.

"They'll probably be tracking us to verify if we do exactly that. Listen when we're onboard Seeker I'll call you to give the ETA and the coordinates and you take care of the pick up"

Sparks motions he wants me to say something to him.

"Hold on they are telling me something here."

I address Sparks.

"What is it Sparks?"

"It has to be the original boat or at least one using the same sonar frequency to make active the buoy."

Good Sparks is on character.

"Sparks is reminding us that...ah OK...good he knows, good then we're set, talk to you when we're underway back to Aruba."

I give the phone back to Capi

"Is he for real or is he trying to set us up again."

"What was all that about?"

"He was talking shop with me like we have been buddies for a long time even confiding in me that someone jumped the gun and eliminated the crew of the pick up boat before he was able to get the coordinates. The guy we met briefly on the yacht, the one who became Mr. Fish Food, he took control of this trip and wrote himself the coordinates he wanted on the buoy. This whole thing was an attempted coup trying to take control of the distribution channel by eliminating us and the Boss. When we made the drop on time, and avoided getting arrested, we not only made ourselves trustworthy to him because unknowingly we saved his skin, we also managed to cause the whole thing blow up on Mr. Fish Food's face. Because when the Doctor inquired who was the source of the information for the warrant, the Cartel found out it was Mr. Fish Food who leaked the info. Capi you were right, it all became a matter of public record once the charges were dropped and the warrant was unsealed."

"That is good news, we're in!"

"Capi, **We're** in but **YOU** are to stay out, strictly business. For you it is touch and go, when we land and get off this jet you are wheels up in five minutes, the G5 can make it to Key West and back without refueling."

"Yes, it can but I'll have to amend the flight plan and request additional fuel it will take another 30 minutes. Go to the terminal and wait out of the sun I'll call you when we're ready to depart."

"You guys go into the terminal I'm going to sweep the G5 before we hop in."

"OK, Sparks good idea."

"Do you always carry your electronic gizmos around?"

Skipper asks.

"I do since after we came back from Aruba. Spook Chick taught me something. In an airplane the only effective bug which may be planted, is a passive bug to record audio but it requires retrieval. To operate, any bug must emit a minimal electromagnetic signal my custom made equipment can detect it."

"Is that all she thought you?"

"The G5 is clean, maybe Spook Chick was supposed to plant the bug and she didn't plant it to protect us. I wonder how she got away with that."

"She did not have to get away with anything. She did record our conversations during the flight in, that is why she remained in Aruba to deliver the recording. She told Capi the plane was clean because she left it clean that is SOP in a handoff. I think the Boss changed his mind about us and decided to return the phones to us at the last minute. On the way back to Panamá there was never going to be bugs on the plane. He probably heard the recording before we arrived at the yacht. When we were leaving he had already decided to trust us that is why he gave us the sat phones, not to bug us he knew we would have to keep the sat phones turned off during the flight. He did it as a show of good faith because he already knew the other crew had been eliminated and he would have to ask the favor for the retrieval."

OVER THE WATER
MANY TIMES

THE RECEPTION AT KEY West was warmer this time, the Station Chief personally met with us and apologized on behalf of the USCG and the Governments of the US and Panamá. There was no mention of Task Force. Seeker went out to sea completely fueled and stocked Skipper plotted a course which will take us back to Aruba within 40 hours with a layover of 8 hours at platform.

"I don't want to cut it so close I'll tell him 48 hours, with the excuse that we don't want to push the engines or that we can't go so fast around the Keys or something."

"Tell him we need to do a shakedown during the trip to make sure the USCG did not plant Seeker full of bugs or crippled any systems. He'll buy that!"

I'm so proud of my TEAM we're all in character now.

"That will do it Skipper, thank you!"

I grab the sat phone and make the call.

"Good day Sir, I have the information for you...yes, a very good flight. Our ETA will be approximately 48 hours from now...sure we could do it in less time but Skipper and Sparks are insisting we do a complete shakedown during the trip to make sure the USCG did not plant bugs or compromised any vital systems...no they are comfortable 48 hours will be enough...OK we will if we need to or even if we can do it sooner...don't you worry these two are very thorough they will inspect every inch. Next, the coordinates, they were still saved on the NAV computer. Ready?...25 degrees north 85 degrees west. OK, bye."

I switch off the sat phone.

"We're still buddies, after he heard about the shakedown he said and I quote: **If the Skipper or Sparks need additional time just call it in!**"

We all laugh together and when we finish we look at each other realizing this is no laughing matter and that we got him.

"OK, now we need to talk to Task Force. Sparks is the second encryptor online?"

"It's but we do not want to eat peanut butter sandwiches!"

"Then make something else!"

"Anything but no peanut butter sandwiches!"

Finally Task Force is heard thru the speakers.

"I heard you the first time Sparks, I was talking to Langley about the spray."

"What's going on with that?"

"They are waiting for confirmation on the test but for some reason it was delayed. Anyway they shipped a drum of the liquid to the platform it will be there by the time you arrive. They also expect to know by then, if the test worked and techs will be there to give you instructions."

"Instructions for what? How to use a little spray can?"

"Spray can? What can? They said it was a drum filled with Brilliance Marker in liquid form. After the techs heard you used compressed air with the material in dust form they tested using the new version in liquid form with compressed air. That is what they are testing. What are you talking about?"

"Spook Chick, she gave us a small can filled with Brilliance Marker and said more would be delivered to the platform, remember the girl in the Customs House, she was the female hostess onboard *El Real* she is working undercover, next to the Cartel Boss, he planted her onboard the G5 on the way to Aruba to listen in on our conversations but we made her, so we were careful not to say anything mission critical in front of her during the flight. Anyway before she left the plane she told Capi **the G5 was clean and asked him to give me the small can with the message about the delivery to the platform.** Are you telling me you don't know about her?"

There is silence *Task Force must be processing the info.*

"She must be working directly for Langley I wouldn't put it past them maybe she has been the source of our Intel all this time but I didn't know about her and I don't get Intel directly from her. In fact, I lost my ears inside, because the other Cartel guy the one who leaked the information for your arrest warrant, he grabbed the only pen remaining, to write on the buoy the coordinates and when the pen did not work on the buoy's surface he threw the pen overboard. We have lost track of him, we will not be able to confirm yet if the information is compartmentalized until we find that Cartel guy."

"You mean Mr. Fish Food?"

"Mr. who?"

"You can stop looking for him. We know his new address it's about 15 nautical miles north northwest of Aruba we witnessed when he was forcefully relocated he was carrying way to much luggage. In addition we have the Intel, the information is now only handled by the crew operating out of *El Real* and it's handed in person to the boat's crew just before departing to make the delivery to Seeker."

"How do you know this?"

"Because I just had a conversation on the sat phone with him and he told me."

"OK, then all I have to say to you is, have a good trip to Aruba and Godspeed to you! Over and out."

THE DRUM WITH THE liquid Brilliance Marker is loaded during refueling at the platform. The techs also deliver a collapsible container to place the merchandise into it during the process of painting, as they called it. The small can had not been delivered for Seeker's crew to use it. It was being returned after the initial application for the test. The test was to confirm the transfer would be **permanent** after the initial application using the liquid version. The target had been painted for more than ten days already and still the Brilliance Marker signal was clearly detected. Multiple points of contact were clear on the target making it easy to distinguish from the initial painter who was displaying a much smaller marker.

During the following several weeks we have made multiple deliveries all the merchandise we handle is painted with Brilliance Marker in liquid form with the compressed air. The tracking of the marked merchandise is active. The Brilliance Marker transfers permanently to anyone handling the merchandise after it has been painted aboard Seeker. Each target painted has to be identified and confirmed to avoid targeting by mistake a person not involved with the distribution.

Langley has decided to classify the tracking information and modified Task Force's mission. We are only supposed to paint the merchandise. The selection of targets is restricted. Handled only by Langley and NSA at the highest levels possible. The same people who are responsible for presenting the request for a Kilo Alpha.

Any interception of the merchandise is carefully coordinated by a very small group of people who selectively **leaked** the information to DEA field agents and other LEO's. In most cases the drug is intercepted before it reached the street but the main goal has been to paint as many people as possible to take action against the painted targets later.

THE INFORMATION NECESSARY to approve a sanctioned Kilo Alpha originates and is handled in the field by the operatives. However, before that information reaches the people responsible for presenting the request, it must be analyzed extensively, cross checked and verified against other sources. Once the request is presented, and before any decision can be made any possible unwanted repercussions have to be laid on the table.

If the action is ever traced back to the US Government, it would seem to be the execution of multiple persons without due process. The due process involved could not be disclosed. Because, the due process is based on actionable intelligence which would expose the covert agents who obtained the information to begin with.

"I can't tell you much more, I'm not getting anything back from Langley I get more information about the drug busts from CNN than I do internally. However, I was able to confirm that Spook Chick is working for Langley, she is or rather was a field operative attached to the tech division she was planted to paint the main target, your Boss. She was planted to gain his confidence so that when the Brilliance Marker was ready for deployment she would paint him and she will be extracted soon. They are just waiting to confirm the transfer worked permanently before pulling her and surely they don't want to burn her so the extraction is in the works to do it cleanly."

"That makes sense. We'll continue painting all the merchandise we handle, there is plenty of marker left in that drum it's still half full. We were just trying to confirm if the marker trace is working or if we had to make any adjustments."

"The only thing I can tell you is that if it wasn't working they would have already jumped down my throat and they haven't. In addition, they would not be talking about pulling assets from the field. If I didn't know better I would think they are preparing to close the channel you might get your request for the Kilo Alpha approved after all. Talk to you later. Over and out."

"Skipper after we complete the drop please plot a course to Aruba. We need to show our faces in Oranjestad and renew the special permit."

"Has it been that long already?"

"Sparks need your help in the galley."

"Aye aye, Chief"

I write on the erasable board on the wall: EARS? But I say out loud.

"We're going to prepare the pasta tonight to celebrate!"

"No, not down hear unless Skipper opens the intercom or we raise our voices."

"That's what I thought but I needed to confirm."

"What's going on Chief? You are scaring me! Are we burned or did anything happen to my mother or Skipper's daughter?"

"No, nothing like that I promise!"

Skipper standing outside the galley door says.

"You better not start lying to us!"

"What are you doing down here? Who is manning the helm?"

"I put it on auto rotation, you have never before asked for help in the galley, I figured something was wrong."

"No, nothing wrong, I promise! Did you leave the audible radar signal on?"

"Yes, and I raised the volume all the way up, because I left the intercom off so that our conversation will not be picked up on the second encryptor."

"OK, quickly, we need to move fast on the plan to place the C4 under the yacht. Langley may be planning to close the channel soon and even approving the Kilo Alpha."

"Task Force confirmed that? I never heard him say anything like that."

"Not in so many words but I know how things work upstairs and the modification of mission to only painting and restricting access to the tracking info are both tell tale signs of wrapping up the show. This is happening. And, you know what? We're celebrating tonight with pasta, after all there is reason to celebrate we're going to start searching for the gold soon."

"I don't know about you but I'll not feel too comfortable exploring for the gold off the coast of Aruba with that murderous son of a bitch operating out of Aruba."

"I agree with Sparks. We need to finish the plan. Hell, we need to place the C4 under the yacht and have everything ready in case he changes his mind and comes after us, we need to be able to blow him up."

"Wait a minute who has his head up his own ass now? We can't do that specially now that we know that Spook Chick is onboard, we need to wait for confirmation she was extracted and we have to wait until the yacht is over deep water and far from land and…"

Oh my God here I go again.

"You sound like you have every detail accounted for already."

I exhale heavily and say,

"I do except placing the C4 and I have not seen a reliable detonator yet."

"You have just laid out the whole plan. First we go into Oranjestad to get the permit, that will put us within one and a half miles from the Marina at Oranjestad from the Customs House, Sparks can direct the REMSO to the Marina and back during the time you and I are doing the paperwork for the renewal of the special permit. Second, I design the placing of the C4 with the imagery REMSO brings back. Third, Sparks builds a detonator…"

Sparks jumps in.

"The detonator is ready."

"Have you tested it?"

"Yes, testing is completed."

Skipper and I both look at him with doubt showing on our faces.

"What? Testing an electrical charge detonator does not require exploding anything. I just needed to confirm the detonator will deliver enough voltage thru the length of the prima cord **and** that it can be triggered it effectively from a remote location. A voltage meter is all that is needed."

"**And** you have already tested that?"

"Yes, you want a demonstration?"

"Yes, I do. Working with prima cord is not easy for a person who has not been trained in explosives."

"Skipper, please turn the knob on the gas burner but do not touch the igniter."

Skipper does as requested and Sparks pulls a gizmo out his pocket pushes the button and the gas burner ignites a second later.

"I just ignited the stove from 44,000 miles away and the shielding provided by the stove is equivalent to the shielding provided by the yacht's hull. Any questions?"

Skipper fills a pot with water and places it on the lit burner.

"Yes, I have one question. Chief, you use salt and oil or just oil for the pasta?"

"What the hell was that?"

"Mr. Electronic genius here found a way to rig a GPS transponder chip to react pushing an electrical charge thru prima cord when it's made active with the satellite signal. You requested detonation from out of this world and you got it."

I'm still doubtful about the detonator and ask,

"Yeah that's marvelous but they will detect the GPS transponder when it is made active."

"They might, but too late by the time they react the Whale will have already farted! Which brings me to the Fourth and most important step, someone has to find a way to dive under the yacht while dragging 600 pounds of C4 the prima cord and the GPS transponder without giving away his position."

"I have that covered I just need some help from one of you two engineering geniuses to design how I achieve neutral buoyancy for the total 600 pounds. I already tested with 60 pounds of lead but when I start releasing the weight the rest starts floating."

"That's easy I'm surprised you have not thought about it. Use a second SEAL CCBC one for you and one for the C4 on a sled."

"A Closed Circuit Buoyancy Compensator?"

"You will dive with Closed Circuit equipment to avoid detection correct? You don't want bubbles rising to the surface giving up your position. We can rig the sled to carry the C4 and the rest of the equipment with a second CCBC and you trim the buoyancy as you install the C4."

"Can you also turn off the stove from the satellite when the water boils or do I have to do it."

I ask with a sarcastic tone in my voice.

"Sorry Chief this works one way only. I did not think there would be any need to turn off the GPS transponder after the explosion."

Sure after 600 pounds of high explosives exploding, there is nothing to turn off.

"Sounds like we have a workable plan. I'll call in to let…"

Skipper interrupts me before I complete my thought.

"No, you are not. We're not going to give Task Force any heads up on this one!"

"No Skipper I'm not telling Task force. I intend to call the Cartel Boss to tell him we're going into Oranjestad to renew the special permit. We all agree on this plan **OUR eyes and ears only.**"

I grab the sat phone on the bridge and make the call.

"Good afternoon, we made the delivery and we're heading into Oranjestad. Just wanted to give you a heads up because we'll go to the Customs House to renew the Special Permit…Yeah that is good to hear tell her I say hello to her too. I didn't want word to get back to you and catch you off base…Boss we have not spotted any tails but I have to assume you have eyes on us when we come ashore. Don't get me wrong we don't mind specially after what Mr. Fish Food tried, we rather you keep us protected from the other Cartels…Great that definitely makes me feel a lot safer, may I share the information with the rest of the crew…thank you and good afternoon."

I switch off the sat phone.

"Just when I thought he would not surprise me anymore!"

"What now? How is he making us safer?"

"The head of the Cartel he works for decided to assign mercy angels to us."

"I'm afraid to ask what a mercy angel is."

"If any of the other Cartel tries to approach us or follow us or even puts eyes on us or any other member of the core group, the mercy angels eliminates the threat. After Mr. Fish Food tried to take over the distribution channel the head of the Cartel became extra cautious and ordered the Boss to handpick his crew including us to become a self contained core group including the mercy angels and the crews of the boats who deliver the merchandise to us."

"Are you sure he is not setting us up again?"

"Let's ask Task Force because **we're not having peanut butter tonight.**"

Task Force hears the clear code and answers on the second encryptor.

"Two times in the same afternoon. Are you trying to make me fall in love with you?"

"No but I need you to make a special request for Intel from Spook Chick before they pull her."

"I'm ahead of you. I already signaled Langley to request the Intel before the extraction."

"Not needed she has the info she was next to him when we were talking on the sat phone I heard her talking to him, she was letting me know she was there and that she heard all the conversation. What you need to tell Langley is to extract her **now** so that she will be able to deliver the info."

"I'll call tonight. Over and out."

"Galley now! Let's serve dinner."

Once everybody is inside the galley again.

"This is going down in the next 72 to 96 hours that is how much time we have to install the C4 and lure *El Real* out to sea once we confirm Spook Chick was extracted."

"What are you saying we're going to go ahead without authorization?"

"No, we will not! However, the authorization will be coming down once they confirm the channel can be closed without leaving any loose ends. We're just going to make it look like one of the other Cartels did the deed. That is the only reason I'm keeping our plan from Task Force so that he will have plausible deniability."

"Understood. Let's eat and punch into Aruba. We have to be there by mid morning."

UNDER THE WATER
A WHALE FARTS

AS WE APPROACH PORT Skipper calls in on the radio.

"This is Seeker, Port Authority of Oranjestad please come in, over."

"This is Port Authority of Oranjestad, what can we do for you Seeker, over."

"This is Seeker, Port Authority Oranjestad please contact Customs House to request permission for docking at their facilities and in reverse, over."

"This is Port Authority of Oranjestad, Seeker our records indicate you have an active Special Permit allowing entrance without clearing Customs, over."

"This is Seeker, Port Authority of Oranjestad if you check your records again you will note the Special permit's due to expire shortly and we need to renew, over."

"This is Port Authority of Oranjestad, Seeker understood but why request docking in reverse? Over"

"This is Seeker, Port Authority of Oranjestad the last time we docked at Customs House facing in, we had trouble coming out due to our LOA so we're requesting permission for docking in reverse, over."

"This is Port Authority of Oranjestad, Seeker understood please hold. Over"

Skipper turns the mike off to wait for the response and Sparks asks him.

"Skipper, why are we really requesting docking in reverse?"

"If we dock in reverse, our stern will be facing that wall concealing you when you drop and retrieve the REMSO."

Over the radio.

"This is Port Authority of Oranjestad, Seeker you request has been approved, over and out."

Skipper gives us a deliberate wink. After putting away the mike.

"Sparks, I got the idea from the suggestion made by the Marina the first time we docked next to the yacht. If the Cartel is monitoring our radio transmission they will not be alerted by the request."

"Gotcha Skipper."

I don't have to worry about these two guys being in character anymore, I think they want to get even with this bastard as much as I do or more.

AFTER WE DOCK FOLLOWING the plan Sparks drops the REMSO already programmed to make a run to the Marina at Oranjestad map the yacht's hull and return to Seeker. I go into the Customs House office to complete the documents required for the renewal of the Special Permit. I purposely make various mistakes to allow enough time for REMSO to return to the barn. Skipper stays aboard Seeker to study the live video feed from REMSO's cameras and start his calculations for the placement of the C4.

When the REMSO returns and is secured in its cradle Skipper comes into the Customs House Office looking for me and alerts me. The REMSO had returned. The renewal is a formality and we are told the new permit would be issued within 30 minutes and we decide to wait.

"Ahoy Seeker, permission to come aboard."

I hear someone calling from the water on a tender.

"Please identify yourselves and state your purposes."

"Chief, the Boss send us to bring you an invitation to dock at the Marina when you finish your business at Customs House I'm here to clear you way into the Marina."

I ask Sparks if he recognizes the person.

"Is that the same crew member who came aboard the first time?"

"Yes, Chief the same!"

"Permission granted please come aboard."

I call out to him and motion with my hand to approach.

"Grab the line, let me help you, grab my hand."

As I extend my arm over the rail to help him climb aboard.

"Greetings"

Definitively the same person now I can see him clearly.

"Thank you Chief. Glad to see you again. The Boss wants to meet with you tonight. Chief, I'm assigned to Seeker during your stay in port."

"Assigned? You mean as our mercy angel?"

When I say that I surprise him.

"Is there any threat we should be aware of?"

Apparently he realizes the Boss must have explained.

"No Chief is just the new security measures for the core group, no threat just new SOP."

I hope you are telling the truth.

"OK, we're waiting for the new permit we will be underway right after it's issued."

"May I use the radio to contact the Marina Skipper?"

"Yes, Sparks please set him up."

Skipper motions to Sparks to help the guest and we all go to the bridge.

"That was VHS channel 19 correct?"

"Yes, Sir"

Sparks calls on the radio.

"This is Seeker, Marina at Oranjestad, please come in, over."

"This is the Marina at Oranjestad, Seeker please go ahead, over."

"You are set go ahead."

Sparks says handing the mike to the mercy angel.

"This is Seeker, Marina at Oranjestad, we're requesting docking instructions, over."

"This is the Marina at Oranjestad, Seeker you are cleared to dock please proceed to parallel slip 82 on your port side as you enter the Marina, over."

"This is Seeker, Marina at Oranjestad, say again did you say slip 82 or 81, over."

"This is the Marina at Oranjestad, Seeker you are cleared to dock please proceed to parallel slip 82 repeat 82 on your port side as you enter the Marina it is empty and it is next to your host, no need to rotate because you are docking on the pier, over."

"This is Seeker, Marina at Oranjestad, roger that slip 82, over an out."

"Chief, you comfortable driving the boat? I need to go to the engine room to check something."

"Sure Skipper no problem"

A Customs House officer from the dockside.—"Ahoy Seeker, your paperwork is ready."

"Thank you Officer."

"We have cleared your departure with Port Authority you may depart immediately."

"Thank you again."

"Always a pleasure Sir, good evening"

"Good evening"

"Sparks secure the lines."

"Aye aye Chief, Lines are secured."

WHEN SEEKER DOCKED at the Marina the Boss and Spook Chick were waiting at dockside and boarded Seeker at the same time the crew member was instructed to go back to *El Real.* The Boss looked nervous which was rare for this man.

"Boss is everything OK?"

"I don't want to alarm you. That is why I asked you to come to meet me, I wanted to tell you face to face. Tomorrow afternoon we will leave for San Andres for about a week, my employer asked me to take care of a situation we need to correct. I need to ask a favor of you."

"Sure Boss what do you need?"

Hugging Spook Chic with his arm as she stands next to him.

"I don't want her to be exposed to what we will be doing in San Andres and I was wondering if she can stay aboard Seeker. I'll also leave the crew member who came with you now, he is assigned to keep you secure."

"Done and done I'll tell Skipper."

"Where is he?"

"He is checking something in the engine room he treats those engines like if they were his babies."

"I have noticed he is a go to man, he does not care if he has to get grease under his nails."

"Not at all, he supervised personally all the work at the dry dock and performed some of the work himself. He is probably making some adjustments to make Seeker run faster."

"More speed great! Thank you for your help and I expect you for breakfast tomorrow morning."

"Definitely, specially if she is cooking, see you in the morning, good night."

I enter the engine room and tell Skipper, the news.

"I hope you have been working on the design for the shape charge and the sled because I have to dive tonight. *El Real* leaves tomorrow for San Andres they will be out one week."

"I'm almost done with the design of the shape charge just have to double check my computations I want to maximize the bubble created by the explosion. I'm going to need Sparks to take care of the sled, after all it was his idea to use the CCBC."

Sparks enters the engine room announcing,

"I heard you and I'm already working on it. After I overheard the Boss requesting accommodations for…"

Sparks pauses looking at my face and realizing I have not told Skipper yet.

"You have not told him yet?"

"Told me what?"

"The Boss asked to leave the mercy angel and Spook Chick with us during their visit to San Andres."

"No wonder Mr. I-Prefer-To-Rent has such a wide grin on his face. You can wipe the grin from your face she will use my cabin and you will sleep on the bridge. Someone has to watch the Mercy Angel in case he has orders to dispose of us."

I'm beginning to feel useless, Skipper is becoming the paranoid one now.

"What? No way Skipper! Well, three months ago I wouldn't have put that past him but tonight I saw it in his eyes the son of a bitch is in love with her."

"How do you know that?"

"Because of the way he was looking at her standing next to him."

"She was here aboard Seeker?"

"Yes, she was standing next to him when he asked me."

"I saw it too Skipper."

"I'll be dammed first we run drugs for him and now we are promoted to baby sit his lover."

"I love to stay and chat but we all have work to do. I have to be in the water before 3:00 AM."

"Why 3:00 AM?"

"Because the diving equipment will only give me two hours of air and I need to be out of the water before sunrise. I'm going to check my equipment and get some shut eye."

"Good night"

WE HAVE SIX HOURS to complete the design of the shape charge and actually prepare it, loading it on the sled and put everything in the water. Seeker's stern is pointing away from the yacht which provides an advantage for deploying the diver and the sled. Skipper has completed his calculations and Sparks double checks all the math, while Skipper starts packing the C4 onto the sled. We finish lowering the sled into the water at 2:30 AM it takes us fifteen minutes. The only noise in the Marina at 2:30 AM is the ripple of the water striking against the hull of a boat in the Marina. Any water splash could be clearly heard by the people standing guard aboard *El Real.* The process is tedious. Sparks dives, more like he crawls down into the water to submerge and adjust the buoyancy of the sled.

During the process he realizes that the placing of the explosive won't be posible for one diver alone if the buoyancy needed to be adjusted constantly.

"What do you think you are doing?"

"Preparing my diving equipment to go with you."

"No, you are not. If they detect me you have to be aboard Seeker to help protect Skipper and..."

He puts up his hand to his mouth motioning me to stop talking and says to me.

"Chief shut up, you need my help, it was very difficult to adjust the buoyancy on the sled you are not going to be able to place the C4 and maintain the buoyancy all by yourself within two hours. Besides, if they make us we're all dead wether we're aboard Seeker or in the water."

"Chief he is right, hell if I could, I would also go, but with my busted ear I'm more useful on deck causing a distraction if anything happens."

They are both right and now is not the time to argue.

"OK but let me explain how the closed circuit breathing apparatus works."

Again he puts up his hand to his mouth motioning me to stop talking and says to me.

"Skipper already briefed me on the particulars I know I can't remove the mask under any circumstances otherwise the bubbles will escape and we all die. Chief we have to do this, let's go."

"Make sure you bring the night vision goggles."

I say to him but looking at Skipper and he nods his head indicating he trusts Sparks will do good.

"Got them let's go it's 2:55 AM."

DIVING AT NIGHT IS different from diving in daylight, under normal circumstances during a night dive we would use high intensity lamps to light our way. However, we're installing explosives on the bottom of the yacht, and we need to hide in the darkness. My SEAL training for underwater demolition kicks in and I have memorized the positions of the C4 but Sparks has no idea where he is or where he needs to go, he will only be able to follow along like a blind man and make sure the sled does not float and hits the hull.

During one hour and forty-five minutes we go thru the tedious process of placing the C4 into the specific positions Skipper has calculated. We also run the prima cord to all the C4. Every time I remove weight from the sled Sparks adjusts the buoyancy, the last item is the installation of the detonator. I decide to locate the detonator behind the housing for the starboard propeller shaft to minimize the danger of having drag tear the detonator prematurely during the travel. By 5:35 AM we're already sleeping in our cabins, we're expected for breakfast with the Boss at 8:30 AM. We will have less than three hours of rest.

"GOOD MORNING EVERY ONE, I hope you all will enjoy the breakfast I prepared."

We're greeted by Spook Chic.

"Boss if I may be so bold. The best part of complying your request, is that we'll have a marvelous cook for the next week. After a while you get tired of peanut butter sandwiches and pasta primavera as the only selections in the menu."

I hear Sparks but I know he is not complaining about my cooking he is looking forward to enjoy time together with her.

"The pasta primavera Chief prepares is exquisite. Why do you complain?"

Is she flirting with Sparks? Back off girl, the mission is not over yet and our lives are still hanging by a thread.

"Try eating it every other day for three months and then ask me the same question."

Everyone laughs as the Boss asks to be excused when a group of men approaches the yacht. He goes to meet them where they stopped. He spends several minutes talking to them but none of them boards the yacht and all avoid presenting their faces to us.

When we were left alone Spook Chick murmurs who the visit is, without moving her lips.

"The older man is the Head of the Cartel, he came to say good bye but he does not want you to meet him, that is why they stayed away."

The boss comes back aboard after a few minutes.

"That was our employer he came to say good bye and give last minute instructions."

"Why didn't he come aboard?"

"He is a very reserved man and he wants to keep the core group as a separate unit from the rest of the Cartel. The way he sees it's that if they don't recognize who you are, you may get closer to your enemy."

"That is a very sound philosophy in this business. I respect him for that."

AFTER THE BREAKFAST *El Real's* engines are started to warm them up and perform the pre departure systems check. The Boss comes aboard Seeker together with Spook Chic and the mercy angel assigned to protect her and us.

"Boss if you are worried about any reprisals because of what's going to happen in San Andres, one man is not going to be enough protection here."

"I can't spare any more men, if anything happens I expect you and your people to assist."

"I'm not suggesting you leave more men and you can be sure we will assist in defending her if it comes to that."

"What are you suggesting then?"

Good he is in listening mode.

"That you allow us to also go out to sea and we remain in international waters until you return. Out there we can deploy our weapons and our radar would alert us if any vessel approaches us, dockside at the Marina we're sitting ducks."

He looks at the mercy angel who is motioning his head in agreement with my suggestion.

"It seems that you always have a better strategy Chief, your military training has already proven to be useful in the past. How much time do you need to before you can be underway?"

Skipper answers that question.

"Sir our engines are turbines they don't need warm up. We can be underway in less than 5 minutes after I start the engines."

"Do it! However, I want you to give her one of your sat phones."

She interjects.

"And a weapon."

"You are not doing any shooting."

He scolds at her but in a protective tone.

"You showed me how to use a weapon and I can to defend myself."

She tries to make a point but he is becoming impatient with her.

"OK, listen you take my sat phone the Boss' number is on speed dial and here is my gun but if we detect any threats you go below deck and call the Boss on the sat phone so that he can come help us."

I try to propose as a compromise, wondering if she did this on purpose to allow me to demonstrate we're going to take good care of her.

"OK."

She surrenders.

"That sounds good to me too."

He surrenders too. *That was easier than I expected. She baited him and it worked, she reads him like a book.*

"Once we're over international waters we will deploy the mini guns and everybody wears life vests always above or below deck."

"I can swim!"

Round two, I hope she is just playing her character because otherwise she is making this too difficult.

"I can also swim but I'm not capable of dodging bullets. Our life vest are made out of Kevlar and they will help protect you from a bullet."

"You will do as he says, it's for your safety."

He puts his foot down and she lowers her head and nods, *wow, she is playing her part this girl is good.*

"Sparks get ready to cast off."

Sparks answers but almost tripping over his own foot, *not now Sparks the mission is not over yet!*

"Aye aye Skipper."

"I hate to throw you out, we do like your company but…"

"I have to go."

"Secure the lines."

"Aye aye Skipper…lines secured."

"Good luck in San Andres!"

She cries out to him. *Keeping in character?*

"See you in a week."

I hope not, I think to myself.

"Miss please follow me below deck."

"Now?"

I motion Sparks to distract the mercy angel

"I want to show you where the galley and your cabin are."

Sparks calls out to the mercy angel who is already comfortable around us and follows.

"Hey buddy can you give me a hand stowing the lines?"

I write on the erasable board on the galley's wall: SAT PHONE IS BUGGED! Pointing at the sat phone I gave her.

"This is the galley and everything you may need to cook should be available thru that door."

She nods back to me indicating she understands.

"Where is my cabin?"

"You will use Skipper's cabin he'll move into the cabin Sparks and I use, Sparks and I'll be taking turns on the bridge during watches."

"Your luggage is already in the cabin and your life vest is hanging inside the door, please wear it!"

"I will, I promise."

"I'll be on the bridge if you need anything."

"Did you warn her?"

"Yes, but we're going to have to figure a way of getting in touch with Toni Foster. Right now we're sleeping with the enemy and bugged."

I ask Sparks as he walks into the bridge.

"Where is he?"

"I left him on deck familiarizing himself with the mini gun. His eyes popped out of their sockets when I showed it to him, he was truly impressed."

"Can you operate the encryptor without being noticed."

"No, I would have to wear the headphones all the time."

"I'm worried if they say they don't want any more peanut butter sandwiches?"

"I have an idea if I rewire the speakers…"

Sparks stops talking in the middle of the sentence and looks at the door. I turn around and see the mercy angel walking in and ask at the same time.

"Any contacts on the radar?"

"No, we're clear, no contacts within 5,000 yards."

"Chief you don't need to worry I love peanut butter sandwiches. However, why would you need to rewire the speakers?"

"I was telling Skipper and Chief that if I rewire the audible signal from the radar to the speakers, we will not need to keep someone on station watching the radar all the time."

Good boy Sparks, you are in character again.

"That would give us an extra pair of eyes on deck, I agree. Do it."

Was he given the authority for this type of decision?

"Don't you want to call it in to clear it with the Boss first?"

"I'll let him know, but he told me I could trust you on tactical matters go ahead with the rewiring."

I'm surprised to learn that the Boss trusts me so openly now.

FOR SPARKS IT WAS a simple matter of substituting the wires coming into the second encryptor for wires from a microphone and a set of headphones and the two way comm channel was established in the privacy of the electrical room behind the galley.

In addition, he wired the audible signal from the radar to the speakers as suggested and it was just as easy. The disadvantage is that Task Force will loose ears aboard Seeker and to make matters worse the Cartel has ears now because the sat phone is active all the time.

"Done, we now have an audible signal over the speakers!"

"Can you test it? Do we need to have a contact?"

I'm not surprised he wants to confirm the work was performed.

"No need that is easy. We just increase the range of the alarm to more than the nearest visible contact and we should hear the signal."

Sparks answers and at the same time motions me to go into the electrical room.

"Do you know anything about radar operation?"

"No but I have always been curious."

"Come I'll show it may be useful that you learn how to operate the radar too."

I write on the erasable board in the galley: NEED YOU AND THE SAT PHONE ON THE BRIDGE NOW

"Can you bring something to drink to the guys on the bridge?"

"Sure."

I try to reach Task Force on the second encryptor

"Task Force come in, over."

"Task Force come in, over."

"Task Force I hope you are recording we were forced to rewire the speakers, sat phone aboard is bugged when active, we will attempt another contact using this channel at 0500 Zulu, over and out."

THAT WILL HAVE TO do for the time being, at least Task Force will know how to act according to the new situation. I turn off the second encryptor and go to the bridge.

"That contact is *El Real*!"

"How can you tell?"

"For various reasons; first, this indicator is reading the heading for the contact it's heading towards San Andres; second, this one reads the speed which within *El Real's* capabilities; third the most important factor, that ever since we departed I designated the contact here as contact Alpha and the radar keeps tracking it as Alpha until I change the designation or the contact goes out of range."

"Wow! That is a whole lot of details to keep track of, I don't think I could do it."

"It gets better, when there are multiple contacts. Heads up guys, when we reach international waters we're going to put the boat on fixed rotation mode and we will deploy the guns and start a watch schedule."

"How can I help?"

"Sparks will tell you what to do."

"Are you used to working with night vision goggles?"

"Not really"

"No problem then, you take the watch during daylight and sleep from midnight to 0600. Its four of us so we can do six hour watches and our cook will serve us chow and coffee."

"When do I sleep?"

Spook Chic asks.

"From 2000 to 0200 overlapping our shifts so you help us keep awake. If that is OK with you?"

"I'm glad to be useful Chief, that takes my mind off the danger."

"That is the whole idea."

THE FIXED ROTATION mode maintains the position of the boat and in addition, it provides a variation to the point of view of the people standing watch eliminating the sun glare and shadows thanks to the rotation thus making it easier to keep an eye on the horizon. During the next five days we watched the sunrise and sunsets over water without seeing land.

From our location, with Seeker's fuel capacity we are able to maintain fixed rotation mode for 30 days if needed and still go back to Aruba at full speed without refueling. The schedule I devise allows the opportunity to contact Task Force when the mercy angel is sleeping.

The best Intel is frequently developed from different sources. When I have the private conversations over the modified second encryptor with Task Force we have been able to fill in the blanks for each other by sharing the information from Spook Chick and the Intel obtained from assets in San Andres.

According to the Intel, the Core Group has gone to meet with the surviving soldiers of Mr. Fish Food's Cartel. Originally they had indicated they were receptive to accepting a merger with the Boss' Cartel, however, when they started showing signs they were changing their minds the Boss' employer ordered the Core Group to be established. When they requested a meeting to find a solution the Boss suggested neutral ground aka San Andres and the Core Group was sent to negotiate a favorable solution.

Legitimate corporate business and Cartel business are handled in similar ways. When a new CEO must be selected usually the person having the most Board members on his side is the one who is appointed. In the Cartel's world the person having the most soldiers usually becomes the new head of the Cartel. Similarities also apply when it comes to mergers and acquisitions, in the corporate world the entity having the most monetary power usually survives. In the Cartel world the Cartel having the most fire power is usually the one who survives.

ON THE SIXTH DAY at Zulu 0500 Task Force informs me there has been a massacre in San Andres the prior evening. Preliminary Intel is that *El Real* has departed from San Andres at approximately 2200 Zulu. The Core Group has eliminated all the opposing Cartel Members but several innocent casualties were caught in the crossfire.

The incident occurred at the same resort where *El Real* had been docked. The Governments of Panamá and Colombia have made backdoor requests to the US Government to take action against the Cartel because citizens of both countries were victims of the massacre. The Commander in Chief had ordered that *El Real* be intercepted over international waters and be brought to Gitmo. The Kilo Alpha has been authorized and if the target presents any resistance, the intercept is authorized to respond with force. Two US Navy frigates and the two US Coast Guard boats were ordered to execute the intercept.

I'm listening to Task Force on the second encryptor very attentive.

"The ships should be intercepting the yacht around 0800 Zulu. Over"

"Hold on I just heard a noise in the galley."

I find Spook Chic in the galley and write on the erasable board: SAT PHONE? At the same time I ask her.

"Can't sleep?"

"I left it in the cabin tucked under the pillow."

"The angel?"

"Sleeping like a baby I dosed his coffee again."

"Come in here for a second."

I talk to Task Force again on the second encryptor.

"Task force I have here the asset hold on another minute."

I talk to her but I make sure I keep the mike opened.

"I can't give you all the details now but we need to know if there is any heavy artillery aboard *El Real.*"

"Yes, I have seen at least four rocket launchers and two ground to air missile launchers all shoulder fired, easy to deploy I suspect they have more."

Again addressing Task Force on the second encryptor

"Task Force did you copy that. Over"

"Yes, I did thank you. I'll notify Langley but I think the boys on those ships are just going to have to be ready for heavy resistance. Over"

"Why not just blow them out of the water with a drone. Over"

"Unfortunately the target is covered by heavy clouds. Anyway, the President wants a visible show of force to send a message that we're taking steps to bring these people to justice. It should all be over in less than three hours. Over"

"Copy that. Over and out."

I turn off the encryptor.

"Go to sleep in the morning we go back home."

I try to tell her the mission is finally coming to an end.

"Home? Where is that?"

I'm surprised to hear her question. But I feel the same way. Have we lost our way like the children in Peter Pan's tale?

"I wish I new."

I go up to up on deck to talk to Sparks.

"How long would it take you to set up the detonation from the time we have Kilo Alpha authorization?"

"What happened?"

"The Core Group committed a massacre in San Andres and the President authorized the Kilo Alpha but he ordered a group of ships out of Gitmo to do the interception around daybreak."

As I talk he listens very carefully and asks.

"So what is the problem? They will catch them!"

"Yes, but it will cost heavily. The girl just confirmed the yacht is carrying heavy fire power, shoulder held rocket launchers and other."

When I answer his question his head snaps and he asks me another one.

"You are sure the Kilo Alpha was authorized?"

"Yes, Task Force just confirmed it to me."

Sparks turns around and looks me in the eyes putting his hand in his pocket and says to me.

"OK. Done."

"What is done? What are you saying?"

ONE AND A HALF SECOND after Sparks put his hand in his pocket a signal comes down from 22,000 miles in space and makes active the GPS transponder chip under the yacht's hull. The activation initiates an electrical charge which travels thru the prima cord detonating simultaneously the 600 pounds of C4 we placed under the hull.

At the same time an alarm goes off on the Cartel's tech's computer indicating a GPS transponder has been activated somewhere on the yacht. Before he can say a word, his body goes down on the deck violently, as a result of the powerful upward push caused by the expanding gas bubble released when the C4 detonates. A fraction of a second later his whole body crashes into the ceiling of his compartment when the gas bubble collapses and the yacht's keel breaks as the vessel disappears underwater.

The shape charge designed by the former Seabee used the yacht's advanced hull deflectors to direct the blast downward and away from the hull increasing the depth at which the bubble was generated thus increasing exponentially the effect of the blast and maximizing the damage.

"A whale just farted!"

As he says those words to me, we hear a shot from below deck, Sparks and I instinctively pull our guns from the holsters and run below deck to find Spook Chick coming out of a cabin with a gun in her hand and sitting down at one of the galley tables. A moment later Skipper arrives. For a long period there is silence, then I take the gun from her hand as she stands up from where she has been sitting.

"Anyone care for breakfast? I can serve it on the rear deck and we can watch the sunrise I have a felling it will be a beautiful one this morning."

She appears to be cool but the hand which held the gun begins to shake.

"What do we do with the body? Lead or freezer?"

I'm surprised Sparks is so calmed.

"Hell man these people are ecology conscientious you know they love to feed the marine life."

Skipper's comment is even more surprising to me.

"We should call Task Force."

I say trying to make sense of what is going around me.

"What for? He probably knows already."

Says Sparks.

"He knows the contact disappeared that is what he knows."

I say.

"No, he wouldn't. You told me Task Force said the intercept would occur at sunrise."

"That is correct."

I say to Sparks and turn around to Spook Chic and ask her.

"Why did you kill the guy now?"

"Because he could have alerted that miserable son of a bitch! Besides Task Force said the Kilo Alpha was authorized."

She pauses for a few seconds and continues.

"It is mission protocol and you were hesitating I heard you talking to Sparks on deck."

She says that but showing clear signs of nervousness now.

"Calm down we're all on the same side here. He attacked you and you had to defend yourself so you shot him in self defense and he fell overboard, end of story, that is how the after action reports will read."

She looks up at me and relaxes. Then she asks.

"What is a whale's fart?"

"That is another story. For you, it's best to have plausible deniability."

"The whale farted?"

Skipper was not aware yet but he is not surprised actually he looks happy from hearing the news.

"Apparently so."

I say looking at Sparks as he pulls the gizmo out of his pocket to show Skipper, with a smile on his face.

"What course Chief?"

"No where, we have been invited to breakfast on the rear deck. We remain here until we're told of the outcome of the intercept. Then we probably will have to go to the platform to deliver the asset we have extracted so that she may be flown to Gitmo and from there…"

I look at her and complete my thought.

"Wherever she needs to go."

She smiles back at me.

BREAKFAST IS SERVED, the sunrise is enjoyed and the fish are fed. Around 0830 Zulu I go to the second encryptor and contact Task Force.

"This is Seeker, Task Force please come in, over."

"Finally I didn't dare contact you with the bugged sat phone and the Cartel Guy aboard. Over"

"How did it go? Over"

"It didn't go. The yacht has disappeared. Over"

"What do you mean it disappeared? They missed it? Over"

"No, the contact disappeared from the Brilliance Tracking with the cloud cover so dense over the target the drones had no visual so we don't know what happened just that the Brilliance tracking says they saw it disappear. At least the tracking has the last coordinates. Over"

"Well, listen we had an incident here the Cartel guy for some reason attacked the girl on deck during the watch and she had to defend herself and she shot him, he went overboard. Over"

"Roger that, just include it in your after action report and head into the platform I want all of you out of harm's way until we're able to sort this mess. Over and out."

"Skipper now we can go, set course for the platform and punch I want to take a long shower with hot water without having to worry about the rationing."

"Sparks any contacts?"

"No contacts within 5,000 yards Skipper."

"Setting course 030 degrees, speed 45 knots."

OUT OF THE WATER
AND ON VACATION

"FIRST ORDER OF BUSINESS, I need you two…"

Task Force is pointing at me and the girl.

"sitting down and writing your after action reports and bring them to me. You two"

Pointing at Sparks and Skipper

"gather all your personal belongings from Seeker because when we're done here, you will be flown to Gitmo and from there you catch a G5 to Albrook. We meet here in 45 minutes."

FORTY-FIVE MINUTES LATER

"Are you sure about this Chief?"

"Yes, sir that's what happened. Sparks and Skipper can confirm."

"What Chief wrote on that report is what happened sir, we were there too, and we helped him turn the asset and kill the Cartel guy, then we fed the guy to the fish, all sanctioned under the Kilo Alpha."

"What are you talking about? That is not what happened I killed him! It's all in my after action report, I shoot the Cartel guy aboard Seeker?"

Task Force turns to the girl tearing her report apart and says to her as he disposes of the paper:

"We don't accept after action reports from assets. The only after action report I have here is from the only CIA operative who completed this mission. This report indicates that you are here because Chief, Skipper and Sparks were able to turn the female steward from the yacht after the

Cartel guy attacked her aboard Seeker. The report also indicates the crew killed him, disposing of his body in the water. It further indicates that you helped to identify the weapons aboard the yacht as…"

Task Force looks at my report

"…some kind of shoulder held guns, big guns. That is what the after action report I have in my hand says. Do you care to dispute anything?"

She looks at me confused and asks.

"Chief?"

"If I'm not mistaken Task Force found out that your cover inside the Cartel was so deep that as far as Langley is concerned you went down with the yacht. They never had a chance to coordinate your extraction and you have become an asset turned by the team of external contractors who work for the CIA assigned to Seeker."

She remained speechless.

"You will go with your team to their safe house for further debriefing and Chief will report anything else he finds out later directly to me. Now then I have bad news and good news. Which do you want first?"

"The bad first please!"

"Seeker stays at the platform this is its home base. As for you guys you are not off the hook yet, just on vacation, the mission infiltrating the Cartel may have concluded but the agreement is not fulfilled yet. Langley still wants the gold, it has not been forgotten."

"That's not bad."

"Let me finish."

"You are on ice for about 18 months but maybe less. The USDOJ is initiating an investigation on the disappearance of the yacht but they do not want it raised until we're certain if the disappearance was caused by one of the other Cartels. That is the main reason why you are going into hiding to protect your cover and yourselves and your families. When the DOJ clears the way, Seeker and its crew, will assist the US Navy in finding and salvaging the wreckage. The gold will be the next order of business after that."

"That is bad news. What are we supposed to do until we can take Seeker out again? Sit on our hands?"

"Sparks you will be consulting for the CIA tech division to put together more of those buoys and the bug detection devices you used during the mission, you will be compensated for your designs and your consultation. Skipper you will consulting for the ship builder to help design the modifications to the new Island Cutters now in production. You will also be on the payroll for that."

"What about me?"

I ask.

"You Chief and your fiancee are going to work with me to devise a plan for the search and extraction of the yacht and the gold. I understand your fiancee is a geologist and an archeologist, we need her expertise to determine if the cause of the yacht's demise was a methane bubble. Or as you called it a Whale's Fart."

"You forget she is in *Antarctica*. Remember?"

"That brings me to the first good news. The USDOJ approved that the protected witnesses be released under the protection of the CIA in a foreign country. Langley authorized the use of covert contractors to protect the witnesses. We need to coordinate your ETA into Albrook so that your arrival coincides with the arrival of WITSEC flight's. WITSEC only agreed if they are able to surrender the witnesses directly to your hands."

Skipper, Sparks and I all smile.

We all exclaim at the same time.

"Those are great news!"

The girl remains in silence.

"Wait there is more. The CI cut up to now, for the drug transactions intercepted, is $18 million but they did not authorize to pay separately USDOJ said it had to be paid to Chief and you handle the split. There will be more coming from future busts."

The room goes silence for a while.

"What about her? What is she going to be doing? She is part of our TEAM now."

"For the time being neither Langley nor the Cartel can know about her. Remember she is dead."

"I understand sir."

"Chief before this goes any further I believe we should consider"

"You don't need to say it Skipper. It's a **four way split on the CI cut** from the drug busts, she is more than entitled to it, she earned it as much as any of us. I assume you have nothing to say about this decision because the USDOJ said we would handle the split."

"I agree 100% with you."

"You are part of the TEAM so we will stay together and protect each other. Having said that, we have to figure how we're going to handle the accommodations. The apartment only has three bedrooms, we're going to be a little tight because the Skipper's daughter and Sparks' mother are also joining us."

"With my share of the CI cut now I can buy the apartment next door."

"And, I can buy the one on the opposite corner. We would only be sharing your apartment for a few days."

LATER THAT EVENING IN PANAMA, everybody except Sparks and Chief had gone to sleep, they were sharing one last drink out on the balcony before going to sleep.

"Did you remember to retrieve it this time?"

"It's in the backpack in my room."

"I still can't believe you left it aboard Seeker in Key West."

"There was nothing I could do, you know they searched us, I barely had time to disconnect it and put next to the stove in the galley, anyway it looks like a regular transistor radio no one even looked at it. When Seeker was released to us, it was laying right where I left it."

"We were so very lucky."

"Will you stop being **The Perfectionist**? Now we're **The Perfect Team.**"

Inter Missions